Bolan heard voices coming from the illuminated box below him

"I don't know what the hell's going on. But there were two men on that roof!"

"J.D. says there was one, a big guy in black."

"Bull! I was on the Criminal Courts Building roof. There was a guy in coveralls, too."

"Probably just a workman, Captain."

"One of those bastards tried to kill the President, Buddy. It was too close. I want to know who the other man was. Are we chasing two guys or one? It's the difference between a lone nut and a conspiracy."

"I still say it doesn't matter, Captain."

"You're young, Buddy—you were hardly born in sixty-three. I was a cop, then, and I never swallowed the official story about Oswald. I'm not saying I know what happened, but I won't let it happen again. I'm going to find those guys and force the truth out of them. This time it's my turn."

Bolan listened with appreciation. The captain sounded like a good man. But the Executioner was also determined to get the truth.

Sorry, Captain, Bolan thought, but this time it's *my* turn.

D0709188

MACK BOLAN

The Executioner

DON PENDLETON's EXECUTIONER
MACK BOLAN
Split Image

A GOLD EAGLE BOOK FROM
W☉RLDWIDE

TORONTO • NEW YORK • LONDON • PARIS
AMSTERDAM • STOCKHOLM • HAMBURG
ATHENS • MILAN • TOKYO • SYDNEY

First edition June 1987

ISBN 0-373-61102-1

Special thanks and acknowledgment to
Charlie McDade for his contribution to this work.

Printed in Canada

Surely as the devine powers take note of the dutiful, surely as there is any justice anywhere and a mind recognizing in itself what is right, may the gods bring you your earned rewards.

—Virgil

I know what's right, and I seek only justice. Share the rewards among the trampled innocents.

—Mack Bolan

THE
MACK BOLAN
LEGEND

Nothing less than a war could have fashioned the destiny of the man called Mack Bolan. Bolan earned the Executioner title in the jungle hell of Vietnam.

But this soldier also wore another name—Sergeant Mercy. He was so tagged because of the compassion he showed to wounded comrades-in-arms and Vietnamese civilians.

Mack Bolan's second tour of duty ended prematurely when he was given emergency leave to return home and bury his family, victims of the Mob. Then he declared a one-man war against the Mafia.

He confronted the Families head-on from coast to coast, and soon a hope of victory began to appear. But Mack Bolan had broken society's every rule. That same society started gunning for this elusive warrior—to no avail.

So Bolan was offered amnesty to work within the system against terrorism. This time, as an employee of Uncle Sam, Bolan became Colonel John Phoenix. With a command center at Stony Man Farm in Virginia, he and his new allies—Able Team and Phoenix Force—waged relentless war on a new adversary: the KGB.

But when his one true love, April Rose, died at the hands of the Soviet terror machine, Bolan severed all ties with Establishment authority.

Now, after a lengthy lone-wolf struggle and much soul-searching, the Executioner has agreed to enter an "arm's-length" alliance with his government once more, reserving the right to pursue personal missions in his Everlasting War.

1

The bridge lay flat and gray in the morning drizzle, its gentle arc all but obscured by the mist and darkness. Three cars, three men in each, sat as if debating whether to cross. In the first and largest car, closest to the bridge, Don Albright, the driver, drummed his fingers impatiently on the steering wheel. This was not a detail he had relished. He was anxious for it to end. Albright was the youngest man at the CIA's Berlin station. He was twenty-six years old and looked even younger. He was getting his first real dose of the romance of espionage. So far it wasn't as glamorous as he'd hoped.

Albright's partner was thirty years older. His leathery, seamed face was a map of the blocks he'd been around. Ralph Collingsworth knew what was what. That was one reason he was assistant chief of station. It also didn't hurt that he had gone to all the right schools. He was sitting in the back seat, next to a large, pasty-faced man who struggled to suppress a smile.

Lighting a cigarette with a disposable plastic lighter, Albright turned to the back seat. He held the cigarette in his left hand, flicking the ashes out the open window. The mist collected in tiny drops on his exposed sleeve.

"Where the hell are they? It's already ten after six. I thought this was supposed to go off without a hitch."

"Relax, I've been through this before. Time isn't important. As long as we can make the switch, things will be all right." Collingsworth tried to reassure his young partner without betraying his own uneasiness. "I was at the big one, this same bridge, as a matter of fact."

"What big one?" Albright asked.

"Abel for Powers. Not long after they put up the wall. It was a half hour late, and I was already chewing on my second fistful of nails when the Russians finally showed up."

The pasty-faced man grunted, then, in heavily accented English, said, "KGB has its own clock. They come when they want. Mostly at night."

Albright looked closely at the Bulgarian and noticed, for the first time, that the man seemed nervous. That was odd. After all, he was going home after spending four years in an American prison. Albright wondered whether it was a peculiarity of the man or if the Bulgarians in the other two cars were equally nervous.

The mist turned suddenly to a heavy downpour. Albright pitched his cigarette out the window and rolled it up, leaving a half-inch opening at the top, just enough to keep the windows from fogging up.

"Damn," Collingsworth muttered, half to himself. "Why the hell does it always rain for these things? Donny, put the wipers on, will you? I can't see a damned thing out there."

Albright clicked on the wipers, and the big Buick engine rumbled under their rhythm, its exhaust mingling with the ground fog swirling around the car and its anxious occupants. He turned back to address the Bulgarian without looking at him. "What's it like over there?"

"Here, there, it's all the same. Germans are Germans." The man grunted with satisfaction, pleased with what he'd intended as a witticism. "There is more color in the West, maybe. Otherwise, no difference to me. I rather be in Bulgaria."

"Don't bet on it, pal," Collingsworth said. "Your KGB buddies are going to ask you more than twenty questions before you get home."

"I have done nothing. I have nothing to fear. Why should KGB bother me?" It was more a plea than a question, and Collingsworth ignored it. The unspoken reply hung in the thick air, increasing the tension in the car.

Behind them, a car door slammed. Albright rolled down his window and stuck his head out into the rain, which was now slackening almost as suddenly as it had begun. Andrew McLintock, the driver of the middle car, was sprinting toward them. Albright unlocked the door and moved into the passenger seat to make room for McLintock.

The CIA man slid into the car, closing the door quietly. His trench coat collar was turned up. To Albright he looked like something out of James Bond. The perfect spy, American-style. But McLintock wasn't a spy at all. He was an intelligence analyst, a paper pusher and number cruncher. He was present this dreary morning only because they needed an extra driver. His face made it plain he'd rather be home in bed. For that matter, so would Albright.

McLintock nodded absently at Albright, his glasses beginning to fog in the humidity of the car's interior. His hair was already thinning though he was only thirty-one, and his complexion was as pallid as the paper he pored over all day long. He turned to Collingsworth, his question already on his face before it reached his lips.

Collingsworth, bored by years of indistinguishable assignments that smacked more of department store floor-walking than intrigue, answered it before it was asked.

"I have no idea where they are. And, no, I don't think there's anything to get excited about. It's like meeting your Aunt Millie at the train station. Sometimes she's late. Go back to your own car. It takes two agents to amuse a fat Bulgarian. You ought to know that by now."

Albright wanted to say something. He looked at Collingsworth and changed his mind. The older man wore a look of tense annoyance. His explosive temper was well-known at the Berlin station. Some even whispered he'd have been COS if he'd had more self-control.

McLintock got out of the car, closing the door so quietly that it didn't latch, and Albright had to reopen it to slam it shut. Suddenly a burst of light splashed across the windshield, smeared by the softly clicking blades. Albright turned off the wipers and strained to see across the bridge.

The twin beams of a car's headlights winked one at a time as someone crossed in front of them.

"Let's roll," Collingsworth snapped, showing signs of life for the first time all morning. He opened his door and gestured to the Bulgarian to follow him. The heavy man slid across the seat, and Albright noticed the large beads of moisture dotted on the man's brow. It wasn't rain. Albright got out the driver's side and walked around behind the car to join the others.

In the darkness behind them other car doors slammed, and two groups of three men straggled toward them through the soft rain.

"Everybody ready?" Collingsworth asked. An unintelligible chorus of grunts seemed to satisfy him. "Let's go get our flyboy, then." He walked toward the bridge, leaning forward slightly, a concession to the improbable trouble he might have to deal with. In single file, the remaining eight men fell in behind him.

Albright thought the procession must look foolish. Nine clowns in a parody of foreign intrigue, they marched sluggishly. No one talked, and the three Bulgarians, alike as sibling peas, looked around them as if drinking in their last glimpse of the West for a long, long time.

At the other end of the bridge, a small group of men moved cautiously forward. At its center, Albright knew, was

David Anderson, walking toward freedom for the first time in four years. Anderson was a pilot, allegedly privately employed, but in reality a contract agent for the Company. Captured when his SR-71 flamed out over Soviet territory and he was forced to land in the middle of a Ukrainian wheat field, Anderson had been neither seen nor heard from for most of the intervening four years.

There were rumors, of course, and the Soviets had claimed to have captured the plane intact. The claims were disbelieved because no evidence had been produced, photographic or otherwise. Unlike the Gary Powers incident, when the Soviets had built a monument out of the U-2 he had been flying, there was little or no reason to believe the Russians had anything more than the charred wreckage of the SR-71. This presumed, of course, that Anderson had done his job and triggered the autodestruct on his plane.

Albright was more than a little awed by Anderson and those like him, who flew planes at incredible altitude and unbelievable speed across thousands of miles of Soviet territory. At the mercy of the elements and protected only by the presumptive technological superiority of the aircraft, such men might as well have been another species, as far as Albright was concerned.

The American team reached the middle of the bridge first. The three Bulgarians huddled together, whispering in their own tongue. Albright couldn't understand the language, but he knew they weren't happy. The Soviets were notorious for holding their agents accountable for their failures. Their punishment sometimes seemed inversely proportional to the degree of the failure, something the Bulgarians would be aware of.

Although the satellite intelligence agencies were nominally independent, there was no one in intelligence circles who didn't know Moscow pulled the strings for them all. The KGB treated the others like lackeys. Often sacrificed on dangerous missions, or used when a direct link to Moscow Central would be undesirable, Bulgarians, Czechs and East Germans were frequently responsible for activities credited to the KGB, as in the attempt to assassinate Pope John Paul II. The smaller states often appeared inept as they took the fall for KGB disasters.

Albright was standing a little apart from the others, watching the Russian team approach. Almost like a flying wedge in football, the Soviet agents had surrounded the taller American, as if to protect him from prying eyes. Albright waited for the moment when the pilot would be released, exchanged for the three chubby, low-level Eastern bloc stooges. He had been wondering about the exchange from the moment he heard about it. It didn't make sense that freedom for a valuable man like Anderson could be bought so cheaply.

He had raised the subject with Collingsworth, but the latter had shrugged it off. "You young guys get more paranoid all the time. You should relax. Understand, this is not much more than a chess game anymore. Everybody knows everybody else. I sometimes think the only reason we bother to keep on going is we've been at it so long we don't know how to quit."

Albright hadn't been able to decide whether that was cynicism or wisdom. Collingsworth was capable of both, sometimes in the same statement. On the other hand, he knew more about such matters than anyone else Albright knew. He was probably right. Maybe Anderson didn't know anything the Russians wanted. Maybe they'd gotten tired of trying to break him. Maybe the Bulgarians were bigger fish than Langley suspected. Maybe all or none of those things were true. As long as Don Albright didn't make the decisions, it didn't matter what he thought, anyway.

As the Russians drew closer, taking their time reaching the center of the bridge, the rain began to pick up again. Albright, the only man without a raincoat, could feel the water soaking through his woolen topcoat. It began to smell the way only wet wool did, and for a moment he thought of New York subways full of people wearing wet wool coats. The cars were so jammed that the passengers not only looked and acted like sheep, they smelled like them.

Albright's reverie was broken by Collingsworth's voice, excessively jovial in the early-morning rain. "So, Sergei, they send you out to baby-sit now, eh?"

The burly Russian, who seemed to be the team leader, smiled bitterly. "Your sarcasm rings a little hollow, Ralph. We are on the same bridge, are we not? And for the same purpose? Or perhaps you couldn't sleep and decided on a morning stroll?"

"At least I've got the Kingston Trio here to worry about. You have only one man."

"Some troika, Ralph. Which one is Trotsky?"

The tension broke then. The team leaders laughed like old friends, ignoring their own men, and the men they had been sent to exchange. Sergei Arkadin stepped to the railing of the bridge, and Collingsworth followed him. Standing out of earshot of the others, they chatted amiably for a few minutes.

Albright watched the two men, shuffling his feet and occasionally squeezing some of the moisture from his coat sleeves. Finally the conversation ended and Collingsworth walked back to his troop. Arkadin did the same. Anderson, surrounded by Arkadin's men, still showed little more than a forehead and a shock of hair above the KGB phalanx. Arkadin barked something in Russian, and the escort stepped aside. The pilot took a few tentative steps, almost somnambulant, then walked briskly toward Collingsworth.

For their part, the Bulgarians looked at one another uncertainly until Arkadin spoke again, more sharply this time. Reluctantly they moved forward in a clumsy ballet, as if each man wanted to be the last one returned to freedom, as the KGB defined it.

The Americans turned their backs, Collingsworth taking Anderson by the shoulder to lead him toward the three cars still idling in the rain. Albright walked beside them while the others, anxious to get home to dry out, sprinted for their cars. "Boy, you must be glad to be home, huh, Mr. Anderson?"

The pilot looked at him curiously, as if Albright had spoken in some language he'd never heard before. After a long moment, he said, "Home is Boise, Idaho. I got a long way to go yet, pal."

Albright, intimidated by the terse response, said nothing more.

As they drew near the car, there was a bright flash, followed quickly by two more. Collingsworth pushed Anderson to the ground and drew his gun. Albright dived forward, concealing himself behind the right front fender of the car. In the dim light, there was nothing to be seen. The only sound was footsteps, someone running in the rain, his feet occasionally slapping in a puddle. Then silence.

"Shit," Collingsworth muttered. "Some asshole photographer. That's all we need. With my luck, the son of a bitch is from the *National Enquirer*."

"Shouldn't we go after him?" Anderson asked.

"You think you have a chance in hell of catching him?" When Anderson failed to answer, Collingsworth continued, "What I want to know is who the hell tipped him off. And if I find out, I'm going to fry his ass."

"What's the big deal?" Albright asked. "We got what we came for. What difference does a picture make?"

"I'll tell you what difference it makes. It means somebody who knew about this little swap opened his mouth. Secret means secret, Donny boy. And as long as you work for me, don't you forget it."

"Maybe it was the Russians," Albright suggested.

Collingsworth snorted contemptuously. "Not a chance, Albright. You think they want it known they gave up a major leaguer for three semipro has-beens? Not too likely."

The angry man stood and opened the car door as if he meant to tear it from its hinges. "Get your asses inside. We're going to Tempelhof. And as soon as I get our flyboy, here, on a plane, I'm going hunting. God help the bastard who's responsible for this fuck-up."

Collingsworth half helped and half shoved Anderson into the back seat of the Buick, climbed in after him and slammed the door. Albright walked around to the driver's side. As he closed the door, an elusive fear, something he couldn't name, caused the short hairs on his neck to stand on end.

2

"It's a colossal screw-up, that's all I know." Hal Brognola, never one to mince words, was more agitated than usual. He slammed a pencil onto his desk so hard that it bounced, then clattered on the floor. Brognola ignored it.

In a formal, straight-backed chair across from him, the man in black remained silent. He knew Brognola well enough to know there was more to the story, much more, and that it would be forthcoming. In due course.

The man from Justice stared at his silent visitor for a moment, the way he might have at a painting he'd never seen before. The eyes were intense, restless, skipping from shoulders to hands to forehead. Finally they came to rest exactly where Mack Bolan knew they would, staring straight into his own unflinching gaze.

"Four years they have this guy—four goddamned years. And he just walks the hell away without so much as a word."

Mack Bolan recognized the pause for what it was, an opportunity for him to ask a question. He did. "What about security? Why weren't they watching him?"

Brognola heaved a sigh, as much of tiredness as of exasperation. "They didn't think it was necessary. The guy was one of our own, after all. Why watch him? He'd be glad to be home. He'd answer questions for a couple of days and get on with the rest of his life."

"Makes sense, actually," Bolan said. "Sure, he might have been pissed at them for taking so long to get him out. Maybe even blamed them for the mess he was in in the first place. But the bottom line is, they got him out."

"You don't mean to say you buy that garbage, Mack? Four years is a long time. Anything might have happened. Maybe they turned him. Maybe they reprogrammed him. Hell, anything is possible."

"Is that what you think happened?"

"I don't know what to think. All I know is, Langley blew it, and we have to get him back. Whether he likes it or not. I mean, Anderson is no rookie. He knows the score. He knows the rules and how the game is played. He owes them a few hours, no matter how half-assed they were about it all. And we have to find him."

Brognola, as was his habit when agitated, got to his feet and began to pace. He thought better that way, saw things more clearly. Some of his acquaintances at Justice thought he was half shark. If he stopped moving, he'd die. They were only half wrong.

And Mack Bolan was more than half shark. A great white one at that. Any of the hundreds of goons who had ever stared into that diamond-hard gaze would testify to it. If they'd survived. Very few had, and those few weren't likely to do much talking to anyone. They'd crawled under the biggest rocks they could find and dug in. For life.

Bolan watched his mentor's restless movements silently. There were things he had to know, but now wasn't the time to ask. Not yet. Brognola stopped pacing and lit a cigar. Its rich fragrance filled the room as small clouds of smoke drifted off to annihilate themselves against the drapery.

"I don't care what it takes, Mack. You have to find David Anderson. And you better do it before those assholes at CIA. I don't buy this thing. Not from word one. It stinks.

Don't ask me why. It's just a feeling, but I've got a nose for a dead rat. There's something wrong here.''

"You think they wanted him out of the way?"

"No, nothing that simple. That would be too easy to arrange, and they're good at that kind of crude arrangement. But I do think they wanted him gone, and without anybody getting a good look at him.''

"Why?"

"Find him, and we'll know."

"All right, give me everything you've got on him. Family, friends, anything that might give me a place to start."

"It's all here," Brognola said, pointing to the thick file on his desk. "And anything else you want, you know where to reach me. Oh, and there's this kid from CIA, Don Albright. He looks like a comer. I think he'll be a big help. I got him on loan from Berlin for two weeks."

"You looked at the map lately, Hal?"

"What?"

"Last time I looked, this was a big country. Lots of corners. Anybody who wants to get lost can do it. And stay lost, if he tries hard enough. Two weeks isn't much time."

"Look, Mack. Anderson is a pilot. True, he flew for the Agency. That means he has some resources. But he wasn't a field agent. He doesn't know trade craft. I don't think he'd know a safe house if he bought one. It shouldn't be impossible to find him."

"Unless he's got inside help."

"Yeah, unless he's got inside help."

"What do you think? Does he?"

"I don't know. My instincts say yes. But my head wants to know why."

"Where can I find Albright?"

"He's at a Company house in Alexandria. He's expecting you at ten tonight. That'll give you a chance to run through Anderson's background, personnel file, clippings about him, the whole shooting match. Your cover name is Michael Baker.''

"How far do I trust Albright?''

"Right now? As far as you can throw the Lincoln Memorial. Later on, it's up to you. The kid seems solid. Not much experience, but that's a plus. He's sharp, but not a practiced liar like the guys he works for.''

Bolan nodded.

Brognola bent to pick up the wayward pencil from the floor beside his chair. With the eraser, he shoved a fat sheaf of papers across the slick surface of his desk. Bolan ignored the gesture, in favor of a question.

"You want to tell me why you think you need me on this thing? I mean, there are better people for it, with less important things to do.''

"That presumes we know what's going on. You show me it's a waste of your time, and you walk away from it, no questions asked. But until I'm convinced it's small time, I need you on it.''

Brognola stood abruptly and left the room, trailing clouds of smoke behind him. Left alone with the papers, Bolan sat motionless, as if in a yogic trance. He didn't much care for this assignment. It wasn't the kind of thing that he felt needed doing. It was too far removed from the real enemies of mankind, the subverters, and perverters, of freedom.

Bolan's war was a lonely one, a trail of blood and fire that crisscrossed the globe like some distorted grid of latitude and longitude. There wasn't a place he hadn't been, a country whose borders he hadn't crossed. And through it all, he had been guided, some might say driven, by the need to wipe the slate clean. Eliminating the lowest forms of humanity, whether they were acting out of greed or a hunger for power, perverted need or, worst of all, the sick pleasure of inflicting pain on the defenseless—that was what Mack Bolan was born to do.

In his lonelier, more reflective moments, he saw his crusade as a kind of biological warfare, probing deeply into the gene pool to cut out the spawn of mutants, the cancerous cells that would ripen into deviant forms of humanity, doomed to rot even as they grew in strength and size. He was a solitary warrior dedicated to the proposition that every man and woman had a right to be free to become the best he or she could be. That right was what America stood for. And what Mack Bolan stood ready to die for.

Tracking down some wayward flyboy, who was, after all, probably on a three-day bender, wasn't exactly going to make the planet a better place to live. But Bolan knew Hal Brognola. The man was his only friend, had been his friend at times when that friendship could have cost the man everything he cared about. And Hal's instincts were sound. If he said this thing wasn't as simple as it seemed on the surface, Mack Bolan wasn't going to disagree. Not unless he was sure. And then, if that time came, it would be Brognola who would cash in his chips, not Bolan.

If he could be stubborn, and he could, Brognola was not bullheaded. He might not often be on the firing line, shoulder to shoulder with the fire-breathing warrior the world knew as the Executioner, but he cared no less passionately about justice. He knew, better than anyone but Bolan himself, how bad things were, and how tough the going could get. Bolan was an invaluable national asset, not carried on any balance sheet. And the bow-tied GS-9s who labored over cash flow and expense accounts had no idea he existed. That told you something about national priorities.

As Bolan scanned the Anderson file, nothing looked unusual, nothing whispered for a closer examination. The pilot had been recruited in the usual way. An aeronautical engineering degree from MIT, followed by a hitch in the Air Force made him a natural hire for Lockheed. Qualified in

F-16s, he went to Lockheed as an engineer-test pilot. Given a crack at the SR-71, he couldn't say no.

Logic said that Anderson must somehow be special. At the time he was captured his bird was the most advanced strategic reconnaissance plane in existence. Its two Pratt and Whitney J58 engines made it capable of Mach 3 speed at altitudes in excess of 85,000 feet over a three-thousand-mile range. A successor to the U-2, it was certainly not the kind of plane you would entrust to a flying cowboy or a yahoo off the street.

Surprisingly, though, there was nothing "special" in Anderson's file. Assuming it was complete, always a risk when dealing with the CIA, there was little or no reason to suspect Anderson was anything more than he appeared to be: a high-flying spy. When he went down over the Ukraine in the early eighties, there had not been much in the press. It was almost as if the Powers incident had sated public hunger for information about such exotic intelligence gathering.

Closing the file, Bolan felt empty. Something was eating at him, whispering to him. That intuitive sense on which he relied so heavily was telling him he was on the wrong track. Already.

Brognola said he smelled a rat. Yet everything on paper said the opposite. A guy who had been in Soviet hands for years decided to take a walk. It was a free country. He had family he hadn't seen in four years, and he was entitled. So why didn't it seem that simple?

Bolan hoped Albright had some suggestions. He also hoped the CIA agent had been apprised who and what Mack Bolan was. The last thing he wanted was to have to deal with some bright-eyed hotshot who decided to make his career at Bolan's expense. Nailing the Executioner would be a coup like no other. Albright could coast for years on a victory like that. Bolan would have to watch his back, keep Albright in sight at all times.

More state and federal agencies than he could count, let alone the intelligence services of half the planet, wanted Mack Bolan. And none of them was particular about the condition in which he was delivered. Bolan was anything but fragile—they all knew that. If any one of them got their hands on him, he could expect all the tender loving care bestowed on a carton of crystal goblets by the US Postal Service.

The reputation was hard earned. And well deserved. No argument there. Ever since his return from Nam and the beginning of his personal war with the Mafia, Mack Bolan had gone at the enemy full throttle. As times changed, so did the targets. His identity wasn't fixed, either. With or without help from the government of the United States, most recently without, he had gone about his work with a grim determination. It was do or die, every goddamned day. And someday, he knew, it would be die. But that was for thinking about some other time. Later. The later the better. There was too much to do, and too little time as it was.

Bolan glanced at his watch. Flexing his shoulders, stiff from sitting at the desk leafing through paper, he stood and left the office. The door closed so softly behind him that he might have been a ghostly apparition.

There were times when Brognola thought so. Something about Mack Bolan, no matter what name he went by, was beyond the real. Brognola didn't know what it was, but sometimes, for just a minute, when he and Bolan were absorbed in something, he would feel a chill. One that lingered long after Bolan had gone. When Brognola got back to his office, he turned up the heat, just a little, against a chill that had little to do with the late November air outdoors.

3

Gunter Vollman had been drawn to photography at an early age. He wondered whether his own nocturnal inclinations had played a role in that choice. The vicarious thrill of peering through a lens, shaping his view of the world in a way no one else could do, gave him a sense of power. But it was the darkroom where he felt most at home. Peering through the gloom, red-tinted and otherwise colorless, silent as the deepest night, he felt at ease as in no other place.

By day, Vollman made his living, a good one, by shooting free-lance news photos. Most days he straggled around Berlin, a heavy bag over one shoulder, three cameras dangling around his neck. It was only the sheer weight of his equipment that set him apart from the tourists. Vollman, a most dispassionate man, paradoxically specialized in human interest photos. A kid feeding ice cream to a seal at the Tiergarten, an old lady protesting the decadence of modern art, a beauty queen cutting a ribbon—these were Vollman's stock-in-trade. And he was good at it.

But Vollman had other interests, as well. His sexual inclinations were somewhat unusual. Indulgence of his odd preferences had brought him into contact with all sorts of night creatures, from the sordid porn freaks to the no-questions-asked types who told him over the phone where to go and what to shoot. He had done a number of straight nude sessions for the slicker European skin mags, and they paid well, but there was no kick to it. He preferred the off-beat, any day.

His latest work was dangling on the light clothesline he used to hang contact sheets. Greta was the model's name. She was voluptuous, of course, but as characterless as most of the girls he'd shot. Her body would keep her in rent for a while, then she'd rush into marriage, one step ahead of sagging flesh and the first stretch mark.

The evening's work had been grueling. Greta had no sense of humor, and getting her to look anything but bored for the camera had been a teeth-gritting job. Vollman had shot four rolls in color, and a roll of black and white, more explicitly posed, for an under-the-counter client. The developer fumes, which always made him irritable, had this time given him a headache. He didn't hear the doorbell on its first ring. Or its second.

When the apartment door opened and closed, he was engrossed in his work. Not until the darkroom door opened, throwing a block of white light against the wall, did he realize he had company. It took him a minute to remember he had not let anyone in and was not expecting anyone. Vollman stepped out of the darkroom a foot or two, and stood framed in the doorway.

The visitor said hello in slightly accented German. Gunter responded automatically. He wasn't thinking straight, and he knew it. It didn't even occur to him to ask the stranger who he was or how he had gotten in. Not that it would have mattered.

The visitor was wearing a rain-spotted trench coat, and Vollman realized it must be raining outside. When the tall, thin stranger reached into his coat pocket, he smiled. When his hand reappeared, it held a blue steel Smith and Wesson .22-caliber automatic. Vollman backed into the darkroom doorway, one hand on either side of the frame.

Casually, with no more thought than a practiced surgeon scrubbing up before an operation, the stranger reached into his pocket again, this time withdrawing a small cylinder, also blue steel.

Vollman watched quietly, fascinated the way he would be by a horror movie, unable to turn away, but wanting to, desperately. The stranger threaded the cylinder onto the muzzle of the automatic. He raised the silenced pistol and pointed it casually at Vollman. He said nothing.

Vollman heard nothing. The slug, traveling faster than sound, struck the photographer just above the bridge of his nose, slightly left of center. He fell to the floor, his face torn between surprise and wry amusement. The tall stranger fired twice more into his victim's forehead, then unscrewed the silencer and replaced it and the automatic in his coat pocket.

From under his coat, he took out a nine-by-twelve manila envelope, already addressed and stamped, and placed it on top of a filing cabinet. Opening the middle drawer of the filing cabinet, he quickly worked his way through the folders until he found the one he was looking for, about halfway back in the drawer. He took three photographs from the folder, inserted them into the addressed envelope and sealed it. After replacing the folder in the file drawer, he closed the cabinet and walked to the door, the envelope under his arm.

He paused for one quick look around, then switched off the light, left the apartment and took the elevator down to the lobby. There he paused to check the address on the envelope before dropping it into the lobby mailbox. He didn't want to make a careless mistake now.

The envelope slid with a hiss into the pile of mail to be picked up in the morning.

Three photographs of David Anderson were on their way to Ralph Collingsworth.

4

Yuri Kuscenko was tired and angry. Thirty-six hours in the woods had done little for his sense of duty. Walking away from the CIA had been easy. Pretending to be David Anderson had been easy. It had been easy at the bridge and easy on the flight over from Tempelhof. Sleeping on the ground had not been easy.

Night was falling again, and he knew they would already be looking for him. He checked the zippered bag slung over his shoulder. There was a change of clothes, some shaving gear and a roll of crisp, new American bills. A small enough load to carry, but a man on the run can afford little more. Anything that weighed him down slowed him down. He had only two weeks to get the job done. It was time to move.

Brushing off his clothes, Kuscenko moved into the thinner stand of trees that bordered the narrow country highway. He knew cars were few and far between after dark. He'd have to catch a ride in the next hour, or risk another night on the ground, another day wasted of the precious few available. And his first appointment was only four days away.

As he drew close to the road, the sun slipped down behind the trees. The highway was in shadow now. To the right, he could hear a large truck, its engine laboring up the slight incline in a low gear. The driver was cautious of the winding turns. The truck would be likely to pick Kuscenko up, but he was in a hurry. A truck would only postpone the real beginning. With any luck, though, there'd be a car or two stacked up behind it.

Making sure no bits of grass or leaves clung to his clothes, Kuscenko stepped into the weed-strewn stretch between the trees and the highway shoulder. The sky was rapidly turning gray, with a fringe of dark blue at the horizon. Nightfall was only minutes away. The truck engine rumbled as the driver downshifted into a tight curve. Its headlights bounced as the heavy load rode with the bumps and dips in the road surface. The lights glanced off the trees and were swallowed by the darkening forest.

The truck was in sight now, a dark bulk behind the headlights. Farther back on the curve, Kuscenko could see three cars, dim shadows following their own headlamps. The truck engine rumbled, its twin stacks spouting dark smoke over the cab. Kuscenko stepped into sight, deliberately too late for the truck driver to spot him. In time-honored fashion, he hooked his thumb into the flow of traffic. The first and second cars roared by, as if sucked along by the truck. The third car, too, sped past.

Kuscenko cursed before he saw the bright red glare of the brake lights. The third driver had slowed, and was pulling onto the shoulder. Kuscenko hitched the strap of his bag more securely over his shoulder and sprinted for the car. It was small and sporty. The brake lights gleamed on the white paint, turning it a dull scarlet. The driver reached over and opened the passenger door. Kuscenko got in and thanked him for stopping.

"Where you headed?" the driver asked.

Kuscenko turned in the seat to face him. "Noplace special," he said, after a pause to study the driver.

The car smelled of new leather. The elaborate dash featured digital readouts rather than gauges. It seemed more like a space capsule than a car. "What kind of car is this?" Kuscenko asked.

"Plymouth Conquest. Nice, isn't it?" The driver smiled broadly, his features tinted green by the dash lights. "Made by Mitsubishi. You don't see too many of them in the States. Turbo powered. It'll do 150, top end. Course, I'd never drive that fast, but it's nice to know you have the juice if you need it."

Kuscenko nodded. The driver was in his early thirties. His short-sleeved sport shirt showed powerful, tanned forearms. Not exactly what Kuscenko had been hoping for, but he'd have to take what came along. "If you get a chance," Kuscenko said, "I have to take a leak."

"There's no gas station for quite a way yet. Want me to pull over? You can go in the weeds." The driver's easy manner was troubling Kuscenko. The guy seemed too comfortable with a total stranger. He'd heard much about the ease with which Americans moved around inside their own borders, but this was more than he had expected.

"I guess, if you don't mind," Kuscenko said. "Thanks."

"No problem." The driver pulled off to the side of the road again.

Kuscenko opened the door as the car came to a stop and slipped out into the weeds at the edge of the road. He glanced back over his shoulder to keep an eye on the driver. The man at the wheel was busy changing tapes in the car's cassette player. Kuscenko reached into the rear pocket of his slacks, made as if he were zipping up, then stepped back to the car. In his hand was a small, flat automatic pistol. He stuck it in through the door.

"Get out, please," he said. His voice was flat and toneless. Uninflected, as if he were talking to a wall. "Now."

"What the hell are . . ." The driver's protest was interrupted by a quick gesture of the deadly looking weapon.

Kuscenko opened the driver's side door. The car's elaborate sensing system chimed its musical reminder the door was open. Kuscenko leaned over the low roof of the car, and gestured toward the weeds. "Put up your hands and come around here, please. Quickly."

The driver raised his hands to shoulder height and moved toward the rear of the car, his eyes fixed on his passenger. The turbo-powered engine was rumbling softly. The driver stumbled, and fell to one knee. Before he could get to his feet, Kuscenko sprang to the rear of the car, ready for any move, however stupid, the driver might be considering.

"I tripped," the driver explained, his voice quavering.

Kuscenko nodded. "This way, please." The small, polished automatic glittered in the garish red glow of the taillights.

The driver thought of a carnival shooting gallery, the way the weapons always looked better than they were. The play of lights and splashes of bright color concealed so many defects. He hoped it would be the same with this gun.

"Into the trees, please." Kuscenko pointed with his empty hand. The driver knew he'd run out of luck. He dragged his feet, but there was little he could do, unless his captor made a mistake.

In the darkness at the edge of the woods, shadows moved quietly. The breeze was silent, barely bending branches as it slipped through the trees. Away from the highway, the sound of the Conquest's turbo disappeared. The woods were absolutely still. The faint squeak of a bat, dipping low for a late-autumn insect, sounded like a gunshot in the darkness. Just ahead, a few boulders were scattered among the trees.

"Here," Kuscenko said. His voice was so close to a whisper, he had to repeat his command. "Stop. This is far enough."

"Why are you doing this?" The question took Kuscenko off guard.

He thought a moment, then said, "You wouldn't understand if I told you." The conversation was making him nervous. He hoped the guy didn't start pleading with him. This was tough enough to do.

Kuscenko's eyes were now adjusted to the gloom. In the darkness, the driver's white shirt seemed to glow, hovering in the air as if unsupported.

"Turn around, please," Kuscenko said. He didn't much care for the sound of his own voice. Unnerved by the closeness of the man, the personal nature of the encounter, he felt himself becoming apologetic, almost obsequious.

"Look, if you want the car, just take it. Hell, I . . ."

"Please be quiet." Kuscenko stepped closer. The driver, his hands still raised to shoulder height, was staring straight ahead, into the dark trees. Kuscenko looked in the same direction. As his eyes no longer focused on the man's white shirt, it blurred into a dull gray and Kuscenko lost sight of the driver altogether, who became little more than a pale shadow, some disembodied apparition, hovering just outside Kuscenko's line of vision.

Kuscenko stepped closer, reaching out with the muzzle of the small pistol, almost tentatively, as if he weren't sure his captive were there. Like a blind man feeling the sidewalk with his cane, Kuscenko stretched the pistol still farther in front of him, until he was almost leaning. He took a step forward and stopped abruptly as the pistol touched the driver's spine, just below the shoulder blades.

Kuscenko's arm shook with the contact, as if two much larger bodies had collided. He suppressed a shiver. None of his previous experience had prepared him for the intimacy of such a moment. He stood, motionless now, as if welded to the driver in some exotic sylvan tableau by Rodin. The figures were dark, brooding in the eerie silence. Kuscenko moved the pistol slowly along the man's spine, as if searching for something.

The driver turned his head, just slightly. "Can I have a cigarette? I mean, you're going to kill me, right? At least let me have a smoke first."

Kuscenko deliberated a moment before answering. "All right, but quickly."

"Thanks," the driver said, reaching into his shirt pocket. The absurdity of the reply hit Kuscenko a moment later. He started to giggle. Annoyed with himself, he tried to control his laughter, but it had a will of its own.

He felt his own will wavering a little, the way ice begins to melt. "Hurry it up." If he allowed too much stalling, Kuscenko knew he'd lose his nerve altogether. But for the moment he was powerless, hypnotized by the static darkness.

The rasp of the flint wheel grated in the dark. As glowing sparks shot away from the lighter's tip, they seemed like a miniature astronomical display. The driver cursed. Again he spun the wheel, and this time the butane caught.

The sudden glare broke the spell. Kuscenko squeezed the trigger twice. The first slug struck the driver just above the hairline at the base of his skull. The second struck just below it. The shots echoed into the trees, fading quickly away. Off in the distance, their reverberations sounded to Kuscenko more like slaps than the small thunder he'd held in his hand.

The driver lay still on the leaf-littered floor of the forest. His last cigarette, its tip glowing dully, lay just beyond his outstretched hand. Kuscenko reached toward it with his foot, then almost as an afterthought bent to retrieve it. He took a quick puff, exhaling through his nostrils, before turning back to the waiting car.

The going was slow. The ground was strewn with numerous small rocks and holes. A misstep in the dark could break an ankle. The undergrowth tugged at Kuscenko's clothes. A thorny vine lashed across his face, leaving two small cuts in his left cheek. He stopped to wipe away the blood, worsening one of the cuts as an embedded thorn caught in his handkerchief and raked across the soft flesh.

As the trees thinned, he noticed a bright glow, oscillating at the edge of the highway. He stopped. Listening, he heard nothing but the rumbling of the Conquest's throaty turbo. The Plymouth's lights were on, but they were fixed. The pulsing light had to be from another vehicle. It could only be a police cruiser.

Kuscenko, struggling to appear nonchalant, stepped out of the trees and walked casually toward the Conquest. A Virginia State Police patrol car was parked right behind it, its lights whirling a garish red smear across the trees. The trooper stood by the front fender. Kuscenko steeled himself.

"Anything wrong, patrolman?"

"That's rightly my line, buddy," the trooper answered. "What's going on here?"

"I had to relieve myself. That's all."

"This here is a lot of car to leave with the keys in and the engine running. You ought to have better sense'n that."

"Well, I suppose you're right. But you know how it is. Nature calls."

"Yeah." The trooper didn't sound completely convinced. Kuscenko knew it. He stepped closer, trying to seem at ease, but his legs felt stiff and heavy.

"You mind showing me your registration?"

"Pardon me?" Kuscenko asked.

"Your registration. For the car." The trooper stepped back from his fender, unsnapping the flap on his holster.

"Oh, of course not. It's in the glove compartment. Let me get it."

Kuscenko walked behind the cruiser to the highway and stepped past the trooper. He leaned into the car and reached across the console for the glove compartment. Suddenly he realized he didn't know where it was or how to open it.

"I just remembered, it's in my wallet." He slid back out of the car and reached into his rear pocket. The trooper eyed him cautiously. Even so, the automatic took him by surprise. The first shot struck him above the left eye. The second missed. Kuscenko knew it didn't matter. The trooper was dead before he hit the ground.

A sudden glare around the bend told him another car was approaching. He would have preferred to conceal the cruiser and the body, but there wasn't time. He leaped to the Conquest and slid behind the wheel. With any luck, he could still manage a clean getaway. If the oncoming car stopped at the scene, its driver wouldn't see Kuscenko's car. If he drove on by, he'd have no idea that a patrolman and another driver had been shot, or that the spiffy sports car in front of him had anything to do with the shootings. At least, not until it was too late to make any difference.

5

Albright was sharp—Bolan knew that immediately. But the young man was inexperienced. As he sat across the room from the Executioner, the contrast between the two men was immediately apparent to both. Albright had been told he would be briefing a Michael Baker. His native instincts, undeveloped as they were, told him the big guy across the room was no ordinary man.

Bolan sat silent, nearly motionless. When Albright finally realized he was going to have to speak first, he couldn't quite suppress the quaver in his voice.

"I...uh...I'm not sure, you know, where I should start," he stammered.

With the barest hint of a smile, Bolan suggested, "Why not try the beginning?"

"Well, uh, okay, sure. Everything seemed normal. At the exchange, I mean. They were late, not real late, about twenty minutes, maybe. It was raining. We made the switch. That's about it."

"Nothing unusual happened?"

"No, well, wait, yeah. There was one thing. The guy who took the picture."

"What picture?"

"I don't know. This guy, he came out of nowhere, right after the switch. Just before we got Anderson into the car, this guy ran out of the shadows, took a couple of pictures and disappeared. We couldn't catch him, and had no idea who he was. Collingsworth was really steamed, but there was nothing we could do."

Bolan recognized the name, but gave no sign of it. "Who is Collingsworth?"

"Assistant COS, Berlin station."

"What did he do?"

"When?"

Failing to conceal his irritation, Bolan snapped, "When the pictures were taken!"

"Well, like I said, he got steamed. There was nothing else he could do. We hustled Anderson into the car and got the hell over to Tempelhof."

"Did he say anything?"

"Yeah, he figured there must have been a leak. He said he would have somebody's ass, if he could find out who was responsible. That's all, really." Albright paused thoughtfully, as if there was something he was trying to put his finger on. "There was one thing strange. But before that. On the bridge, he talked awhile to the KGB guy. It was like they were old friends. You know, sarcastic, wisecracking."

"That's all?"

"Yeah. All I can think of, anyway."

Bolan stared off into space. The silence was making Albright uncomfortable. Rather than dispel his discomfort, Bolan sat back, using the silence. Albright might remember something else, and Bolan could mull over what he'd just heard, sifting through it for anything of significance.

The conversation at the bridge he dismissed immediately. The bravado implicit in such exchanges was common practice. Men who shared a trade often felt a bond that overcame enormous differences. Bolan himself had felt it on occasion. It was even possible under some circumstances to develop an admiration for your enemy. Honor and courage were not exclusive to one ideology. Even the Mafia, for all of its evil, numbered brave men among its members, men who had the courage to honor its code, no matter how perverted.

Recognition by an enemy of those mutual virtues was no guarantee of salvation, but it did earn a grudging tip of the hat. Bolan knew that some KGB men respected him, but that respect wouldn't stop them from killing him if they got the chance. Still, there was more than one kind of death, and there were ways to honor an enemy even as you watched him draw his last breath, heard the death rattle in his throat. Bolan knew. He had been there, more than once.

Albright had by now conquered his discomfort and he stared curiously at his companion. There was no mistaking the raw power, the energy that radiated from the man, like electricity crackling just under the skin.

"All right," Bolan said, startling the young man. "Track me on this. We give up three low-level Bulgarian turkeys in exchange for a hotshot pilot who has ten times the intelligence value. Am I right so far?"

Albright nodded.

"At the exchange, there's nothing unusual except a mystery man taking pictures. The flyboy comes home. Twelve hours later, he's gone. Now, either he doesn't like the new TV shows, or something's up, right?"

"Right."

"So what can it be?" Bolan's blue eyes grew steely, boring into the young man even more intently. "Any ideas?"

"Well...I guess, if you start with the disappearance, there's only two ways to go. Either he went by himself, for reasons unknown...or he was forcibly removed by persons unknown." Albright smiled, pleased with himself. When Bolan's face remained stony, he continued, "If I had to guess, I'd say it was the latter."

"Why?"

"Well, it doesn't make sense any other way, does it?"

"Maybe not."

"Well, you said yourself, he was worth ten times what those fat guys were. I figure the Reds just snatched him back."

"But if that's the case, why bother? Why take the risk with a valuable property like that and get nothing much for your trouble? Is there something about the Bulgarians we don't know? Something that makes them more important than we thought?"

"I can't imagine what."

"I'm sorry to hear that. I thought you guys were paid to have imaginations, vivid ones at that."

Albright swallowed a chuckle when he realized Bolan wasn't joking.

"I've got a job for you tomorrow. Check out the Bulgarians again. Read the files over and over, until you can recite them from memory, if you have to, but make sure we didn't miss anything. Brognola's right. Something stinks here, and I don't have a clue what it might be."

"What are you going to do?" Albright asked, struggling to control the quaver that had crept back into his voice. He knew a no-bullshit guy when he saw one, and Michael Baker had the lowest tolerance for crap he'd ever seen. That was now the only thing he was sure of about his current assignment. "If you don't mind my asking..."

"No," Bolan said, getting to his feet, "I don't mind."

The door closed behind the big man.

If something from Moscow smells, the first place to look is under the rocks where the KGB lives. Much is said about KGB agents using diplomatic cover at the Soviet embassy in Washington, the UN in New York and a variety of cultural and technological missions around the United States. True as all that may be, the really dirty laundry is worn by the KGB's illegal residents. They are not protected by diplomatic immunity, but their illegal status gives them unparalleled freedom of movement. Connected in no overt way with the Soviet Union, they come and go. Their safe houses are numerous, and few are known to anyone outside KGB circles. But that ignorance did not extend to Mack Bolan.

Brognola's hunch was sufficient to make Bolan uneasy, but vague enough to leave him without a real thesis to explore. The Bulgarian angle was interesting. The KGB used Bulgarians for everything from carrying messages to arranging the assassination of a pope. But, interesting as that angle was, he'd have to wait until Albright got back to him on it. In the meantime, he had one avenue to examine. It was an idea without much logic behind it, and what little there was was less than compelling. That meant the Executioner would be going hunting. He was not ill-equipped.

The Bulgarian legation sat back from the edge of V Street. Like most embassies, it was more ostentatious than necessary and more lavish than the citizens it represented could afford to support. On the other hand, diplomats did have their perks, and in this the Bulgarians were no different from any other nation.

Bolan would not enter the legation itself. Not only was it, strictly speaking, the sovereign territory of Bulgaria, it was also well guarded. Neither of these impediments could have kept Mack Bolan out if he had wanted in. He had overcome more imposing obstacles many times. But he knew that what he was looking for wouldn't be in the legation at all. Sooner or later, however, someone from the legation would lead him to what he wanted. If there was anything at all to the notion that the Bulgarians were up to something more than US intelligence suspected, they would have to make contact with the KGB.

The Russians, gifted in the science of intelligence, would not entrust their instructions to cable or telephone. They knew only too well how easy it was to intercept such transmissions. And codes, though increasingly difficult to crack, were unnecessary encumbrances. Especially when all you had to do was get in a car and drive a few miles to deliver your message in person. So Mack Bolan sat. And waited.

The probability was high that any Bulgarian operation would be controlled by a KGB illegal resident. Washington was bound to have more than one. Bolan knew he was playing a shell game, with high stakes. If he followed the wrong man, another could leave the legation, deliver his message and return before Bolan was any the wiser. Patience was the only tool he had—that and the unfailing instincts that had kept him alive through his one-man war. So far.

Wearing black, Bolan watched from a rented Dodge under some trees down the block from the legation. He was not quite sure what he was watching for. He would know it when he saw it, he hoped. There wasn't much traffic in the late hours, but his hunch was that would be the time. The more inconspicuous the person, the more likely he'd be the courier, if there was a courier at all. After midnight, he would probably be one man alone, on unofficial business. The last thing either party would want was to attract attention.

At one-thirty an official car, flying the Bulgarian flag and probably carrying the legate, glided to a halt at the wrought-iron gate and waited for the guard to admit it. No doubt it was returning from one of the endless round of parties that seemed to be the main business of diplomacy. Expensive food and drink, shared with expansive gestures amid glittering surroundings, were of little use, as far as Bolan was concerned, in solving international problems. For the men and women who practiced the refined art of diplomacy, Bolan had no use at all.

The car disappeared almost silently, the gate clanged shut and shadowy serenity returned to the quiet street. For the next hour, nothing much happened. An occasional car passed by, and a few entered tree-lined drives leading to the large private homes with which the legation shared the block.

At three o'clock, the small gate adjacent to the guard-house swung open so quietly that Bolan almost missed it. A man in a woolen overcoat that was a little too heavy for the autumn temperature walked swiftly up the sidewalk in the direction of Bolan's car, but on the opposite side of the street. He was obviously in a hurry, and just as obviously trying to conceal the fact. His pace quickened unconsciously until, aware that he was supposed to seem casual, he would slow down too abruptly for a man out for a late-night stroll. Bolan had his man. He was certain. The tight knot in his gut was all the proof he needed.

Bolan's problem was to follow without revealing himself. On foot, it would be relatively easy, but if his quarry was meeting someone with a car, or if he managed to hail one of the infrequent cabs, Bolan would lose him. There was no way around it. He had to use the car. Waiting for the man to clear the corner, he cranked up the rented Dodge and cruised past the legation, turning left at the first corner and making the next left, as well. He could make good time when he was out of the man's sight, but speeding past would kill any chance to keep tabs on him.

As Bolan reached the next intersection, he glanced to the left, the man had already passed the corner. Halfway down the next block, he was walking at a rapid pace. Bolan was about to pull out when he spotted a cab coming. Keeping an eye on his man, he waited for the cab to pass the intersection, hoping the Bulgarian would flag it down.

The cab slowed as it approached, obviously anticipating a fare. The driver wasn't disappointed. The man in the overcoat caught sight of the taxi and hailed it, unnecessarily, with a shrill whistle. Bolan sighed with relief. His quarry would relax a little, and the cab would be easy to tail.

Now, if only the man were going to a house. If he were meeting his contact in a park or some other public place, Bolan would be only one knot closer on the string. His sixth sense told him he didn't have the time to haul in his prey hand over hand, a foot at a time, like a fisherman pulling in a lobster pot. He wanted a target, someplace likely to contain documentary evidence, or someone who knew where such evidence could be found.

The cab was making good time heading down Sixteenth Street. At Scott Circle, it turned onto Massachusetts Avenue, toward the eastern corner of the District. At Union Station, the cab slowed, and Bolan thought for a moment his string had snapped, but the cab picked up steam again and sped through Stanton Square. Once across the Capital Street Bridge, it moved at a steady clip.

Minutes later, they left the District altogether. Bolan dropped back. There was little traffic and it wasn't difficult to keep the cab in sight. They passed through Carmody Hills and after several minutes in open country, they were on a narrow secondary road.

About fifteen minutes out of the District, they came to the entrance to a winding lane, shrouded by foliage. The entrance was marked by a pair of fieldstone pillars, but no street number or name identified the place. The cab pulled over, its right front wheels narrowly avoiding a broad ditch at the side of the road. Bolan had been hanging back quite a distance on the lightly traveled road. Now, two hundred yards behind his quarry, the car's lights extinguished and engine off, he hoped the Dodge would be hidden by the shadows.

The Bulgarian in the heavy coat opened the rear door of the cab, little more than a dark gray bulk at this distance. He paused to pay the driver, and watched the cab out of sight. Glancing up and down the deserted road, he missed Bolan's Dodge. Satisfied he was alone, he walked up the narrow, winding lane, his faltering step betraying his trepidation. Bolan was fifty yards behind him, keeping to the trees. The Bulgarian knocked diffidently on the door of a rambling fieldstone farmhouse. And Bolan knew what he'd be doing tomorrow night.

6

Don Albright was getting bored. The prisoner exchange had been the highlight of his career, so far. For the first time since joining the agency, he had felt an adrenaline hit. Like a jolt of electricity, the current running through him that morning had seemed like a harbinger of things to come. Meeting the big man in black was another high. It had looked as if he was finally going to get a taste of excitement. What a joke.

Reading carefully through the files of the three Bulgarians was the pits. He had come to think of them as the three little pigs. Only none of them had built a house. They weren't even that interesting. There was nothing in the files that suggested anything out of the ordinary. He was making his third pass through the papers. So far, he wasn't even sure they were spies at all. The papers were so clean that he'd guess, if he didn't know better, they'd been prepared by the other side.

Pushing paper wasn't his idea of intelligence work, anyway. In the past when spending long hours on some boring research project, he'd tell himself that it was better than sitting at home alone staring at the tube. With no family, no one to go home to, he hadn't minded staying in the office all night. He'd done that more than once, sleeping on the cheap Naugahyde couch in the reception area. But now that he was back in the U.S.A. pushing paper, his German assignment seemed more like a passport to oblivion than a step up the career ladder.

Disgusted, he closed the file of Little Pig Number Two and pushed it away. There was nothing there that hadn't been there on the first two passes. He leaned back in the desk chair and stretched his arms over his head, suppressing a yawn. He stood up and walked to the reception area, where the nearest window was located. His watch told him it was 11:00 p.m., but that could be an illusion. The small office in which he worked was so cut off from the real world that it could have been any time at all. And, anyway, he wondered, what difference did it make? He was getting nowhere fast. The parking lot below was virtually empty. There were a few cars belonging to the skeleton staff on duty at night and to the security people, but they looked lost, helplessly adrift on a sea of asphalt.

Albright wasn't a careerist, just an eager beaver. He cared about things, passionately. That kind of devotion wasn't as fashionable as it used to be. Some of his former classmates at college were already working on their second BMW, had cabinets full of stereo components and trendy original paintings on the walls. Maybe they were right and he was wrong.

He stared into the polished glass and saw a ghostly image of himself, transparent and ephemeral. He had been staring right through it a second before. How fitting, he thought—I might as well not be here at all, for all the effect I have on things.

Struggling to suppress the despair beginning to gnaw at him, he yawned. He really should go back to the cubicle and get to work on the file of Little Pig Number Three. He knew his pass at it would be as fruitless as the other two, but he had signed on, and he was a good sailor.

What troubled him most was the suspicion that the Bulgarian angle was a red herring. If it was, they were all on the wrong trail, and Mr. Baker was in trouble. Albright figured the big guy was checking out an angle of his own. He hadn't said what it was, but if the files were as innocent as they seemed, and the three fat Bulgarians as inconsequential as the files, there was something seriously wrong, something that smelled like a plot.

But what plot? Albright asked himself. Of whom and for what purpose? The answers were elusive, floating just outside the reach of logic. It might be too late to help Baker, but he'd be damned if he'd give up without a try. He'd read the papers once more before checking out for a few hours' sleep. If he was wrong, or if luck was with them, he and Baker would have a chance to discuss it. He hoped.

To bolster his confidence, Albright gave his image in the glass the thumbs-up.

It didn't work.

WHILE ALBRIGHT PUZZLED his way through the paper palace, Mack Bolan was working his own side of the street. He was skeptical of the luck that had brought him to so secluded a place so easily. But you don't fight a war like Bolan's by being too careful.

The house was dark and quiet. It was relatively isolated, the nearest houses situated several hundred yards to either side. Unlike its neighbors, Bolan knew, it harbored KGB agents, and probably did not resemble any other house for miles around once you got past the front door. He parked the nondescript Dodge even farther away than he had the previous night. If he had to move out quickly, he wanted some distance between himself and any pursuers before he had to stop for the car.

Dressed in black from head to foot, he was an imposing shadow, justice forsaking its stately robes to walk abroad in casual wear. On his hip rode the stark silver of Big Thunder, his .44 AutoMag, more than a counterweight for the lighter but no less deadly Beretta 93-R. A KGB safe house was no place to go unarmed.

The last light had gone out nearly an hour ago. Quiet surveillance from shrubbery across the broad lawn had confirmed that the house was inhabited, but by how many people, he didn't know. The place was almost aggressively silent, as if its residents were determined to avoid calling attention to themselves. Bolan would have bet a bundle that last night's visit was an unusual occurrence.

For the first hour he watched, Bolan wasn't even sure there was anyone inside. The lights going on and off could have been controlled by timers, available at any hardware store. It wasn't until a faint shadow moved against a heavy shade that he was certain. And it was a half hour after that when he was certain it was time to move in.

Getting inside wasn't going to be easy. What happened when he did would depend on what he found. There were too many possibilities to plan for them all. Mack Bolan knew only that he wouldn't kill anyone unless he had to. The best course would be for the penetration to look like a random burglary. Even a quiet, rural neighborhood was not immune to such crimes. If he could get in and get out undiscovered, he would even muss up a few things and take a TV or silverware, anything to make it seem as if the intruder had no idea the house was different from any other.

The front door was the best bet for entry, because it was the one place that had to appear normal. It was where the mail would be deposited, and the newsboy would come to collect. The odd salesman, relic of a bygone era in mall-ridden America, still might pay a call. Any safe house worth a damn had to seem to belong to ordinary people.

It all came down to details, the little things that made all the difference. You fitted in or you didn't. If you were a KGB illegal, you had been trained, and very well at that, at the school in Balashikha. You were more American than your neighbor and holier than thou, or you wouldn't last six months.

Mack Bolan knew the value of details. Attention to them had kept him alive this long. God willing, they'd keep him alive a while longer. And it was detail that got him inside. From the middle of the lawn as he crossed it toward the house, he noticed the crack under the garage door. The garage just might be unlocked. And it just might have another door that led to the interior of the house.

Sprinting swiftly on the grass, he knelt in front of the garage door. It was unlocked. Lying flat, he pushed it up slowly, its rollers barely moving in their tracks, until he had an opening he could slip through. Once inside, he pulled the door back down. The torch at his belt was dim, by design. In its feeble glow, his eyes still adjusting to the darkness, he almost missed what he was looking for.

The two cars inside were as ordinary as you could hope for. A three-year-old Cutlass Ciera and a banged-up Nissan, old enough still to be called a Datsun. And to the left, by the Ciera's front fender, was a door. He knew it wouldn't be unlocked. They couldn't be that careless, and they weren't expecting him. Or were they?

Moving quickly, he reached the door, pressing himself flat against the wall within reach of its knob. He laid an ear against the wallboard, but heard nothing. Reaching for the knob, he turned it gently. It gave only slightly before stopping. It was locked.

So intent on the door, Bolan failed to hear the rustle of footsteps on the cement driveway. He twisted the knob harder, hoping it would give, and knowing it wouldn't. Suddenly he was blinded as the garage was flooded by light from overhead. With a rush, the garage door flew up.

"You looking for something?" The voice was almost too American, like that regionless dialect spoken by radio and television announcers in the early days.

Bolan whirled to find himself staring into a pair of ugly
pistol barrels. Each looked about as large as the mouth of a
fifty-five-gallon oil drum. They were Smith and Wesson
.38s, as American as apple pie. As American as the men
holding them were not. The taller of the two stepped into the
garage. The other followed, stopping long enough to lower
the door.

"I asked you a question." It was the taller man who had
spoken. Obviously the superior. Perhaps the same man who
had received company in the early hours of the previous
night. When Bolan didn't answer, the man continued,
"Something tells me you are no ordinary burglar. Am I
right?"

The shorter man smiled. He approached Bolan carefully,
making sure his partner had a clear line of fire in case the
intruder made a sudden move. As he got within reach of
Bolan, he yanked the AutoMag from its holster. He stepped
in a little tighter and began patting down his captive very
professionally. He found the Beretta immediately.

Stepping back, he placed both guns on the hood of the
Cutlass with a clank. Bolan glanced quickly at the guns,
calculating the odds. They were dismal.

"Move over to the other corner," the tall man said, gesturing with his weapon. Bolan did as he was told. "Anton,
open the door."

He spoke with the casual authority of a man used to being
obeyed. Bolan studied the man, while Anton searched for
the keys to the inside door. He was perhaps an inch taller
than Bolan. Slender, with pale, thinning hair, he appeared
to be in his late thirties. His hands were large, almost too
large, and strong looking. Casually dressed, he seemed no
different from any other man who might live in the neighborhood. He was probably in better physical condition, and
certainly spoke at least one language other than English. His

skin was tanned, but only slightly, the product of one short vacation, Bolan would bet.

Anton produced his keys, and rattled them until he found the right one. As the door opened, Bolan spoke for the first time.

"Look, I didn't mean anything. I was just...uh, you know—"

"Buddy, I don't know who you are, but there's no way in hell you were just anything. Nobody doesn't mean anything with a cannon like that on his hip. Who are you, and what do you want here?"

"I told you, I—"

"I know what you told me. Now, if you would be so kind as to follow Anton inside, we can continue our little interview in more comfortable circumstances. Before we call the police."

The last thing Mack Bolan needed was to be hauled into a police station on what would certainly be presented as an attempted burglary, even though the tall man knew it was much more than that.

There were no prints on file, not anymore. But Bolan couldn't afford to have any taken. And once the cops came, he'd have a hell of a time getting away. His only hope was to keep the two interested long enough for him to figure some way out, before they placed the call. If he gave them a little, baited the hook, they'd bite. And as long as they were nibbling, they would have no more desire to bring in the police than he had.

Bolan stepped into a small foyer, the tall man right behind him, bringing Bolan's weapons with him. Anton was against the opposite wall, his gun trained on Bolan's middle. The door closed behind them, and Bolan was inside. But not exactly on his own terms.

Anton stepped through a doorway to his left, clicking on a light. Prodded by the .38 at the base of his spine, Bolan stepped into the room. It seemed like an ordinary suburban living room. In many ways it was. Bolan looked around, taking it all in as quickly as he could.

"Shit, you guys don't even have a TV," he mumbled.

"Hell, Mikhail, maybe he is just a burglar," Anton said.

The tall man laughed outright. "Somehow I don't think so."

Anton sat in a leather wingback chair, his gun held carelessly in his lap. He gestured to a couch against a windowless wall, and Bolan crossed the room and sat down.

"You guys aren't really gonna call the cops on me, are ya? Hell, I didn't even steal nothin'."

Mikhail sat down in an easy chair near the door they had just entered by. There was a sideboard next to him, and he placed the AutoMag and Beretta down, leaving them within easy reach.

Mikhail looked at Bolan for a long, silent moment. When he spoke, his voice had taken on a harder edge, as if his true self were closer to the surface, now that they were safely inside. "I'm going to ask you once more, who are you and what are you looking for?"

"Nothin'. You know, a stereo, a TV. Places like this are usually pretty easy to hit. For a guy like me, they're usually pretty safe houses, you know?"

Mikhail flinched, just slightly, but Bolan caught it. His fish was on the line.

"What do you mean, 'safe houses'?"

"You know, no burglar alarms or anything. Usually I don't get a lot of stuff, but it's in and out, you know. I mean, it don't take a lot of intelligence to pull off. And the risk ain't too great. Usually."

Mikhail narrowed his eyes. If he had had any doubts that Bolan wasn't what he was trying so hard to seem, they were gone. He continued to stare at Bolan in silence. When Bo-

Ian said nothing more, Mikhail asked, "But why this particular house?"

"It's quiet, you know, around here. I mean, it didn't have to be this one. It coulda been next door. Up the road. This kind of neighborhood, that's all."

"And nobody sent you—is that what you expect me to believe?"

"Do I look like I work for somebody? What, you think rippin' off TVs and silverware is big business? No way. I fence shit, I get about a dime on the dollar, if that. I rip off a five-hundred-buck color TV, we're talkin' fifty bucks. You got any idea how heavy a set like that is? You think it's easy luggin' one around? Try it sometime."

Mikhail stood suddenly, and walked threateningly toward his captive. He stood in front of Bolan, as if trying to stare him down, the .38 clenched in one white-knuckled fist. Bolan's foot was planted firmly in the tall man's crotch before Anton realized anything was wrong.

Grabbing the .38, Bolan dived across the floor, rolling on one shoulder and coming to his feet with the gun leveled at the smaller man, who was still in his chair, his jaw agape.

"Gently, now, Anton, gently. Put the gun on the floor and kick it over toward me."

Mikhail was bent double, holding his groin and moaning. Bolan stepped up behind him and kicked him again, this time at the base of the spine. The tall man tumbled onto the empty sofa and lay writhing.

"Now, Anton, I got a few questions of my own." Bolan stepped to the sideboard, holstered the Beretta and the AutoMag, all the while keeping his captured .38 pointed in Anton's direction. For the moment, Mikhail was no threat. He was interested in only two things, both of which ached like hell.

"If you think I'm no burglar, you must have some reason. I want to know what it is."

"Don't tell him anything, Anton, I'm warning you," Mikhail groaned from the sofa, gritting his teeth so that the words were barely intelligible.

Bolan ignored him, continuing to bore in on the weaker link in the two-man chain. "You know any pilots, Anton? Somebody told me you knew a pilot who could fly me someplace without anybody knowing."

"I don't know any pilots. I don't know what you're talking about."

Anton was lying, and Bolan knew it. And Mikhail knew that Bolan knew. The whole exercise was pointless. Bolan wasn't going to get anything out of these men. And he couldn't let them walk away. Whatever was going on, if they were involved in it, they knew now that he was on to them. And if they weren't involved, someone above them who was would soon know.

There was only one way out, and Bolan took it. The Beretta was in his hand, and quietly spat its deadly poison. Anton fell to the floor, a small round hole in his forehead. The leather of the wingback wasn't as neat. Small chunks of brain tissue clung to the smooth surface for an instant then fell to the chair seat. The blood was more leisurely, moving slowly down the shiny brown calfskin.

Mikhail was next. Two slugs from the Beretta ripped away the left side of his head. He stiffened and went limp, all in an instant.

Quickly Bolan moved from room to room, looking for something, anything he might use. But the place was clean. Nothing to suggest it was not what it appeared to be—a suburban house. His search was tiring, and Bolan was getting impatient.

He ripped pictures from walls, looking for a safe. He searched the basement for some sign of a hidden room for electronic equipment. And at the end of it all, there was nothing. It almost seemed as if he were supposed to be here.

If he hadn't known better, he'd have thought he *was* an angry burglar. The only signs of a KGB presence in the house lay dead in the living room. And yet . . . they were there. He had been set up. For sure.

There was a purpose to this diversion. It led straight back to Moscow center—of that Bolan had no doubt. Somebody was working both sides of the street, laying so much smoke that nobody could see straight. Somewhere in the smoke was the end of a chain. Pull it, and somebody would be yanked right out of his shoes. No one was better qualified to pull it. Mack Bolan would rattle a few cages before this was over. But first he had to cover his ass. There would be time to think about tonight's business later. Maybe Albright had come up with something. But until Bolan got his ass out of this sling, it wouldn't matter.

He ripped open drawers, scattered papers and piled a small compact stereo unit and a set of sterling ware together in the center of the floor. He quickly went through the rest of the house, making it look as if the two men had surprised a burglar.

Then he slipped back into the garage, tearing the knob from the door as he did. The KGB trap had failed. Three minutes later, he was back in the Dodge. It remained to be seen whether his own ruse would work. He might never know. Neither would Anton or Mikhail. But for them, it didn't really matter anymore.

7

The ringing seemed to go on for a long time. Coming awake slowly, Albright reached for the phone. The voice on the other end of the wire dispelled the remnants of sleep in a hurry.

"What did you find in the files?"

"They were clean. The three little pigs were nothing more than they seemed to be—a little industrial espionage here and there. Enough to get them a couple of years in jail, but that's about all. How about you? Did you find anything?"

"Not for long."

"What do you mean?"

"Never mind. Meet me in an hour. I'll be on a bench in Dupont Circle. Take a cab." The phone clicked before Albright had the chance to say a word.

Albright showered and dressed, not bothering to shave. He had less than forty minutes to make the appointment by the time he got to the street. It took him five minutes to get a cab. Praying there was no traffic, he directed the cabbie to Dupont Circle. On the way, he wondered what Baker would look like. He would certainly not sit around in a public place dressed as he had been the first time they met.

Three blocks from his destination, he jumped out of the cab and sprinted to the circle. Something told him there was a reason for this meeting that Baker had not cared to trust to the telephone.

Threading his way through traffic, he stepped onto the curb and started to walk the perimeter of the circle. There were just a few benches, but almost all were occupied. Albright knew better than to appear to be looking for someone. Instead, he strolled around the circle as if looking for a place to sit without the harsh sun in his eyes, preferably on an empty bench.

Halfway around, he spotted Baker. He knew it even before he could see the man's face. Suppressing the urge to hurry, he continued his casual stroll. Baker was alone on the bench, and Albright wasn't surprised. Even when he wore conventional clothing, there was something forbidding about the big man. The tweed jacket, immaculately pressed and precisely tailored, was taut across his broad shoulders. Albright smiled at the incongruity of the man's appearance and his work.

Albright sat down at the other end of the bench. Baker reached into his coat pocket and pulled out a pack of cigarettes, then patted his pockets as if looking for a light. He turned to Albright and asked for a match. Each man slid toward the center of the bench as Albright withdrew his lighter and bent forward to light the dangling cigarette.

"You made good time," Bolan said.

"You didn't really give me a chance to argue, did you?"

"The Bulgarian angle is a dead end," Bolan said matter-of-factly. Although Albright had come to the same conclusion, he was surprised by the big guy's equanimity. He wanted to ask what had happened, but knew it was pointless. The soldier would tell him, or not, as he saw fit.

"That's not why we're here, is it?"

"No."

"Then why?"

"A friend of ours got some interesting mail," Bolan said.

"Oh, what is it?" Albright felt that same adrenaline jolt he'd noticed at the spy exchange.

"I'm not sure, but we're going to find out right now. We'll take my car."

The drive took them out into the Virginia countryside. It was pleasant, the afternoon clear and crisp. The foliage was turning color, and Albright wondered at the incongruity of the natural beauty he saw at every turn when compared to the career of the man who sat beside him. How could nature have produced such life and such death? And if there was a God, did he wonder about it Himself?

"What is this mysterious mail we're going to find out about?"

"Photographs."

"Of what?"

"Not what, who. And I don't know. That's what we're going to try to find out. Just sit back and enjoy the ride. I have a feeling things are going to get a whole lot worse."

Albright took the cue. He turned to look out the side window. He studied Bolan's reflection in the glass as they drove on in silence. The man driving the car seemed so ordinary in so many ways. That he wasn't ordinary went without saying. No one had told Albright, on or off the record, that the man he'd be working with was the Executioner.

Albright had heard of him and his exploits, of course, and had heard that half the CIA wanted the man dead. He had known, as soon as he met the man called Michael Baker, who he really was. He didn't let on, of course, but he knew. And Bolan, without asking, knew he knew. Albright wasn't dead certain himself, but lately there had been some rumors that Company operatives were instructed to back off where Bolan was concerned.

Albright cast another surreptitious glance at his companion. Bolan was bigger than most men, but not by all that much. And he was certainly powerfully built, and kept himself in good condition. But he was a man, for all of that.

So what was so special about him? Albright had wondered. And he'd realized it was the one thing you can't measure with the eye: heart. Judging by the things he'd heard, Albright knew Bolan had more than his share of heart.

After a half hour, Bolan turned into a narrow country road. There were no signs to indicate where they were, and Albright didn't have the faintest idea. There was no way in hell he'd be able to find his way this far again, he thought, let alone to wherever they were going. The narrow road was paved in tar and gravel. The smell of the tar filtered into the car, the fresh gravel crunching crisply under their tires, a low, steady grinding thunder.

They headed into a long stretch of road bordered by trees in single file on either side, their branches interlaced overhead, and their leaves aflame. It was like roaring through a tunnel of cold fire. Then the road curved to the left, and the trees were all behind them. Nothing now but rail fence and open field to either side. They were deep in the countryside, and Albright, the city kid, was overcome.

"It's beautiful here. Where are we?"

Bolan didn't answer. But Albright knew that he, too, was aware of the beauty surrounding them. Albright guessed the steady, unflinching gaze fixed on the green expanse was probably as close as Bolan ever came to prayer. And maybe it was as close as anybody needed to get.

Bolan found himself thinking back to what this place used to mean to him. It was Stony Man Farm. A flood of memories washed over him suddenly, some good, some bad. He put them out of his mind, concentrating on the mission at hand. Besides, he had a very good reason for coming back. There were people here who could help him. In fact, with his new sanction he had no doubt that he'd be visiting this place in the future.

Hal Brognola met them at the entrance, as prearranged, and ushered them down a long corridor.

Near the end of the hallway, Brognola steered them into an office humming with electronic equipment. The big Fed walked to the center of the room and peered over the shoulder of a stocky man seated in a wheelchair at a computer console. It was Aaron "Bear" Kurtzman, resident computer genius who was crippled from the waist down during an attack on the facility a couple of years before. Kurtzman turned as Bolan and Albright entered.

"Striker, good to see you again. Sorry I can't stand," Kurtzman said, a mischievous glint in his eye.

"Bear, how are you?" Bolan inquired, smiling. He realized it wouldn't be a good idea to remain too solemn, because he was certain that Kurtzman had reconciled himself to the idea of a life in a wheelchair. The amenities over, Bolan got to the point.

"Anything yet?" he asked.

"Nothing certain, but we're making headway."

"What's going on?" Albright asked.

"That mail I told you about," Bolan said. "We're taking a closer look at it."

"What is it?"

"Photographs. Of David Anderson."

"What kind of photographs? Where from?"

"All kinds. But the most interesting ones were taken that morning of the exchange."

"Where the hell did they come from?"

"Somebody was kind enough to mail them to Mr. Collingsworth," Bolan answered. "We don't know who, and we don't know why. And we never will know, probably. Somebody killed the man who took them."

"Let's get going," Brognola said. "Bear, do it."

Kurtzman turned back to his keyboard and punched in some numbers. He pressed a red button and a large TV screen on the desk lit up. "This is the last batch, the ones you just got," he said. "So far, everything is just what you'd expect. All the photos of Anderson show slight differences commensurate with aging, minor variations due to weight change and so on. Now, let's see what we got here."

He hit some more numbers on the keyboard, and the image on the screen leaped forward. He was zeroing in on certain key features of facial construction. "There, look at that. Just like in the preliminary analysis. See that jawline? And here, look at the ear. Wait, let me get you a comparison." His fingers flew over the keyboard again and the screen image divided. Two ears were displayed.

"Look at that pattern of whorls. Just like fingerprints. Except you can't get rid of them," Kurtzman said, looking meaningfully at Mack Bolan.

"All right, Aaron," Brognola said. "What are you trying to say?"

"The man you brought back from Berlin wasn't David Anderson."

"You're sure?" Bolan asked.

Kurtzman turned off the equipment and the screen went blank. He pushed back his wheelchair and laced the fingers of both hands together, cracking his knuckles. The room was absolutely silent.

"I'd bet the Farm on it."

RICHARD LANDIS DIDN'T LIKE bad news. There were some in the Berlin station who swore he didn't like good news, either. But what he liked least of all was rumor. And Berlin was the home of rumor. What he was getting lately was all chaff and no grain. As the CIA's chief of station in the most sensitive city on the European continent, he wanted to know what was going on, every minute of every day. Lately, he wasn't sure from minute to minute whether he knew anything at all.

For a long time, he hadn't been happy with the way things were slipping, slowly but surely in his estimation, out of control. Landis had a superstitious streak, a remnant of his days as captain of the baseball team at Yale. Right now, he saw omens everywhere he looked. Ever since the spy swap and David Anderson's disappearance, he had been trying to shake things up, and so far nothing had worked. It was funny about superstition, he mused. It was easy to settle on a formula when things were going well—if you won a ball game, you wore the same shirt until you lost. But nobody had ever been able to tell him how to put an end to an unlucky streak.

He was going over the morning field reports. Each one, in keeping with long-established custom, was neatly typed and stapled, with a summary sheet paper-clipped to the top page. If all around you was chaos, he believed, you didn't have to tolerate it in your own sphere of influence. More than one analyst had been bounced back to Langley for failure to accept that notion. Landis was a shrewd man, despite his idiosyncrasies, and he hadn't gotten, and kept, this post by being a buffoon.

What disturbed him was the prevalence of assumption and speculation in the summary sheets. He would check the reports themselves, just to make certain no one had been cutting corners in the summaries. Nevertheless, the lack of hard information was distressing. Intelligence, as he saw it, was the art and science of winnowing the real from the probable, divorcing the probable from the merely possible, and altogether disregarding the unthinkable.

This particular morning, that was no easy task. Rumor ridden though they were, the morning reports were full of the unthinkable. Source after source had heard that the KGB had managed to pull off the impossible. As unlikely as it might be, the prevalence of the theme was more than upsetting. It was downright alarming. Yet there it was, in typographically perfect black on white. Over and over again.

He knew the KGB was gifted in the area of disinformation. He knew that disinformation was frequently employed and was often marginally helpful to the Soviet scheme of the moment. But he had never seen it spring as it had this morning. If it were disinformation, he was sure there would have been sporadic early warnings. Little tidbits here and there would have come to the surface like bits of cork, bobbing on the tidal wave of data that ebbed and flowed on a daily basis across his desk.

This time, though, there had been no such early indications, the usual, inevitable consequence of judicious planting by the KGB, a source here and there given the same myth to tell and retell. They would crisscross the dark underbelly of Berlin, embellishing as they went. This time, too many people knew too much, too soon. This time, Richard Landis feared, the unthinkable might not only be thinkable: it might be true.

He skimmed the raw field reports, quickly riffling through the neatly typed pages. When he was certain the common thread was no accident of uninitiated analysis, he buzzed for his assistant COS.

Ralph Collingsworth knocked once and walked into his superior's office.

"What's up, Dick?" he asked, plopping down in the armchair across from Landis's desk.

"You getting anywhere on those pictures?"

"Not so far. We know the general area of the city where they were mailed, but that's all we've got. It isn't much."

"What about the photographer? Anything?"

"Zip. Gunter Vollman was about as clean as you can get. He had a variety of sleazy clients for pornography, that sort of thing, and I guess he could have met somebody who was using him, but so far there's no evidence of that. We can't link him with any intelligence service at all. Unless, of course, one of ours isn't leveling."

"It wouldn't be the first time," Landis grunted. He leaned back in his own chair, and stared at the ceiling. By now, he knew every defect in its acoustic tile. When stumped, he'd made a habit of designing constellations by linking the flaws together. He imagined it was a process not unlike that of the early astronomers, searching the sky for meaning.

"We're still digging, of course," Collingsworth reassured him. "But I don't think we'll find much. Even luck isn't going to help us on this one. We need a miracle."

"The whole thing makes no damned sense at all. Somehow, the guy knew about the exchange. Somebody, obviously somebody who knew the details, tipped him off. It had to be either us or the Sovs. But why?"

"That's what makes it hard to get a handle on, Dick. Why even bother? Anderson wasn't a big deal, and the Bulgarians were nobodies. Why bother to leak news that isn't news? And what the hell were the pictures for?"

"I've gone over it again and again. Every time I come up empty. The pictures don't show anything. I mean there's absolutely nothing in them of value to anyone. Not even the *National Enquirer* could make anything out of them."

"Maybe there's nothing there...."

"Then why kill the guy who took them, Ralph? If they're worthless, the man was killed for nothing. And somebody went to an awful lot of trouble to send them to you. Whoever it was must have known who you are and what you do for a living in this wasteland of a city. There's a piece missing somewhere, a big one. The puzzle will never fit without it, but I don't even know where to look."

Collingsworth nodded silently. After a moment, Landis continued. "Well, whatever, we should be hearing from Langley in a few hours. Maybe they'll come up with something. They can worry about it for a while."

"They'll just toss it back, you know."

"I know, Ralph, but I'm stumped on this one." Landis tilted his chair back to level and picked up the topmost print. It showed David Anderson in profile, part of the Buick in which he had been driven to Tempelhof, a stolid Ralph Collingsworth and little else. Landis turned the photo ninety degrees and examined it for what must have been the hundredth time since Collingsworth dumped the originals in his lap the day before.

Unable to quell the suspicion that there was a relationship between the photographs and the recent field reports, Landis was growing uneasy. When he factored in the inexplicable disappearance of David Anderson, he grew nearly paranoid.

"Have you seen the morning reports?" Landis asked his assistant.

Collingsworth nodded.

"What do you think?"

"Disinformation, most likely. We've seen it a thousand times. Why do you ask?"

"Because I think it's all connected. There's just too much unexplained about each of these things to disregard the possibility they're all part of a larger pattern."

"With all due respect, Dick, I think you're nuts. No way those field reports hold water. I don't give a damn if we have two dozen more saying the same thing. It just doesn't seem likely."

"And you don't see connections among the photos, Vollman's death and the disappearance of David Anderson?"

Collingsworth got to his feet and began to pace. He paused for a moment to light his pipe, then resumed his restless shuffle. "I suppose it's possible there's a connection of some kind. But without any reason that explains it, however convoluted, I'd have to say no. There *is* no simple explanation that takes account of all the facts."

"We'll see."

Collingsworth nodded. "Let me know if you get anything on those photos, will you?"

"First thing, Ralph. We have a three thirty, anyway. We should hear by then, if there's anything significant."

Collingsworth left his superior's office, and went to his own. Left alone, Landis leaned back in the chair again, and stared at the ceiling. Something was chewing at him, nagging the back of his consciousness. If he sat long enough, it would chew its way through to daylight.

The one thing he couldn't explain was the role of Anderson in all this. Somehow, he knew, it was crucial. Anderson was at the heart of the puzzle, and all the other pieces dangled just out of reach of reason. It was as if the vanished pilot were the bar that supported a mobile. Perhaps that was the key, Landis speculated.

He had been thinking of the affair as a jigsaw puzzle, an unknown number of cleanly cut pieces that could be assembled into a coherent, rational image. But a mobile was different. It didn't require a single image. It depended instead on balance. A series of discrete pieces, carefully placed and only tenuously connected, could still yield information and form a meaningful construction. Perhaps there was a way to balance what he had in such a way, still leaving room for additions.

Distillation of information from such a notion would, of course, be much more difficult. There would always be room for additional pieces. Gathered in groups, they could be distributed without disturbing the established order, simply adding to it. Added singly, they would be more difficult to place, but it was still not an impossible task. The only impossible thing about such an assemblage was knowing when you had all the pieces.

Landis turned his concentration back to the photos on his desk. Again taking the topmost print, the one that most clearly showed David Anderson, he turned it this way and that in his hands. And then the idea struck him, like a runaway freight.

He remembered the controversy that surrounded photos of the Texas School Book Depository, ever since the assassination of John F. Kennedy. Some of the pictures, he remembered, could be placed precisely in time, because there was a clock on top of the building that appeared in the photos. What was significant about those photos was what they *didn't* show. In several, there was no one in the window that had supposedly harbored Lee Harvey Oswald. Since it was difficult to explain how that could be the case if Oswald was the lone assassin of the president, those photos had disappeared, as completely as David Anderson seemed to have done. Maybe the key to these particular photos was what they *didn't* show.

But how can you tell whether something is missing when you don't know what is supposed to be present? He turned on the green-shaded banker's lamp that stood at the corner of his desk, reserved for moments that required close concentration and minute scrutiny. He pulled the lamp toward him and placed the photo flat on the desk, directly beneath it.

One more time, he examined the picture, his mind automatically breaking the flat plane into separate, contiguous regions. Inch by square inch he pored over it, looking for some emptiness, some absence. There had to be a reason for the photo in the first place. It would help if he knew who had arranged for its taking, and still more if he knew why it had been sent to the CIA. But he knew neither. He was on his own. And so far that wasn't good enough, not by half.

It had to relate to the coup pulled off by the KGB, but how? It had to explain some aspect of David Anderson's disappearance, but what? Angrily, Landis slammed his fist into the desk top, rattling the windows of the office and provoking a visit from his secretary.

"It's all right, Grace—never mind." The woman stared at him a long moment, uncertain whether to believe him. When he ignored her to turn his attention back to the picture, she left him alone, closing the door softly behind her.

8

Sitting in the fortresslike office at the electronic intelligence analysis laboratory, three men stared at a fourth. What he had told them moments before was barely credible. Don Albright, perhaps because he was the youngest, seemed to take the news the hardest.

"How can that possibly be true? That man was David Anderson. I saw him. I *know* it was." He paused a beat, to let his opinion sink in. There was not a flicker of agreement, no sign that he had even been heard. And Albright continued, "All right, then...if it wasn't Anderson, who was it? What's your machine got to say about that?"

Hal Brognola, sympathetic to the younger man's position, even sharing a little of his incredulity, said, "That's not up to Aaron to tell us. What we have to do is get some other photos, pictures of other possibilities. He can analyze them for us and tell us whether we have a match."

Albright stood, his hands waving wildly. "Other possibilities? *What* other possibilities? There *are* no other possibilities. Don't you understand?" He looked at Mack Bolan, hoping to see some little sign of agreement, or at least encouragement. Somebody had to be on his side.

But Bolan said nothing. Instead, he leaned back against the sofa, the big muscles rippling under the rolled-up sleeves of his shirt. He seemed to be in a trance, almost as if his mind were elsewhere. Albright, in desperation, turned back to Kurtzman.

"Are you absolutely sure?"

"To a mathematical certainty." Kurtzman, used to having his work disputed by those uncomfortable with its result, smiled. "Look, Don, I know it's hard to accept. How the hell do you think we feel? It's not a personal thing, and you can't afford to take it like one. It's out of our hands now. We know what didn't happen, and now we have to find out what did."

"And why..." Bolan's words, his first since the discussion began, hung in the air.

Brognola shifted uncomfortably in his chair. "I'm afraid we already have some idea. The National Security Agency has been monitoring some traffic. Nobody's sure yet what it means, but it looks like the KGB is up to something."

"Such as?" Albright, unused to Brognola's ways, asked the obvious question.

Bolan, impatient, shushed him. "Let's get this over with. I've got a feeling I'm going to have plenty to do before this is all over. Hal, I told you I didn't like this whole thing."

Brognola nodded. "And the smell I noticed is getting a lot stronger. The cable traffic seems to conform to some CIA intel from the Berlin office. Nothing certain, just rumors, or so it seems. But there are too many points of congruity."

The big Fed paused to bite down on the end of a cigar. But he didn't light it.

After he had moved the stogie from one side of his mouth to the other, Brognola continued. "The gist of CIA field intel is that the KGB has pulled a fast one. Nothing specific, just consistent reports. Too consistent to be disregarded. The cable traffic, some of it still indecipherable, is more opaque. But there's no doubt about it. We've got a penetration."

"What are they up to?" Bolan beat Albright to it. The words sent a chill up the young man's spine. The room seemed several degrees cooler.

"Assassination."

"Target?"

"Unknown."

"Who is he?" Bolan had lowered his voice. The last question was nearly a whisper.

"A specialist. We have his code name, but don't know any more than that. That, and the fact that he looks like David Anderson. Enough like him to fool us. Maybe he wouldn't have fooled us for long. That's most likely why he bolted the first chance he got."

"How do you know he's an assassin?" Albright leaned forward to hear the answer to his question. For a moment, Bolan was puzzled by the young man's eagerness. It seemed as if he were excited by the prospect of an assassin on the loose. An assassin who was already well on his way, and whose pursuers had no idea where he was going.

Then the warrior relaxed. He understood Albright's eagerness. The kid *was* excited, but it wasn't because he thought he was in the middle of a game. It was because, like Bolan himself in his younger days, he saw a chance to do something. Something useful. They had a chance to strike back, for once, instead of sitting back and letting things happen. A chance to act instead of react. The soldier smiled.

Brognola placed the soggy cigar into an ashtray before answering. "We know he's an assassin because he's taking orders from the old Thirteenth Department of the KGB. It's got a new name, Department V, Directorate S, but nothing else has changed. It's still the department that specialized in what our friends in Moscow call 'wet affairs.' Assassination."

"What's the code name they've given him?" The question was Bolan's.

"Petrov."

"Mean anything?"

"Not as far as we can tell."

Bolan leaned forward. "I don't get it. Why the hell would they go to all this trouble? There are lots easier ways to get a man inside the country. Ways that don't call so much attention to themselves. Hell, they could just sneak him in from Canada or Mexico. Papers are easy to fake, and a lot less important here than they are in Russia. They're up to something. You're right, Hal. This whole thing stinks."

"I agree. But what are they up to?"

"Maybe they want us to know about this," Albright suggested.

"Not likely," Kurtzman said.

"No, maybe Albright's got something," Brognola said. "Maybe they want us to be looking for this guy."

"Yeah," Bolan said. "Or maybe *that's* what they want us to think. If we think they're up to something else, and this is just a cover, we'll run around looking for something that doesn't exist."

"Why would they do that?" Albright asked.

"Things aren't always what they seem," Brognola said. "It's like a nest of Chinese boxes. You pull one open, and there's another one inside. You have to open every one before you know how many you've got. If you don't, the last one might have what you're looking for. It's sitting right there in front of you, and you don't even know it."

"Counterintelligence have anything to say?" Bolan asked.

"Not yet. This stuff is too new. And you know what they're like. Nothing means anything until they've torn it into so many pieces you can't put it back together. Half the time, things are all finished happening before they even decide something might."

"It's still worth a look, isn't it, Hal?"

"Yeah. I'm pulling some strings, see if I can shake something loose."

"I'll see what I can do about it," Bolan said. The warrior got to his feet. "Let's go, Don." Bolan was through the door before Albright even realized he was being asked to go along.

YURI KUSCENKO FELT comfortable in the Pontiac Gran Prix. Out of the dozens of American cars available at the KGB training facility at Balashikha, he had taken a shine to the sporty Pontiac. Now the used car salesman smiled as Kuscenko took the car through its paces. He knew by the driver's smile that he had a sale on his hands. The smile grew as the car wheeled through some tight turns in a wooded stretch of highway outside of Richmond, Virginia.

"She's a few years old, but I'll tell you, I hardly ever get one in such good shape. Only twenty thousand miles on 'er. I swear, I'd tell you she belonged to a little old lady, 'cept I know you wouldn't believe me." Lance Purvis expected the driver to laugh. When the man at the wheel didn't say anything, Purvis wondered what was wrong. The line always got a chuckle.

Kuscenko continued to push the Gran Prix through a series of tight turns. The car handled well. It was a few years old, a plus, because it would pass unnoticed through much of his trip. The salesman was getting on his nerves. If it wouldn't call unwanted attention to him, through the car, he'd as soon shoot Purvis and take the car as pay him for it. But he needed anonymity.

Kuscenko wheeled into a dusty patch by the side of the road, narrowly avoiding the closest trees as he spun the car into a 180-degree turn.

"Christ a'mighty!" Purvis said. His teeth were clenched and he grabbed the dash with both white-knuckled hands. "You test-drive a car, you sure as hell test 'er, don't you?"

"Sorry if I upset you," Kuscenko said. He turned to face Purvis. "But I know what I want, and what I expect. This is what I want. I just had to be sure it would *do* what I want. I'll take it. If the price is right.''

Kuscenko remembered the seemingly endless lectures about the greed of capitalists, American-style. He now knew he had to run through the usual ritual. Bargain, bargain hard, and try to get the car for less than it was worth. Typical of people who cared about money more than anything else, Americans would cut corners any way they could.

Purvis relaxed his grip on the dash. ''Well, now, how 'bout we get on back to the office and discuss it.''

Kuscenko nodded. He peeled out onto the highway, throwing the salesman hard against the bucket seat. Secure in the knowledge that he had a sale, Purvis didn't mind the hard ride.

An hour later, all the paperwork completed, Kuscenko peeled three thousand dollars in crisp, new hundreds off a roll in his jacket pocket. He slid them in a neat pile across the desk to Purvis.

''You can go register the car right now,'' Purvis said. ''There's a motor vehicle office right down the block. Them temporary plates are only good for a couple of weeks.''

Kuscenko nodded. ''Thank you. I'll do that.''

Purvis stood and reached across the desk to shake Kuscenko's hand. ''You take good care of 'er, son. You hear? She's a good little buggy.''

''Buggy?''

''The car, boy. Hellfire, I know you're young, but you ain't that young. You never heard a car called a buggy?'' Purvis shook his head. ''I must be gettin' old.''

Kuscenko smiled. ''I was just thinking about something else, that's all. All I heard was buggy.''

''Now, son, you don't have to try and make me feel better. We all get old. I just didn't think it'd sneak up on me so fast. Been a pleasure doin' business with you, Mr. Anderson.''

Kuscenko walked to the door, opened it and smiled at the car. He had waited a long time. This assignment was going to be more fun than he had thought. There were, after all, compensations for the long hours of training, the deprivations, the bone-crushing discipline. A few days with his favorite American car would make up for a lot. But not everything.

He juggled the keys in his hand, descended the pair of wooden steps to the gravel of the used car lot and walked around the Gran Prix once, running his hand over the smooth, polished metal. He got in and drove carefully out of the lot. It would no longer do to call attention to himself. From this point on, he had to be as inconspicuous as possible, and try to blend in with his surroundings.

He drove slowly down the streets of the quiet, midsize American city, getting used to the feel of the car. From now on, it would be his sole means of transportation. As much as he had disliked the unctuous demeanor of the car salesman, he had had to make the purchase. He wouldn't need the car for long, not as long as the temporary plates would last, and he didn't want to sign anything. No car rentals, no airline reservations.

He'd used Anderson's name, as he'd been instructed. But it didn't come easily to him. The less he had to identify himself, the better off he'd be. He'd left a small trail, not untraceable, but small enough. Anderson was not an uncommon name. Someone would have to look pretty hard to find his trail.

Yuri Kuscenko smiled as he left the city limits of Richmond. The open country made him feel less trapped. The countryside was more reminiscent of his homeland than the confines of the city. He felt less alien, more human. There was an elemental, almost prehuman, pleasure in being his own boss. It was only for a short time, he knew, but that wouldn't stop him from relishing the freedom.

He turned on the radio and idly twirled the dial, looking for something he could relate to. The rock music that blared out of the car's stereo speakers was raucous when compared to the tame, state-sanctioned version permitted for the consumption of Soviet citizens. It made him nervous. The wild guitars and thumping bass were too primitive for his taste, unaccustomed as it was to the American top thirty.

Now it was time for the next step. In a way, he almost regretted it. Not because he disagreed with the plans, but because carrying them out would signal the end of his freedom. Wild as the music was, there might, after all, be something to be said for a country where you could buy a car in an hour instead of signing up for a four-year wait.

Well, one step at a time. One foot in front of the next. He'd get where he was supposed to go. Or not. It was, after all, a free country.

9

Mack Bolan was getting impatient. The thing he hated most was waiting. There was too much to do in a war like Bolan's. Waiting time was down time. But cancer didn't sleep; it ate away at the guts in the dark, and that peculiar cancer embodied in the KGB was no different from any other kind.

Now, as he waited for Albright to check with counterintelligence, there was nothing else he could do. The tools of his trade lay cleaned and ready on the motel night table. Bolan thought he could hear them rust as he paced around the room. Boundless energy confined was the cruelest form of imprisonment, and Bolan was, at this moment, a prisoner. Trapped by the slowly moving wheels of bureaucracy, he felt angry, frustrated. He turned off the light and lay down in the semidarkness.

Frustration was his worst enemy, and he knew it. It could make him careless, sloppy in his work. And carelessness could cost him his life. But he was anxious to get on with his one-man war. Every moment he waited was a moment irretrievably lost, while the cancer grew, its silent corruption gnawing away at America's vitals. In the quiet twilight of the motel room, its inexorable advance grew to a roar in his ears.

Albright would need some time. Bolan accepted that, but wished there were something he could do. He needed action, craved it like a junkie his next fix. There is a fine line between dedication and obsession. Bolan's dedication had been taken for obsession by more than one bureaucrat. It accounted for his presence on the shit list of more than one organization supposedly dedicated to the same goal as he was.

Yeah. Dedicated. Some of these lazy bastards were content to sit back and draw a check, waiting for retirement. Others were too blind to realize how securely their hands were tied by the system they sought to serve. But the worst ones, the ones for which Bolan had nothing but contempt, were those whose dedication was available to the highest bidder.

Somewhere at the heart of the conundrum, Bolan believed, there was such a man. Someone was orchestrating events from a vantage point too close to home. Whoever he was, he was close enough to see things clearly, perhaps even control them. Not totally, maybe, but enough to make a difference. There was nothing Bolan could do about it now. But there would come a time when he could. When all this was over, that man was a dead man. Bolan would see to it.

Personally.

He had almost drifted off into the restless sleep that comprised most of his rest. The thump was so soft that it could have been a shoe falling to the floor a couple of rooms down. Maybe a car door closing in a nearby garage. But Bolan left nothing to chance. There was something too bizarre about the entire sequence of events so far to take anything for granted, anything at all. Bolan sat up slowly, his ears cocked in the direction of the sound.

Leaving the bed, he grabbed the Beretta 93-R from the night table and moved to stand beside the doorway to his room in stocking feet. There was a second thump. This time there was no mistaking it. And by its sound, Bolan knew it wasn't anything innocent. No way.

Whoever was making the sound was trying to be quiet. Bolan leaned away from the door and pulled the curtain back from the window. The pavement outside was stained a dull orange by the setting sun. The color glinted off the chrome of several cars parked at an angle across the front of the row of motel suites. Bolan dropped the curtain and listened again.

The silence was overwhelming. He remembered Vietnam, and how quiet it would get just before all hell broke loose, as if everything in the jungle had fled. In a few minutes now the sun would be totally gone. Whoever was stalking him was waiting for that moment when the sun would disappear before making his move.

Bolan waited impatiently. The action was so close now, and still he was forced to sit on his hands. There was another thud, this one from the back of the building. Bolan deliberated for a few moments before risking a peek out the back way. The last thing he wanted was to be caught in the middle of the room. No duck was deader than a sitting one.

The faint orange smear at the edge of the curtain was growing darker. Deciding he had to make his move immediately or stay where he was, Bolan stepped softly across the floor to the bathroom door. He stepped into the humid room, aware of the faucet dripping in the tub. There was a scraping sound at the window, followed by the tinny rasp of a screen hitting the ground. A muffled curse and a cautionary hush told Bolan what he wanted to know. There were at least two men at the back.

They were certain to try to open the bathroom window next, and Bolan accommodated them, reaching up under the curtain to silently release the hook that held the window down. He drew back. The next step was to slip out of the bathroom and block its door.

Bolan was banking on coordination as a key ingredient in the assault. Anything he could do to disrupt it would buy him precious time. Once in the bathroom, the men would be slowed down. Dragging a metal-legged chair over, he propped it in place under the knob. The door opened inward, but the top of the chair, wedged tightly against the frame, would prevent it being yanked open in a hurry. Satisfied the chair would hold long enough, he grabbed Big Thunder from the nightstand and strapped it on. Even in the dimness, there was an evil glint to its polished steel.

Free now to concentrate on the front, Bolan positioned himself across from the bathroom. He could keep his eye on the front and, time permitting, throw a couple of slugs into the bathroom through the door. With any luck, he'd nail one of the bastards. At least he would slow them down a little.

Lying on the floor under the window, Bolan prepared for the assault. There was another thud in the bathroom, this one heavier. One of the raiders had landed inside. The moment was coming. Bolan felt the tingle in his combat-honed nerves. With a crash, the front door burst open. Two men were momentarily framed in the pale blue glow from the motel sign. Bolan didn't wait. Aiming carefully, he squeezed the Beretta's trigger, almost caressing it. There was a soft spitting sound, followed immediately by another. The lead man dropped to the floor, his body tossed aside by the impact of the 9 mm parabellum slugs. His forehead was gone.

The second intruder stopped, puzzled. He seemed disoriented, and bent to help his friend to his feet, as if he had simply tripped and fallen. Bolan's next slug shattered the skull of intruder number two, just in front of the hairline at his temple. With the sound of a ruptured pomegranate, the second raider's head slammed into the floor.

The Beretta's whisper was too low for the men in the bathroom to hear. The doorknob rattled, and the chair started to shake. Anxious to turn the tables, Bolan sped in a crouch across the floor of the small room. He was so close to the carpet that he could smell the chemicals used to clean it, and the years of cigarette smoke that lay securely in its fibers.

As he reached the wall beside the bathroom door, a slug ripped through the door panel and slammed into the opposite wall. The doorknob stopped rattling for a few seconds. Since it was too risky to try anything else, Bolan reached out with his foot and kicked the chair loose during the lull. The knob rattled again, and this time the door came open. The raiders were taken by surprise, and the man closest to the door fell backward, momentarily losing his balance. Regaining it, he cursed and came bounding out of the doorway. Bolan's leg was extended across the entrance, and the man tripped and fell heavily. His gun slipped from his grasp and skittered across the carpet. It landed with a thud against the baseboard.

The second man fell over his partner. He tried to rise, and Bolan shot him once in the back of the head. He fell prostrate, pinning his struggling ally to the floor long enough for Bolan to knock the latter unconscious. The racket had been minimal, but the Executioner had to make sure no one had heard enough to call the motel manager or the police. He kicked the yawning front door shut, closed the bathroom door and checked the curtains. There was no indication that anyone had heard a thing. He clicked on the small reading light over the bed to examine the carnage. The unconscious man started to groan, rolling his head from side to side.

Bolan sat with his back to the wall, facing the door and keeping one eye on the slowly awakening gunner. He knew it was possible that the four were not alone. If they had company, and failed to return, one of two things would happen: backup would come bursting through the door, or they'd hightail it to the nearest secure phone.

Bolan knew what he'd do in their shoes. On the other hand, there were a lot of unknowns about this situation. It was best to wait for Albright. But he couldn't let the young agent walk into any remaining hitters outside. Bolan slipped on his shoes, knelt behind the still-groaning gunman and rapped him solidly behind the left ear with the butt of his AutoMag. He slipped out through the bathroom window and made a quick sweep of the motel grounds. None of the cars in front was occupied.

As he rounded the back of the long row of identical units, he caught a glimmer in the trees behind the motel. Some-one had lit a cigarette. Bolan stepped into the darkness, his element, without a moment's hesitation. In a small clearing among the trees, he spotted a van. From his vantage point among the trees, he could see two men, both in the front seat. Without a doubt, they were waiting for something. Waiting for someone. And they wouldn't have to wait long. They were about to receive an unexpected visitor.

Circling through the trees, Bolan approached the van from the rear. He knew he didn't have much time. He also knew he had to make certain the men in the van were con-nected to the attack on his room. He worked his way among the trees, stepping carefully, until he was directly behind the vehicle.

Stopping to listen, he could hear muffled conversation. The van was still too distant for him to hear clearly, despite its open windows. Bolan dropped to the ground and slith-ered forward until he could reach out and touch the rear bumper of the dark gray Volkswagen. Listening again, he could hear what the men were saying now. They were ar-guing whether to wait, to call for help or to go on in them-selves. Bolan knew what he needed to know: the argument was in Russian.

The faint illumination of his watch dial told him Al-bright was scheduled to arrive in only fifteen minutes. That left very little time to do what had to be done. The Execu-tioner checked his Beretta and hauled himself to one knee. Pressing himself flat to the rear of the van, he debated which side to hit first. As he watched the driver's side, he noticed an arm extend out the window, just long enough to flick ashes from a cigarette. It was long enough to make up Bolan's mind.

Between the conversation and the cigarette, the driver was less likely to be alert, relying on his partner for vigilance. Bolan paused until he heard the conversation begin again, raised the Beretta to shoulder height and rushed along the van's left side toward its front.

Abreast of the door, he heard a muffled shout of alarm. The window began to roll up as he reached in and pressed the muzzle of the 93-R against the driver's left mastoid process. The ordinary whisper of the automatic pistol was more silent than usual. But no less deadly.

The driver, his brain tissue spattered all over the dash, slumped forward. The Executioner took aim at the second man and squeezed off a 3-round burst. Fragments of all three slugs starred the closed window behind the passenger. Rags of blood wiped across the glass, darkening it to the color of the woods outside. In the van, nothing moved.

Sprinting around the corner of the motel, Bolan headed for the door to his room. As he opened it, a car pulled up. He turned as the driver killed the engine and lights at the same time, opening the door almost immediately. When the dome light came on, Bolan recognized Don Albright. The young agent slammed the door of the car before he noticed him.

"Wait until you hear what I found out!" Albright said. He looked flushed, but Bolan couldn't tell whether it was from excitement or exertion. He pushed the young agent through the door into the motel room, closing the door just as Albright clicked on the lights.

"Jesus! What the hell happened here? Are you all right?" The questions tumbled over themselves in Albright's anxiety to get them all out at once. "Who are these guys? How did they know you were here?"

"I was about to ask you the same question," Bolan said, gesturing toward one of the room's two chairs. "Sit down."

10

"All right," Bolan snapped. "We don't have much time. Tell me what you found out, and then I've got a package for you to deliver."

Albright gulped. Looking around the dimly lit room, his eyes were bulging. For a long moment he stared at Bolan as if transfixed, then he bolted for the bathroom. The sound of retching was nearly drowned out by the running water, as the young CIA man yanked the toilet flush valve and held it wide open. The sound seemed to go on forever, and Bolan waited, sympathetic to the young man's situation. It was probably the first time he'd seen a man shot to death. Three at one time was more than most stomachs could handle.

The sounds died away as Bolan sat, waiting patiently, in his chair. In a few moments, Albright reappeared, wiping his mouth on the shabby towel, the faded monogram of the motel crumpled in front of his face.

"I...uh, I'm sorry. It's just that I..."

Bolan silenced him with a wave of his hand. "Forget it, Don. It happens to everybody the first time. Me too."

Albright looked at Bolan as if seeing him for the first time. "You too?"

"Yeah. I'll tell you about it sometime, maybe. Right now, we've got things to do. What did you find out?"

"Okay, first the hard stuff. Our man Anderson, or whoever he is, bought himself a car in Richmond."

"You're certain of that?"

"Yeah. After he left Langley, he must have hidden in the woods awhile, then hitched a ride. He killed a guy named McGuire, and a cop. He drove McGuire's car to Richmond and left it on the street."

Bolan stood up. "Did he rent a car in Richmond? Take a bus?"

"They were checking out rental agencies and bus stations the last I heard. But sit down, there's more. Not hard, but much more interesting."

Bolan remained standing, but waited for the young man to continue.

"I've got a friend in counterintelligence. He couldn't tell me everything, you know—they're pretty strange guys. But he told me a lot that I think is relevant to what's been happening. It seems like we have an internal argument going on."

"What kind of argument?" Bolan made no attempt to disguise the impatience in his voice.

"I'm not sure exactly—the guy was pretty vague. As near as I could make it out, though, what's happened is this: in the past two years, there've been two major defections of high-ranking KGB types. One came over to our side in Berlin right away. The other stayed in place for eighteen months. Then it started to get hot, and the agency had to get him out in a hurry. They smuggled him in through Mexico. Trouble is, the defectors contradict each other. One says black, the other says white. Nobody knows for sure which one is telling the truth, or if either of them is."

Bolan busied himself with the Beretta while he listened. He slammed a new clip home as Albright paused. He stared at Albright expectantly. After a moment, the young agent realized he was supposed to continue.

"Counterintelligence is split into three factions. One bunch trusts the first defector, a guy named Balanov; a second, which includes my friend, thinks Balanov is a plant, so they believe the other defector, Korienko. Everybody else believes neither one of them is genuine. Their thinking goes something like this: it's too much of a coincidence that we get two fish in so short a time, when we can go yours without a nibble. According to this theory, both defectors are here for the same purpose—to confuse things to the point of total paralysis."

"Any reason to believe the third group is wrong?"

"Yeah, plenty, depending on whether you're a Balanov fan or a Korienko booster. Both men have given some pretty valuable intel. Balanov gave Berlin enough information to roll up two strings, one in the West German BND. Korienko blew a string in London. MI6 had been looking for a heavy-duty leak for more than a year. Korienko's information gave them enough to find it and plug it."

"Could they both be genuine?"

"Yeah, they could. But nobody wants to believe that's possible, so nobody openly admits it. My guess is there are some people who think so in each of the three groups. They've been working on Balanov since he came over. Nearly two years now. So far, there's a lot of contradictions in his story, but not enough to hang him with. They keep giving him rope, and he keeps dangling, but nobody's been able to spring the trapdoor on him. If you've been under interrogation for two years, it's pretty hard not to contradict yourself."

Dolan nodded. This was all alien to him, a side of the war he seldom got near. He knew the mechanics, and appreciated the subtleties of thought, but it didn't seem to have much to do with his current problem.

"I don't see what any of this has to do with Anderson's disappearance. Whoever he really is."

"That's the interesting part. My friend Alan—Alan Mitchell, the guy who gave me all this background—thinks the KGB wants to take out the other guy, Korienko, because he's genuine.''

"Why? Why not let counterintelligence stew for a while? If they can't decide what to do, they won't do anything at all.''

"Because if Korienko *is* genuine, when we're finally sure of it, he'll be a gold mine. This presupposes Korienko knows something the KGB can't protect.''

"Such as?'' Bolan asked. He already knew the answer, but he wanted to hear someone else say it.

"A mole—at least that's what Mitchell thinks. Somebody so deep they can't dig him out in time to save him, and somebody so important to them they don't want to lose him, either.''

"Why doesn't somebody just ask Korienko?''

"Because half the time these guys know things they don't realize they know. They walk around like time bombs. If we learn as much as we can from them, and cross-check it against other information, pieces fall into place. The guy with the key piece doesn't even have a clue. Alan thinks Korienko is a smoking gun.''

"Did he tell you why?''

"No. He said he couldn't.''

"Any ideas?''

"Just one: we lost our own mole recently. The first one we'd ever been able to get into the KGB. There are rumors, unconfirmed of course, that he was blown. The problem is, there's a dozen people who could have been responsible. Backtracking takes time—more time than we have.''

Bolan exhaled softly, cursing under his breath.

Albright continued. "There's one more possibility.''

Bolan waved him on.

"There's a series of public appearances by the President scheduled for the next two weeks. If the imposter Anderson is an assassin, the President could be his target. In the absence of any other information, we have to treat it as a real threat."

"What I want to know is where this guy has gone. How the hell could he just disappear? I'm no rookie when it comes to moving around underground, but this guy just fell off the earth."

"Unless he has help," Albright suggested.

"Which brings me to my next question. How did our friends here—" he gestured toward the dead men "—know where I was? Did you mention to anybody where I was staying?"

"Of course not."

"I have to tell you, I don't like it. Only you and Brognola knew I was staying here. I know Hal wouldn't let it slip. I also know, though, he might have reason to pass the word informally, because of the situation."

"What are we going to do with the bodies?"

"Leave them."

"Here?"

"Where else?"

Albright paused. There was something about this business that seemed less than human. The brutality he had been exposed to in the past few days was about as far as you could get from the dispassionate analysis of raw data that had been his reason for joining the agency in the first place. His inclination to use logic to draw conclusions seemed like a tool of fairly limited utility. The CIA was interested in his skills, and few others seemed to care. But now he wasn't so sure he'd made the right career decision. He wasn't cut out for slaughter, no matter what the cause or how pressing the justification.

"We do have one who's only sleeping," Bolan said. It sounded like a grim joke, but when Albright looked at the soldier's features, there was no trace of a smile.

"Sleeping?"

"Yeah. The guy on the bottom isn't dead. I think it might be useful to ask him a few questions."

"Like what?"

"Brognola will know." Bolan stood up and walked over to the pair of hitters nearest the bathroom door. "Grab an arm." He yanked the dead man on top, spilling the body in a heap in the corner.

"What about this guy?" Albright nodded at the unconscious man.

"I'll tell Brognola where he can be found. He'll take it from there. And he'll take care of the other two—don't worry."

"What do you want me to do?"

"Go outside and around behind the motel. I'll hand the package out to you."

Albright stood as if he didn't believe what he'd just heard.

"Get moving," Bolan snapped.

Albright backed toward the door and opened it without looking. For a moment Bolan thought the kid would cut and run. He watched the young agent struggle with his sense of decency. Duty was hard-pressed to justify what lay on the floor. It was that way for most rookies. Even in Nam, Bolan remembered good soldiers, the best, who had trouble the first week.

The raw, elemental brutality of that war had been a trauma for some and for others a cauterizing fire. For Bolan himself it had been even more. He had learned there the skills that, unbeknownst to him at the time, would become the foundation for the rest of his life. As long as he lived, he would never forget the train of events that had brought him so far in so short a time. The blood and fire he had waded through since Vietnam, more often than not up to his neck, had so far left him scarred but intact. The next few minutes would tell him whether or not Albright would be a reliable ally in the next few days.

As he wondered, Bolan stripped wire from the larger of the two lamps in the room, and from the television set. Taking the still-unconscious man by the collar, he dragged him clear of the dead man and tied the hitter's hands behind his back. Working quickly, he doubled the wire and brought the man's legs together, tying them securely in place. With the heavier wire of the television set, he bound the man's limp legs to his wrists, then, grunting softly, he hauled the prostrate form to its knees.

Dropping to his own knees, Bolan hoisted the sleeping form to his shoulder and moved smoothly into the bathroom. Without ceremony, he tossed the unconscious man through the bathroom window. He heard him land with a thud.

"Jesus, give a guy some warning," Albright cursed.

Bolan stuck his head through the window. The young CIA man was kneeling on the ground, checking the wires that bound the gunman. "You could have popped the wires loose. Don't you know anything about physics, for Christ's sake?"

Bolan laughed for the first time in days. "I thought maybe you might not be there."

"Like hell," Albright said. "I'm in this one for the long haul. There's no way you can handle everything by yourself. Although I have to admit you haven't done badly so far. But I have my orders, and unless things have changed lately, orders are orders, as wacky as they might seem."

"Wacky isn't the word I'd use to describe what we're into here," Bolan said.

"Shit," Albright answered. "You know another word, I'd love to hear it."

Bolan dropped softly to the ground, just to the left of the deadweight he'd hefted through the window. Without another word, he reached down to grab the hitter under the shoulders. Albright, he knew, was going to be all right. And

Bolan was going to need all the help he could get before this one was over.

Albright grabbed the other end of the package without being told. "Where are we taking him, or will I know when we get there?"

"There's a van behind those trees."

"That what they used to get here?"

"I don't know. There were two more men in it. I don't know if they were backup or transportation."

"Two more?" Albright almost lost his grip. "You mean you killed five men since I spoke to you on the phone?"

Bolan said nothing. When presented so starkly, it seemed inhuman. At his recent trial, down in Texas, he'd admitted to killing more than two thousand people. Everything from mobsters to Kremlin lackeys. The sheer weight of the numbers seemed to numb everyone in the courtroom, not excluding Bolan himself. As with the Holocaust victims, totals that large seemed somehow to dehumanize the grim facts. But three, five, even a dozen...those were small enough numbers that the mind could wrestle with them on a human level.

More often than not, Bolan avoided thinking about such things. But from Albright's perspective it was all new. The five dead men might as well have been the first instead of just the latest. As they approached the van Bolan signaled Albright to stop. Whether to spare Albright's feelings or because of some tacit recognition of the young man's perspective, Bolan lowered the burden to the ground more gently than he might otherwise have done.

While Albright waited in the trees, Bolan slipped up to the van to check it out. The men in the front seat lay as still as they had when he left them. Moving to the back of the van, Bolan tried the door and, as he expected, found it unlocked. He left the door ajar and slipped back to Albright. Together, they covered the last few yards in a hurry. Sliding the unconscious man into the rear of the van, Bolan closed the door.

"You have a gun?" He looked at Albright.

"Yes."

"Good, you stay here. Make sure nothing goes wrong. I'm going to call Brognola, let him know where to find the van. When he gets here, you tell him all the rest, about the defectors and that I want him to look for leaks. I'm not going hunting, even for an assassin, with my back exposed. I'll be heading for Richmond next, but tell Brognola I'll call him tomorrow morning for anything new on Anderson."

Albright nodded. He watched the big man disappear back into the trees. He moved so comfortably in the dark, Albright knew, because that's where he lived.

It was where he belonged.

11

The following morning, Bolan called Brognola early. His night's sleep had been fitful, and he kept seeing the look on Albright's face as the young man first took in the carnage strewn about the motel room floor. Bolan was worried *for* Albright, not *about* him. The kid had shown him something the night before, something he liked. A lot.

But there was work to do, and Bolan was getting antsy. He knew Brognola would have gone right to work. The goon sent to him gift wrapped via Albright would not have got a good night's sleep, either. And Brognola would have pulled out all stops. They needed something about the phony Anderson, and they needed it now. Bolan was hoping for that one slip, the little smudge on an otherwise blank sheet of paper. Without it, there was virtually no chance they could catch the assassin until it was too late. Especially for his victim.

The big Fed sounded groggy when he answered the phone. "Hello. Who is this? What time is it?"

"It's me, Bolan, and it's six-thirty. You got anything for me?"

"For Christ's sake, man. It's not even light out yet."

"I do my best work in the dark," Bolan said. "What have you got for me?"

"Not much, I'm afraid. We worked on our friend all night long. The guy wouldn't say a thing. Nothing. I only got in an hour ago."

"They still working on him?"

"Not anymore."

"Why the hell not?"

"He managed to kill himself somehow. Shellfish toxin, they think. Like the stuff Powers was supposed to use. Nobody knows how he managed to smuggle it into interrogation with him. But he sure as hell did. And he's sure as hell dead."

"Damn! What about Anderson after he ditched the car he stole?"

"A Mr. David Anderson bought himself a dark gray Gran Prix in Richmond. A guy named Purvis, Lance Purvis of Richmond Motorama, sold it to him. It had temporary plates. I'm waiting for the number now."

"What else?"

"That's it. He paid cash and moved on."

"I'll call you from Richmond."

Bolan hung up without saying goodbye. He finished dressing and strapped on his AutoMag. The stainless steel .44 rode calmly on his hip. When the Beretta was in place, he slipped into a gray tweed jacket and sprinted for his car. The Dodge was old and nondescript, but its powerful V-8 engine would come in handy.

The car's throaty rumble drowned out the squeal of rubber as Bolan left a patch on the asphalt and pulled into the nearly empty streets. Richmond wasn't that far away, and with any luck, he'd know where the hell he was going before noon. The freeway system of Washington, D.C. wasn't arranged in the most logical pattern, but with little traffic, the only thing he had to worry about was the speed limit. Once out in the open country between D.C. and Richmond, even that wouldn't be a problem.

The trip was more than 150 miles by the most direct route, and Bolan intended to swing to the west, circling around the heavily populated easternmost reaches of Virginia. Hard pushing would get him to Richmond by ten o'clock.

The Dodge rumbled reassuringly as Bolan passed into the wooded mountains. It felt good to be moving at last. God help Lance Purvis if he'd taken the day off. There was so little time, and so much of it was slipping by to no purpose. Purvis, of course, might not have any idea where the bogus Anderson was headed, but he might have noticed something that could provide a clue, and if he had, Bolan was going to make sure he remembered it.

As he drove, he had the time to mull over several nagging questions. Somebody was leaking information about him, somebody who knew more than he could afford to have known. He had trusted Brognola with his life far too many times for him to suspect the man from Justice. The kid was an unknown quantity, but there was good stuff there—Bolan had seen it. He knew Albright would be right there at the end, and on his side.

The range of alternatives wasn't large, but every one of the possible leaks was unthinkable . . . unless Mitchell's theory was correct, and there was a KGB mole high up in the agency. If that were the case—and there was no reason to discard the possibility at the moment—the only answer would be complete and perfect cover. Bolan would have to dig as deep as the mole, even deeper. He'd go underground, where he was no stranger, and stay there until this job was finished.

It would mean lying to Albright, and making sure Brognola said nothing to anyone. Bolan hated the prospect of the former, but had relied on the latter enough to know it would be no problem. The questions were too important to be ignored: why had he been led to the safe house by the Bulgarian? How had anyone known he was staying at the motel? Who had killed Gunter Vollman, the photographer? Why had the pictures been sent to Collingsworth? Where had the KGB goon gotten the poison to do himself in?

On and on, one question to the mile, it seemed. As Bolan drove, the flurry of puzzles circled in his brain like a swarm of angry bees. The more he paid attention to them, the louder they buzzed. And there wasn't an answer in sight, not even to the simplest of them.

By the time he reached the outskirts of Richmond, Bolan was weary. The uncertainty took its toll on him, as it always did. It was the toughest part of his chosen career. This warrior, unlike most soldiers, made his own command decisions. The ultimate responsibility lay solely with him. He wouldn't have it any other way, not when so much was riding on any decision, but it wasn't the easiest road to follow.

Downtown Richmond was less than fifteen minutes away now. Bolan pulled into a gas station to refuel. As the attendant gassed up the Dodge, Bolan hit the head and engaged the gas jockey in conversation when he returned. It didn't take him long to learn the location of Richmond Motorama. It was the largest used car dealership in Richmond.

As soon as he'd paid for the gas, Bolan headed straight for the car agency. He pulled into the lot in a spray of white gravel, stopping in front of the office. Inside, a receptionist told him Lance Purvis was out on the lot and invited him to take a seat. Bolan was through the door before she finished speaking.

"Mr. Purvis?"

A ruddy-faced man was bent over the windshield of a Chevy Camaro, checking the price sticker. He leaned in to look at the mileage on the odometer, then turned to face the newcomer. "That's me, partner. What can I do for you?"

"I need some information fast."

"I sell cars, friend. You want information, try the library."

Bolan reached out to take the salesman's tie in one large, tanned fist. "You don't understand. The information I need is something you might have." He jerked the tie, and it began cutting off the salesman's wind. He jerked it again, and Purvis turned a brighter red.

"Hey! Let go of my tie." He reached out to grab Bolan's arm. The fat fingers of his right hand found something that seemed made of steel. He decided he'd made a mistake in assuming a belligerent attitude. "All right, for Christ's sake, let go. How the hell can I talk to you if I can't breathe?"

Bolan let go of the tie with a final tug. Purvis reached up to his collar, struggled with his chubby hands to loosen the tie and undid his collar to rub his neck, now vividly marked with a narrow white band where the tie had bitten into the red skin.

"What kind of information you looking for?"

"You sold a car the other day, a dark gray Gran Prix. About four years old."

"What of it?"

"I need something."

"Like?"

"The man who bought it."

"You a cop?"

Bolan reached out for the tie again, playing with it idly while he stared into the salesman's frightened face. "Does it make a difference?"

"Not to me. I got my money in cash. Hey, wait a minute. That was your money, wasn't it? Them bills he paid with, I should have known. You ain't no cop, that's for sure. What are you, a drug dealer? They was brand-new bills."

"Where is he?"

"How should I know?"

"Think about it. Did he say anything about where he was going? Anything at all?"

"We didn't talk much. He was kind of surly. I knew there was something funny about him."

"What do you mean?"

"You know, I made a joke. He didn't get it. About the little old lady owning the car. He looked at me like he'd never heard of it before."

Bolan nodded. "He hadn't. Did he ask anything, directions, anything at all? Mention where he was going?"

"Like I said, he didn't talk much. He had a couple of maps, though. I seen 'em when he test-drove the car. They was on the seat."

"Maps of where?"

"New Orleans was on top. I didn't see the other one, though. There was two of 'em."

"That's all?"

"That's it. Listen, you a cop, or what?"

"No."

"I didn't think so. I know lots of cops. You ain't like any of 'em. It's kind of funny. You're more like he is than anybody else I ever seen. You guys partners or something—is that it? He burn you on a deal?"

"Not yet," Bolan said. He turned abruptly and strode toward the Dodge. "And if I can help it, he won't."

"I bet," Purvis called after him. "Listen, I can make you a good deal for that there Dodge. You want to deal, you all come back. Anytime."

New Orleans. New Orleans and someplace else. But where? There were a number of large cities between Richmond and New Orleans. Memphis, Nashville, Lexington. Hell, even Cincinnati wasn't that far out of the way. The map didn't even have to be a city. The only thing to do was go with what he had. And he had New Orleans.

The guy was driving, and had a big lead. He was probably already there. Driving after him would be too slow. Bolan headed back to D.C., this time taking the most direct route. He broke the speed limit most of the way, slowing down only when he reached the outer edge of the District.

Unlike most men, the Executioner couldn't just throw a few things into an overnight bag and carry it on the plane. His profession was specialized, his tools exotic.

He'd have to pack a few things into a bag for the luggage compartment of the flight. But this was it. From this point on, he was down, and he was going to stay down until it was over. There was too much monkey business going on. He'd stay in touch with Brognola by phone, but nobody, not even the big Fed, was going to know where he was or where he was going.

As he packed, the warrior realized he was engaging in the oldest form of warfare. A hunter was stalking another hunter who was, in turn, stalking him. Round and round, an endless dance that whirled them both along in its own momentum. Reaching deeper and deeper into the head and heart of each man, the contest would command every resource, every last reserve of courage and stamina. Until, in the end, a solitary player would remain.

Bolan had played the game before. And, as always, he wondered if it would be his last. Seldom, if ever, had the odds been so firmly against him. He had little knowledge of his adversary, less of what the man's intentions were. Field experience was useful, to a point, but it was purchased at an exorbitant cost. Only time would tell whether Mack Bolan could afford the price.

And if he couldn't, he would never know.

12

The flight from Dulles to New Orleans was uneventful. When you live life on the scale of Mack Bolan, there's not much in coach to make you raise an eyebrow. As the plane landed, Bolan was already planning his first move in New Orleans. Before takeoff he had touched base with Brognola and let the big Fed know he was going underground.

Brognola had wondered aloud whether Bolan suspected Albright was the leak, but the Executioner had put his mind at ease on that score. The kid was solid. Inexperienced, sure, but Bolan was happy to have him on board. Even so, he knew it was going to be a long haul, and the kid was going to ride the bench. Bolan would pinch-hit him somewhere along the line. In the meantime, he was a gofer.

Brognola had no more news about "Anderson." Further photo analysis of the man pretending to be David Anderson had only confirmed that the man flown in from Tempelhof wasn't the American spy pilot. He was believed to be a Soviet assassin. Nobody knew who the hell he was. Flying blind wasn't high on Bolan's list of favorite hobbies. He'd do it, but he sure as hell wasn't going to learn to like it.

As the carousel churned its endless cargo of luggage, Bolan waited impatiently for his own. The bag looked nondescript. Its contents were anything but. Unable to carry the Beretta or the AutoMag on the plane, he had been forced to pack them. Since there was some room left in the bag, an

Uzi filled the vacuum rather nicely. In a smaller case, the long-range Weatherby Mark IV traveled first class.

When the bags finally appeared, Bolan made his way to the car rental counter. He wanted something with a little muscle, and had phoned ahead for a Buick. The big cars were no longer fashionable, but they served a purpose. You never knew who or what you'd be chasing. Something that handled but could take a heavy beating was ideal. Especially if it blended in well with a crowd. The Buick was as American as baseball, and just as unobtrusive.

The tall blonde behind the counter took her time, spending long minutes in mooning conversation with a slender dark-haired man. She obviously couldn't wait to finish her shift. Processing rentals was a low priority. When, finally, the paperwork was finished and she handed Bolan the keys, she seemed to notice him for the first time. She smiled, showing a lot of teeth. When her smile was ignored, she shrugged and drifted back toward the end of the counter where her friend was loitering.

As soon as Bolan was out of sight, the "friend" left the counter. He knew what Bolan was driving. He'd gotten what he came for.

Out in the lot, the Buick was nearly lost in the sea of small foreign knockoffs and American compacts. It was the biggest car in its row, and easy to spot. Not so easy to get to. Bolan handed the keys to an attendant and asked him to move the Buick out into the ramp area. While he waited, he watched the pedestrian traffic that seemed to flood out of the terminal. Everybody in New Orleans was renting a car, it seemed.

A face flashed by that attracted Bolan's attention. It was familiar, but he couldn't place it. The man called attention to himself by the way he was trying to avert his face without taking his eyes off Bolan. Then it clicked. It was the guy at the car rental counter. So Bolan was expected, then. It wasn't the first time in this strangest of assignments that Bolan's whereabouts were known to the enemy. If things ran to form, it wouldn't be the last.

The lot attendant screeched to a halt, and left the Buick while it still rocked on its springs. Bolan tossed his bags in the back seat and left in a cloud of burning rubber. If he was going to be followed, he wasn't going to make it easy. The airport traffic was heavy, as Bolan maneuvered the big car in and out of the fast lane.

Keeping an eye on the rearview mirror, Bolan noticed nothing unusual. He pushed the big car through narrow gaps in the triple line. A small red Honda Civic was dogging him, but the driver seemed more intent on taking advantage of Bolan's skillful driving by tailgating, much as a running back follows his blockers.

As he watched the line of cars ahead, a movement caught his eye. A passenger in a light blue Oldsmobile in the left lane was talking into his hand, as if he were in radio contact, probably with someone behind him. He kept peering back over his shoulder.

Bolan decided to find out if he was the subject of the conversation. He nudged the Buick forward, sliding in between two smaller cars, threaded his way past a jitney in the extreme right-hand lane and was abreast of the Olds. Drifting dangerously close, Bolan stared at the driver of the blue car, who muttered something to his passenger. Inadvertently, the latter jerked his head to look, and Bolan winked.

The passenger mouthed a curse and reached into his coat. The driver, moving quickly, grabbed his companion with his right hand, steering with his left. The movement was costly.

The road veered to the right, but the driver's attention was on other matters. The blue Olds bore into the concrete divider. There was a shower of sparks as the left front fender of the car ground its finish into blue dust against the abrasive barrier. Then, as the fender crumpled, the tire gained traction and the car flipped, skidding on its roof for several yards before coming to a halt. With screeching tires, the following traffic braked, but not soon enough. A green Toyota plowed into the rear end of the Olds, crumpling the trunk of the inverted vehicle and mashing its own engine compartment.

Bolan watched the pile-up in his side-view mirror. He felt sorry for the drivers of the following cars, but there was little he could have done to prevent the accident, and he had learned some valuable information. He was, after all, expected.

And if he was expected, it raised the distinct possibility that his presence had been engineered. Mack Bolan was beginning to feel like a puppet on a string. It was a feeling he was not used to, and one he definitely didn't like. But most troubling was not knowing who was pulling the strings.

Or why.

THE RIVERVIEW HOTEL was unexceptional and unexceptionable. A little off the beaten track, situated on Chartres Street on the fringes of the French Quarter, it catered to budget-conscious tourists and high-priced call girls. At first blush, it was an unlikely combination, but when he thought about it, Bolan realized working girls were no less concerned about the state of the dollar than anyone else.

His room was reasonably priced. The staff was courteous but not in the least pushy. He could get what he needed without having to fend off a bellman or a maid every fifteen minutes. And what he needed was time. Time to himself, to think things through. This maze was beginning to exhaust him. Every turn seemed to lead to a blank wall. Every time he thought he'd figured out what was going down, he found a new wrinkle.

The bogus Anderson was supposedly heading to New Orleans. All right. New Orleans it was. Now what? The watchdogs were all the evidence he needed that he had been expected. But now that he had arrived, and they knew it, what was he supposed to do?

New Orleans was not exactly a small Southern town. Anyone determined to get lost could do it easily. And just as easily stay lost. As skilled as he was at working the underground tunnels that underlie every large American city, Mack Bolan knew he was looking for a very elusive needle in a shifting haystack of colossal dimensions. Somehow he knew that if he found David Anderson's impersonator, it would not be accidental. The real secret was to make the most of it, to know in advance what he would do if he found him. Bolan had to find some way to climb the puppet strings and bite the hand that led him.

The broad window of his room looked out on a row of office buildings. With the light off, he stood near the glass and wondered where the elusive view of the river might be found. Just above the parapets of the lower buildings, he saw a narrow band of dark, shimmering blue. Typical of the way things had been going lately, his view had been obscured by someone's construction.

Drawing the curtains to shut out the descending night, Bolan crossed to the bed and lay down. On the dull, white ceiling, he sketched scenario after scenario, replaying the past three days like a videotape. Scene after scene passed before his eyes, as vivid as they would have been if he were drowning. And that, in more ways than he cared to admit, was exactly what he was. He was going down for the third time, and there was no one around to throw him a line.

Again and again, he ran through the scene on the highway. There was something about the occupants of the blue Oldsmobile that didn't seem to fit the rest of the picture. Whoever those guys were, they weren't KGB. He was sure of it. He didn't know why he should feel so certain, but they just didn't fit the pattern that had been developing so far.

Before he could pin down the impression any further, the phone rang.

Convinced that his success in avoiding importunate staff had come to an end, he listened to the phone without making a move to answer it. Finally, when the noise began to grate on his nerves, he lifted the receiver from its cradle just long enough to establish a connection, then replaced it. He waited for the jangle to resume. It didn't.

Three minutes later, there was a knock on the door. Drawing his Beretta, Bolan dropped to the floor and rolled under the bed. The knocking was insistent. Whoever it was was neither trying to be discreet nor inclined to take no for an answer.

Too bad.

After a prolonged assault on the door, he heard voices in the corridor. There was more than one person in the corridor. The knocking died away, its echo just a dull ache in his head. Then, unmistakably, the sound of a key grating in the lock. Sliding forward, he angled himself under the bed and waited. The door swung open, a block of light splashed on the floor and disappeared as the overhead light was clicked on.

There were three men. He could see three pairs of shoes, one of which needed a shine badly. Another, he knew by the uniform pants, was a hotel employee. He wore tasseled loafers.

"Bolan? You here?"

The voice wasn't familiar. The speaker repeated his call. Still Bolan waited.

"I thought you said he answered the phone?" the same voice demanded.

"Yes, sir, I did. I thought so, anyway. I mean, it stopped ringing. It sounded like someone answered and hung up immediately."

"Well, he's not here. Listen, you know where to reach us. If he comes in, I want you to give him this, and call us right away. You got that?"

"Yes, sir, I got it."

Bolan couldn't see what was given to the bellman. But he damned sure was going to get a look at it.

The shoes withdrew, and the room returned to darkness. For a long time Bolan lay on the floor. When he was satisfied the three had gone, he slid out from under the bed. He had his hands on the string. Now all he had to do was haul himself up, hand over hand, to the top.

Bolan strapped on Big Thunder and the Beretta, grabbed a jacket and stepped to the door. He listened for traffic in the hall, heard none and softly turned the knob. Getting out of his room might be the toughest part of the job. It was not uncommon for the opposition, whoever they might be, to take a room directly across from their quarry, with a team taking turns watching through the peephole.

Palming the Beretta 93-R to hide it as well as he could, he pulled the door open while flattening himself against the wall, then counted to five. Nothing. Not a sound. Quickly he slipped out and pulled the door closed. At either end of the hall was a stairwell. He wanted to walk down, but knew someone might be waiting for him on the stairs.

Stopping in front of the elevator, he pushed the up button, then stepped into the alcove housing an ice maker and several vending machines to wait for the car. It arrived quickly, with a soft electronic tinkle. He stepped in and rode up three floors, then got off.

If anyone was in the stairwell, Bolan should now be above him. He sprinted to the door at the south end, opened it softly and stepped into the well. The pale illumination of low wattage fluorescent lamps threw dim shadows on the walls and stairs.

The stairs were the flattened spiral type, and he leaned over the rail to look down. Sure enough, one flight above his own floor, someone stood, watching the door below him.

Bolan slipped off his shoes, tipping them up against the door as a makeshift alarm and began his descent. The Beretta was no longer concealed. Stepping cautiously, he angled along the rail, keeping his eye on the waiting man, whose attention was focused on the door below him. Another curl in the stairwell, and the man was directly in front of him. Bolan tiptoed the remaining steps, but the man sensed something and began to turn. Bolan was on him, leaping the remaining three steps and pinning the man's arms to his sides as they collided. The impact carried them both down the stairs to the landing below.

The guy was strong. He squirmed until he was facing his attacker and struggled to free his arms. Bolan released his bear hug and brought the butt of the Beretta down sharply across the bridge of the man's nose. The bone gave with a crack, and the man went limp. Quickly searching the unconscious man, Bolan found his wallet. There was thirty-odd dollars in bills, a handful of photos, probably family, and identification. The man was a U.S. government employee. CIA, to be precise.

And Mack Bolan pulled himself up another foot on the string. The next step would be to find the bellman. Leaving the prostrate man on the landing, Bolan raced back to get his shoes, then bounded down the stairs to the lobby. At a newsstand, he bought a couple of papers and fell into a plush-covered easy chair to watch. And wait.

13

Bolan took the envelope from the bellman, ripped it open and read the note three times. It was a message from Albright.

Motel man broke. Anderson is Yuri Kuscenko. Rooming house at 312 Avenue Bonaparte. Good luck. Don

Bolan smiled. Finally things were breaking his way. Whether or not the note was from Albright, its author was obviously unaware that Brognola had already told Bolan that the prisoner from the motel killed himself before reveuling anything helpful. And since Albright must know that, too, by now, he would be unlikely to have incriminated himself with such a blunder. So the note was not from Don.

But the message itself just might be true.

Bolan read the note three times, then burned it. He hurried to the parking garage, opened the trunk and took out the attaché case containing the Weatherby. Tossing it in the back seat, he jumped in and started the car. A quick glance at a street map told him Avenue Bonaparte was two blocks from the river, an area of broken-down rooming houses, flophouses and sleazy dives.

The big Buick rumbled through the cavernous concrete interior of the underground garage as it climbed toward street level. As he broke into the open, rain spattered his windshield. Bolan clicked on the wipers and made a quick left. The trip was a short one, but it might be a long night. Kuscenko was somebody he wanted to meet. Personally.

Too much had gone down in the past few days that needed some explanation. Kuscenko might not have it, but he might be the key. Hired guns seldom knew who employed them, political hitters like Kuscenko seldom knew why they did what they did. But Kuscenko alive was worth something more than Kuscenko dead. How much more would have to wait until they nailed him.

The rain got heavier as Bolan drove through the deserted streets. It was after eleven, and the weather had chased most of the pub crawlers indoors. Rather than wander from bar to bar, they'd curl up for a good drunk at one venue on a night like this. The air was chilly for New Orleans. The rain and littered streets gave it an ugly face, one that Bolan had seen in more than one city over the years. He was entering the twilight zone where strange things live and anything goes.

Hitting Avenue Bonaparte at an angle, Bolan swung to the left and looked for number 312. It was three blocks down, a ramshackle boardinghouse that saw the coroner more often than the painter. Cruising past, Bolan started looking for a place to leave the Buick. He wanted a close-up look on foot before planning his attack.

A block away, he spotted an alley off to the right, lined with weatherbeaten garages and small businesses. The pavement was cracked and broken, and the buildings had long since seen better days. There was a niche next to a Dumpster just large enough to accommodate the Buick, and Bolan parked the car hurriedly. As he got out, a small platoon of rats scurried under the Dumpster with a rattle of damp paper.

Walking quickly back toward the avenue, he took stock of the surrounding area. Just behind the rooming houses lining the avenue and parallel to the alley, was a gray, weathered-wood fence, a few flakes of paint still clinging to it, that looked like a row of hurdles in some long-forgotten track meet.

The avenue itself was a dreary stretch, the occasional streetlight dimmed by the neon flashes announcing the presence of rooms to let. The rain-slick pavement bounced the light back into the air, glazing the asphalt with rainbows. The whole flickering vista seemed otherworldly. Bolan was already soaked to the skin, as the rain continued to beat down, drumming on the roofs and hoods of cars lining the curb.

Number 312 was a four-story brownstone. Its cement steps were chipped and broken and worn to a rounded valley in the middle from countless footsteps. Bolan mounted carefully, entering the hallway to get out of the rain. Inside the door was a row of bells and broken mailboxes. Kuscenko would not be listed under any name. There wouldn't have been time. And of the ranks of transients who passed through, it was unlikely more than a few had ever put their names on the useless receptacles.

Ticking away in the back of Bolan's consciousness was the knowledge that this was a setup. The CIA presence at the Riverview proved nothing about whether the assassin was really here. After all, he knew the note couldn't be from Albright. But somebody wanted Mack Bolan at 312 Avenue Bonaparte. He'd be damned if he'd disappoint them.

The best way to run down a place like a rooming house was to start at the top. That way there were no surprises. If you spooked your prey and he ran for it, you could always chase him, but if you walked into an ambush from below, there wasn't much you could do about it. So Bolan climbed the rickety stairs, littered with cigarette butts and empty beer cans.

At the top of the stairs, a small window looked out over the rear of the building. The two lower floors were deeper than the top two, and covered by a slanted roof that reached almost to an alley intersecting the one where he'd left his car. The boardinghouse was more of a rat trap than he'd seen in a while. And if he were Kuscenko, he knew where he'd be. The third floor, with access to the roof. It was the one escape hatch available.

The floorboards creaked as Bolan walked toward the front of the top floor. At each door he listened, then knocked softly. Receiving no answer, he tried the knob. The first two rooms were vacant. The third was occupied but unlocked. An ancient man with gray hair lay snoring on a cot. The floor was littered with newspaper, and a table, covered with days-old dishes, stood against one wall. There was no chair. The old man must have eaten standing up.

The fourth room was locked. A muffled curse greeted Bolan's knock. "What the fuck you want?"

"Steve?" Bolan asked, in a half whisper. "Steve, that you?"

"Go away. No Steve here."

"Steve? Open up." Bolan persisted. As expected, the knob rattled and the door swung open on a large, disheveled and very drunk man. He was not happy. Nor was the woman on the twin bed. Her bare legs dangled to the floor as she struggled to cover herself with a gray sheet.

"Told you, there's no Steve here, buddy." The man was as surly as he was large.

Bolan stuck the Beretta in his face and pushed, gently. "Back up, now," Bolan whispered. The gorilla thought it over, was considering whether to make a move for the gun, and Bolan pressed a little harder. Wisdom won. The gorilla backed up resentfully, one step at a time, staying just ahead of the pressure of the Beretta's muzzle against his upper lip.

"What the fuck is this?" The big man seemed confused. Given his drunken state, it was a wonder he could stand, let alone have any interest in his female companion.

"I'm looking for someone," Bolan said.

"Unless it's me, you got the wrong room." The gorilla had a sense of humor.

"No, not you. Anybody new here?"

"How new?"

"The last couple of days . . ."

"Who wants to know?"

Bolan pushed forward with the Beretta, muffling the last part of the man's response. "I do."

"All right, all right, get that fucking thing outta my face, would ya?"

Bolan eased off the pressure, paused, then put the gun away. Reassured, the big man relaxed somewhat.

"Yeah, there's a new guy. Came night before last. In the back, 3D, right at the top of the stairs."

"Blond guy, about six one?"

"I guess. I only seen him once. Could be."

"That won't cut it. Could be is not what I need to know. Is he a blonde, about six one? That's what I need to know."

"Yeah, yeah. That's what he looks like."

"All right, now I want you to stay in your room. And not a sound, understand?"

"Hey, man, I mind my own business. That's all the trouble I need."

"Good boy." Bolan tapped the big man gently on the cheek. "Let's keep it that way just a while longer, okay?"

The gorilla nodded, and Bolan backed out of the room. He heard the door close gently behind him as he walked back toward the head of the stairs. Descending quietly, he approached the door to 3D. The room was quiet. He placed his ear to the door and heard nothing. But he felt something.

Somebody was waiting inside. For him.

Stepping back for leverage, Bolan planted the sole of his foot against the middle of the door in a well-aimed kick. The door gave with an earsplitting splintering and screech of screws wrenched from the wooden frame.

There was a burst of gunfire, and the frame was chewed by the rain of slugs. Two shots plowed into the age-softened plaster behind Bolan as he dived for the floor. He couldn't tell how many men were inside, but at least the fire was all from handguns. What he lacked in numbers he didn't have to match in firepower.

Getting to his knees, he braced himself for a rush. Whoever was expecting him hadn't gone to all this trouble just to wait inside. They were certain to press the attack. There was a whispered conversation, followed by another burst of fire. The slugs went high into the wall, and Bolan knew a body would come flying through the door any second.

With a rush, two men dived through, landing on their stomachs in the hallway. One of them, closest to the stairwell railing, lost his grip on his weapon. The gun skipped across the floor, slid between the banister slats and landed with a crash on the stairs.

The second man was luckier. He had his gun, a large-caliber automatic. Bolan didn't wait. He aimed carefully and squeezed. The 9 mm slug caught the first man just above the left eye. His death spasm squeezed off a round, the slug narrowly missing. It plowed a groove along the plaster just above and behind the Executioner.

The second gunner scrambled to his feet and ran for the stairs. Bolan aimed low, catching him in the middle of the back, just to the right of the spine. The guy staggered once, nearly losing his balance, then lurched to the head of the stairwell. He was completing his turn when Bolan fired a second time. This time the gunner was unluckier still.

He pitched forward, landing face first on the stairs, a large red stain spreading high across the back of his suit jacket. The second shot had passed clean through, tearing a large hole in the shiny gabardine.

The next step was getting inside the room. Neither of the dead hitters was Kuscenko. Of that he was sure. The assassin, if he was there at all, had to be inside. Setting the Beretta for a 3-shot burst, Bolan got to his feet, debating whether to rush the room or wait. The latter was too risky to consider for long. Even in this neighborhood, the sound of automatic weapons would bring the police.

Eventually.

Before he could decide, there was another rain of fire. The second team took the field. A small man, not much more than four feet in height, burst through the door. He carried an Uzi, and knew how to use it. Bolan squeezed off a burst as the Uzi opened up. The hellfire weaved toward him like a drunk on the sidewalk, its zigzag path gouging the floor with holes whose ugliness was apparent even in the squalor of the boardinghouse hallway.

As he fired, Bolan leaped for the railing, just clearing it as the Uzi stopped its hammering. As he sailed to the stairs below, Bolan saw three small holes tightly grouped in a triangle around the small man's heart.

The Executioner's fall was cushioned by the body of the fallen gunner, his feet landing squarely on the dead man's shoulders. The blow jarred the body loose, and it slid forward, taking the warrior's balance with it. Bolan broke his own forward fall with extended arms, and grabbed a splintered stair to stop his backward slide.

There was a rush of footsteps at the top of the stairs. Bolan looked up to see Yuri Kuscenko for the first time. The tall blond man wore a crooked smile. He pointed a small-caliber automatic in Bolan's direction and fired once, the slug taking Bolan just below the shoulder in the fleshy part of the upper arm. Before he could stabilize himself enough to return fire, Kuscenko vanished. There was a crash, followed by a tinkle of raining glass. A cool breeze blew down the stairwell as Bolan struggled to regain his feet.

Rushing up the stairs, Bolan reached the window in time to see the assassin leap from the edge of the roof into the alley below. Still woozy from the hit, Bolan staggered through the window after the Russian hit man, feeling the steady rain wash over him with its coolness. The groggy sensation left, and he sprinted toward the edge of the roof.

In the alley, two stories below him, Kuscenko was already running for the intersecting alleyway. Bolan wanted him alive. He dropped to his stomach and lay flat on the slanting roof, then pushed backward until his weight pulled him down. He clung for a moment to the eaves, swinging back away from the wall and let go. The height wasn't that great, but in his weakened state, the impact jarred him, and he staggered for a few steps before recovering.

Kuscenko had already turned the corner. Bolan listened. He heard no footsteps, but in the distance, there was a wailing siren. Bolan sprinted down the alley. The intersection was empty. He stepped to the center of the larger alleyway and listened again. Still nothing. He moved ahead a few steps in the direction Kuscenko had taken. The siren was drawing nearer.

Turning toward his car, he heard the roar behind him and turned back just in time to see the careering car shoot into the mouth of the alley. Its tires hissed loudly under the screaming engine, and it barreled straight toward him. He dived for the wooden fence on his left, just hauling his legs up to cling to the horizontal strut as the car's bumper smashed into the fence. Through the windshield as the fence tottered, he saw Yuri Kuscenko, wearing a predator's smile.

When he hauled himself out of the ruins of the shattered fence, Kuscenko's car was still in sight, barreling straight for the river. Bolan ran to his own car and cranked it up. The tight K turn took just enough time for Kuscenko to reach the alley's end.

The Buick roared down the alley, fishtailing on the slick pavement. The taillights of Kuscenko's car veered left and vanished.

14

Kuscenko's car was just a pair of twinkling red lights, as Bolan's Buick sped in pursuit. On the slick streets, with the rain falling more heavily, Bolan tried to close the gap. Kuscenko was a skillful driver. The dark gray Gran Prix was little more substantial than a fast-moving cloud in the rainstorm.

Taking advantage of every twist and turn, cornering suddenly and secure in the knowledge of his own destination, Kuscenko wove his way through the darkness. The Gran Prix was a match for the Buick in muscle, and more maneuverable.

As the seamy part of New Orleans fell behind them, the two cars seemed connected together by an invisible string. Neither was able to gain ground on the other. The sporty Pontiac was three hundred yards ahead of Bolan's Buick and stayed there. On I-90 leading out of New Orleans, Kuscenko opened it up. It was late and even the police seemed to have stayed inside on a lousy night.

The car was heading in the general direction of Lake Salvador. Bolan had some knowledge of the area, and he didn't like to consider the possibilities. If Kuscenko lost him in the wilderness, he'd be impossible to find. Flooring the gas pedal, Bolan felt the big car strain, its engine groaning with the effort. Still Kuscenko stayed ahead. The road began to wind, and traction was hard bought on the rain-slick surface.

The terrain grew rural, buildings few and far between. Bolan had to keep the Russian in sight. If Kuscenko slipped into a side road, he could get lost in a matter of seconds. Gradually, barely perceptibly, the gap began to narrow. All of a sudden it seemed as if Kuscenko were uncertain of where he was going.

Up ahead, a deserted truck stop lay rotting at the side of the road, its sign rusting away beneath the neon tubing announcing EATS, as if from some disease. The building was faded white, its sun-bleached clapboard siding like something carved from bone.

The Gran Prix roared into the parking area and spun in a tight one-eighty. Bolan, wary, slowed as he approached. Had Kuscenko decided to make a stand at some roadside OK Corral?

There had been too many inexplicable events in this latest chapter of Bolan's one-man war. The last thing he wanted to do was walk into a trap any idiot would have seen from a mile away. As Bolan slowed to a crawl, drifting closer, the lights on the Gran Prix were extinguished. Bolan waited for the telltale dome light, but nothing happened. Kuscenko was still in the car.

Stopping a hundred yards away, Bolan extinguished his own lights. And waited. The foliage on either side of the road was ghostly, draped in Spanish moss and full of shimmering shadows. Out behind the nearest row of trees, Bolan knew, was a no-man's-land. Mercenaries of all kinds had been training in the area off and on for years. Even the CIA had used it to train some anti-Castro Cubans in the early sixties. Bolan had been there once or twice, but he was on shaky ground.

Rolling his window down, the Executioner listened. His arm was throbbing from the glancing bullet, his sleeve sticky to the touch. It wasn't a serious wound, but it should be attended to. But not now. No way was he going to walk out when he was this close.

The deep, throaty rumble of a male gator echoed among the trees. The chorus of tree frogs and crickets stopped for a beat, then continued in a more subdued manner. Kuscenko's car sat still and dark. It was too far away to tell if its engine were running, unless Bolan shut off his own. The Gran Prix could have been a mirage. Nearly invisible against the darkness behind, it was only given away by its chrome trim. An occasional flash of lightning threw it into bolder relief, but so quickly that you'd have missed it if you didn't know it was there.

And Mack Bolan was getting tired of the stand-off. The two of them could sit like this for hours—forever if it came to that—and nothing would change. Somebody had to make a move. Never backward about the philosophy of the first strike, Bolan reached up with a free hand and popped the cover off his dome light. He twisted the bulb free and put it on the seat.

He shut the engine off and waited. If Kuscenko's car were running, Bolan would hear it, and if it weren't, Kuscenko would have heard Bolan's engine shut down. Through the chatter of insects and ominous basso continuo of large life forms in the forest around them, Bolan heard the steady pulse of an engine. The Gran Prix was still running.

Show time.

Mack Bolan slipped out of the Buick on the driver's side, opening the door just wide enough to pass through. Crouching behind the car's bulk, he crept to the rear of the Buick. There was a fringe of undergrowth along the perimeter of the clearing. Its closest approach to Bolan's car was fifteen feet, but that was behind the car. If he kept down, he could make it without being seen.

There was a flash of lightning, and Bolan moved, hoping the contrast would lend him extra cover as the darkness returned. He dived for the undergrowth. Once in the bushes, he could make his way slowly and deliberately toward the assassin's car. The route was circuitous, and he'd have to cover two hundred yards at a minimum. Moving a little deeper into the undergrowth to conceal his movement, Bolan began his approach.

The rain slackened momentarily, then resumed harder than before. The steady downpour hissed through the leaves as the wind picked up. The tree branches began to whip wildly, some of the more slender trees bending under the onslaught. The Gran Prix sat still. The going was sluggish, mud and swamp water beneath Bolan's feet slowing him down. The footing was treacherous.

Half the distance covered, Bolan stopped to reassess. He was beginning to wonder whether Kuscenko had slipped out of the car. Straining to see through the murky night, he peered intently at the windshield and the driver's side window. In a brilliant flash of lightning the assassin was clearly visible at the wheel. A loud crash of thunder broke, and the concussion dulled Bolan's hearing for a few seconds.

Almost as if the thunder were a signal, a second car pulled into the vacant lot. Ignoring the heavy downpour, four men got out and raced to the Gran Prix. Kuscenko rolled his window down and one of the men, the shortest of the four, leaned down to converse.

The odds had changed. Drastically.

Before he could move closer, Bolan saw two of the men run back to their car. The first one opened a back door and leaned in. He handed something to his companion, then withdrew a second stubby, bulky shadow for himself. Holding the objects in front of them, they crouched low, and in another flash of lightning, Bolan recognized the ugly shadows for what they were: Kalashnikov assault rifles. There was a crackle, like a distant electrical discharge, and a series of flashes. The two men raked Bolan's Buick with their fire. Two small explosions signaled two flat tires.

The next lightning flash showed a smear of rainbow where the windshield had been. The engine, still cooling down after its heavy push, spewed steam into the air through the grillwork and around the hood.

Being outgunned and outnumbered was nothing new to Mack Bolan, but seldom had the odds been so heavily against him. Already deprived of transportation, he was cut off from everything but the battle in front of him. That, too, was nothing new.

Circling farther along the perimeter, he knew what he had to do. He had to strike first and fast, taking out as many as he could in the first attack. If he failed, he would be worse than outgunned, he would be unarmed. He had the Beretta and Big Thunder, and some spare magazines for each, but at the best of times and in the best of hands, they were overmatched by Kalashnikovs.

There was a new noise, just beyond clear hearing, and Bolan waited for it. As it drew nearer, it was unmistakable: a chopper. A better place for a rendezvous would be hard to imagine, Bolan thought.

One of the remaining two men sprinted over to the two gunmen. The three then returned to their own car, opened the trunk and removed something. Each walked to a different vertex of a rough triangle. A moment later, the clearing was garishly lit by sputtering red flame. The flares smoked and sizzled in the hellish light. The chopper drew nearer.

Now was the time. The only time.

Bolan unslung Big Thunder and drew a bead on the nearest man, who was facing away from him and looking at the sky. The man was large and heavily muscled. His lumbering movement suggested he was the slowest and, ideally, could be left until later. But beggars can't be choosers. The heavy AutoMag barked once, then again. The big man pitched forward onto his face. Bolan got a break. The heavy body, in its soaking coat, fell across the flare, snuffing it out. The man had been one of those with a Kalashnikov, but there was no chance for Bolan to retrieve it. Not yet.

The others were stunned by the shots, but the sound had ended before they could pinpoint its source. The dome light of the Gran Prix winked on, then off. Kuscenko, more than likely accustomed to selective fire, and attuned to the sound of weapons in a way the others could not be, had been able to place the shot. He yelled something and pointed in Bolan's direction.

Bolan hit the deck, just ahead of a spray of automatic weapons fire. The slugs chipped away at the undergrowth above him, raining bits of leaves and twigs over his prostrate form. It was only a matter of time before the enemy charged into the bush. Bolan, without rising, pointed the AutoMag in the general direction of the Gran Prix and squeezed off three quick rounds.

One struck metal and whanged off into the night. The next two seemed to miss everything. While his opponents were off balance, Bolan wriggled through the underbrush, looking for deeper cover. The muddy water felt cold and clammy as it seeped through his clothing and soaked him to the skin.

There was a second wave of fire, this time more widely dispersed. Kuscenko must have been directing the others. They were fanning out, trying to nail Bolan by chance if possible, and making sure he kept his head down. Bolan decided to hit them head-on, something they wouldn't expect. Wriggling around to face the clearing, he scooted forward until he was just behind the last stand of cover.

In the flickering red light, shadows danced grotesquely as the confused men alternately scanned the sky and searched the bushes. Bolan noticed they seemed disinclined to enter the bush after him. They seemed more intent on receiving the chopper, which was drawing nearer. The unmistakable whup-whup-whup of the rotors was almost overhead.

The chopper spotted the flares and turned on its landing lamps, flooding the clearing with light. Bolan got to his feet and fired three quick rounds. The short man, standing next to Kuscenko at the front of the Gran Prix, went down, and the others hit the deck.

The chopper swooped in low to the center of the clearing, hovering there a dozen feet off the ground. Kuscenko waved it to one side, and Bolan realized what he wanted. The chopper moved to hang just beyond the second car, a large sedan. Kuscenko sprinted for the car while the remaining two men raked the bushes with rifle fire.

The chopper's engine was roaring to keep it steady. Kuscenko reached the sedan and leaped onto the hood, then the roof. He reached high for the helicopter's nearest landing strut. Swinging his body in an arc, he hooked his feet around the strut and the chopper began to rise. Bolan emptied the magazine of the AutoMag at it, but the shots glanced harmlessly aside. The chopper veered away, and Bolan watched helplessly as two pairs of hands reached down to haul Kuscenko in.

The two men remaining on the ground stopped firing long enough for Bolan to sprint to his first victim. He tugged the Kalashnikov from under the fallen body and swept it in a broad arc. The hammering of the weapon sent flashes of pain through his wounded shoulder. One of the two men charged forward, his own AK-47 spitting sudden death. Several slugs chewed the ground around Bolan's ankles when one of Bolan's shots caught the advancing man in the chest. He went down heavily, landing with a splash in a large puddle at the center of the lot.

Bolan was startled by a sudden flash, as the Gran Prix swerved and lurched across the parking lot. He threw a couple of slugs its way, then the magazine ran dry. Tossing the empty assault rifle to one side, Bolan dived back into the undergrowth and unholstered the 93-R. He had to nail the last man before he hightailed it.

The last man was either brave or stupid. Perhaps both. He advanced on Bolan's position steadily, more like a fireman with a hose than a soldier with a gun. He fired short bursts, sweeping the rifle from side to side in a tight arc. The slugs screamed and whined through the leaves. And the Executioner waited.

As the man reached the edge of the woods, Bolan rose and fired a short burst at point-blank range. There was no way he could have missed.

He didn't.

15

When the last man went down, Lake Salvador was quiet again. The sound of the chopper was long gone, but its echo lingered in the air. Bolan scrambled for the enemy's car. His own was useless now. He grabbed the Weatherby in its attaché case and tossed it into the back seat of the late SWAT team's Cadillac. The keys of the sedan dangled in its ignition.

The next step was...where? Bolan had to get to a phone. He had noted the number of the chopper. If he could reach Brognola, and if the man from Justice could find out where the chopper came from, where it was headed, there might still be a chance to stop Kuscenko. He was miles away now in the dark night sky, his purpose still unknown. Except that it was to kill. And Bolan had no idea who his target was.

The big car was sluggish, its engine missing irregularly. Bolan wondered whether it had taken a stray slug during the firefight. As it limped along, barely able to manage the speed limit, the big man watched for a light, any sign of life along the road. Fifteen miles through the rain, hoping the engine wouldn't give out, paid off. A roadhouse loomed ahead. There were a few cars in the lot, and its blinking neon sign was more welcome than he could have imagined.

The car coughed to a halt against the railroad ties used to mark the edges of the parking lot. Inside, the rain was drowned out by a full-tilt boogie band. The amps didn't seem to have a number less than ten on their dials. The music was a raucous blend of blues and country, and it was good. Too loud, but damned good.

Bolan caused a few heads to turn as he walked in, but everybody was either drunk or hell-bent on catching up with those who were. The few who noticed soon turned back to their beers. There was a phone booth in one corner, its small blue-and-white light the quietest thing in the house. Bolan dropped a dime and dialed. As the phone started to ring, he held his breath. After a half dozen rings, a duty clerk got on the line. When Bolan asked for Brognola, he heard a click and found himself in the limbo of static and silence known as "hold."

After what seemed like forever, Brognola got on the line. The buzz and whirr told Bolan they had patched the call through to the big Fed's home.

"Where the hell are you, Striker?"

"South of New Orleans, near Lake Salvador."

"What the hell are you doing there?"

"Someone sent me a lead."

"What lead?"

"Someone who says he's Albright sent me a note, via the CIA, to tell me where Anderson was."

"First I heard of it."

"Well, it was from someone who didn't know the guy from the motel was dead. But it panned out. The guy's name is probably Kuscenko, Yuri Kuscenko. He was staying in a dive near the waterfront. He slipped by me, but I tracked him down. Almost had the bastard."

"What happened?"

"A chopper picked him up. And he had a flying wedge running interference. By the time I took out the blockers, he was gone. I want you to track the chopper, if you can."

Bolan gave Brognola the details, sketchy as they were, and made arrangements to call back in two hours. The next step was back to New Orleans, but getting there wasn't going to be a snap. He couldn't take a chance on the crippled Cadillac.

Out in the bar, he asked the bartender if there was a taxi anywhere nearby. The laugh he got in response was no louder than he expected.

"Fella, you are a *long* way from home. Look here, you think any a these boys is in any shape to drive? Iffen he *had* a taxi?"

"I got a car, and I ain't drunk." The voice was soft, Southern fried and, most important, sober. "Where you need to go?"

"New Orleans."

"I can take you."

"Let's go."

"It'll cost you, though."

"I'll pay it, whatever it is."

The tall, lanky farm boy at the bar got up and led the way out of the bar. Bolan stopped at the moribund Cadillac for his attaché case, then followed the kid down the long row of mud-splattered pickups and rusty hulks. He wondered what godforsaken rattletrap it would be his luck to ride in. At the end of the line, behind a battered Volkswagen van, sat a surprise—a candy-apple-red '55 Chevy. Gleaming chrome lakers and wire rims vied for attention with the high-gloss, metal-flake finish.

"She's a beauty, ain't she?"

"Last thing in the world I expected to see," Bolan said.

"I need the money to get her in shape for racing season, otherwise I'd drive you cheaper."

"Forget it. As long as I get there, it'll be cheap at twice the price. In fact, you make it by 3:00 a.m. and I will pay twice the price. Plus any speeding tickets you might get. Fair enough?"

"Get in, buddy. And make sure you wear your belt. This mother moves."

BACK AT THE RIVERVIEW, Bolan raised a few night-shift eyebrows on his way through the lobby. The elevator seemed slothful after the dragster, but it was only 2:45 and he had time to spare. The drive had cost him a hundred dollars, but it was money well spent. He slammed the door to his room and got Brognola on the horn.

"What have you got for me?"

"Some answers. First of all, you're right that Albright never sent you a message of any kind. He's never heard of Kuscenko. That's one. The chopper your boy got on? Air Texas, a company proprietary. They set it up with the DEA to use against drug runners in the Southwest. That's two. It's based in Brownsville, but was in Dallas for an overhaul. That's where it's supposed to be, and I'll bet my last dollar that's where it is in the morning. It's a CIA chopper."

"Speaking of CIA, what do you figure is going on about the phony note supposed to be from Albright and delivered by a genuine CIA man?"

"You know the theory about the mole in the Company? I figure it's on the money. The guy's running scared. He's high enough up to know about the defectors, and he figures he's got nothing to lose."

"Okay. Where do we go from here?"

"That's my last bit of news. There's a presidential motorcade in Dallas the day after tomorrow. If your man is an assassin, and I don't doubt that he is, that could be his assignment."

"The Soviets wouldn't dare," Bolan said. But as he spoke, he knew he was wrong. There were some, in and out of the CIA, who were convinced the KGB was responsible for the assassination of John F. Kennedy. They couldn't prove it, but nobody had disproved it, either.

If the Pope was fair game, a U.S. President was not exempt. The real question was whether it would be a sanctioned operation or whether a rogue faction would be acting on its own. Either was possible. And there was a Bulgarian connection, just as there had been in the attack of John Paul II. Bolan felt a twinge of nausea. Then he made up his mind.

"Hal, I'd better go check out Dallas. But look, I have no confidence in the security on this thing. I want the Company out of it. You're the only man who should know where I am."

"Fair enough. What about Albright?"

"We can use him, but keep him dark. He can't do much on his own, and anything he says could get into the wrong ears in a hurry. If there is a mole, he knows a lot more than Albright. He can read between the lines. I can't afford that."

"I agree."

"I'll call you tomorrow from Dallas. I'll have to check out the motorcade route as soon as I get there."

"Shall I inform the Secret Service?"

"Negative. They don't do such a hot job at the best of times. I don't need them mucking around in this. The only way to get Kuscenko is to keep it quiet. If the motorcade is canceled, we're out in left field again. Who knows what the hell his backup plan might be. If I can't find him in Dallas, we'll never find him. Not until it's too late."

"You're playing a dangerous game, guy."

"I know, Hal, I know. But it's the only game in town. We have no choice. None."

Bolan called the airport for flight information, then packed hurriedly. When he finished, he called a cab and went down to the lobby, paid his bill and checked out.

The cab pulled up two minutes after Bolan walked through the broad bronze doors and set his bags down. He tossed them into the cab and hopped in beside them. Twenty minutes later he was at the ticket window. The flight was due to depart in fifteen minutes. He rushed his bags through and

HIT
THE JACKPOT
WITH GOLD EAGLE

Scratch off the 3 windows
to see what you'll get—FREE!

Then peel off Sticker, affix it to your Scorecard
and mail today to claim your Free Prizes!

IF YOU HIT THE JACKPOT, YOU GET 4 FREE BOOKS AND A FREE POCKETKNIFE

The free gifts shown on the slot machine Sticker are yours to keep forever—even if you never buy another book from Gold Eagle. But wait, there's more . . .

SCORE A BIGGER BONANZA AS A GOLD EAGLE SUBSCRIBER

Life is a game of chance, but you can be one of its lucky winners. How? By getting the world's hottest action-adventure novels delivered right to your home on a regular basis.

As a Gold Eagle subscriber, you'll rack up an unbeatable combination of benefits and privileges:

- You'll get 6 brand-new titles every second month (2 *Mack Bolans* and one each of *Able Team*, *Phoenix Force*, *Vietnam: Ground Zero* and *SOBs*) hot off the presses—and before they're available in stores.

- You'll save a hefty 12% off the retail price—you pay only $2.49 per book.

- You'll get our newsletter, AUTOMAG, *free* with every shipment.

- You'll get special books to preview or purchase at deep discounts.

YOUR NO-RISK GUARANTEE

As a subscriber, you can always cancel, return a shipment and owe nothing—so how can you lose?

RUSH YOUR ORDER TO US TODAY!

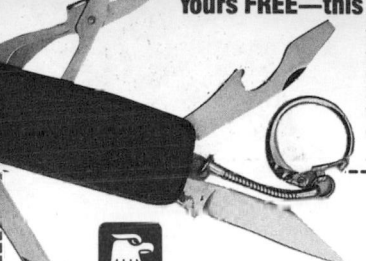

Yours FREE—this stainless-steel pocketknife.

Talk about versatile! You get 7 functions in this one handy device—screwdriver, bottle opener, nail cleaner, nail file, knife, scissors and key chain. Perfect for pocket, tool kit, tackle box. And it's yours free if it appears on your slot machine Sticker.

® **GOLD EAGLE READER SERVICE**

YOUR SCORECARD

Did you hit the jackpot with 4 Free Books and a Free Pocketknife?

PEEL OFF STICKER
FROM SLOT MACHINE
AND PLACE IT HERE

☐ **YES!** I hit the jackpot. Please rush me the free gifts on the Sticker that I have affixed above. Then enroll me as a Gold Eagle subscriber with all the benefits and privileges outlined on the opposite page, Including a no-risk money-back guarantee if I'm not satisfied.

166 CIM PAJ9

Name _____ (PLEASE PRINT)

Address _____ Apt. _____

City _____

State _____ Zip _____

GOOD LUCK

SEND NO MONEY. MAIL THIS CARD TODAY.

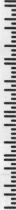

sprinted for the gate, his boarding pass clutched tightly in his fist.

The terminal was nearly deserted, except for a few other anxious departures, scrambling for their flights. Nobody seemed to hang around Southern airports in the middle of the night, the way they did in railroad and bus stations. Bolan was acutely aware that he had been manipulated and misled from day one on this assignment, and he kept a watchful eye for anyone showing undue interest in his hasty progress.

But he didn't notice the heavyset man in a gray pin-striped business suit, a topcoat over his arm, who got up and waddled after him to the boarding gate. At least, not immediately. But the fat man caught his eye as he hurried through the gate into the boarding tunnel. The sudden haste of a man who had been placidly reading the *Times Picayune* seemed odd. So, too, did the furtive eye movements of the bulky man. He was obviously looking for someone, and just as obviously trying to disguise it.

He flinched for just a second when he glanced at Bolan on the way past his seat. The warrior's gray eyes were locked on his own. His ruddy cheeks developed a sudden pallor. He'd been nailed, and he knew it, but to leave now would only acknowledge it. Regaining his composure, the man bustled past, taking a seat a few rows behind Bolan.

Whoever was pulling the strings was also pulling out all the stops, Bolan thought. Using a guy this inept meant you were spread thin . . . or that you wanted to draw attention away from something else. Toss a dog a bone, and he might not notice the beefsteak on the table.

The preflight rigmarole began, and Bolan patiently waited for the full panoply of instructions and demonstrations, including the use of the seat cushions "in case of an unscheduled landing on water." There were damned few scheduled landings on water, Bolan thought. Although, the way things were going, this plane just might have one on its flight plan.

The seat belt light went on, and the floor shivered as the engines of the jet revved up. The plane began to taxi away from the terminal. Bolan could feel the eyes of the fat man behind him, but he had decided the guy was a throwaway. He was more interested in who else might be watching him.

As soon as they were airborne, and the warning light extinguished, Bolan released his belt and wandered toward the rear of the plane. He smiled at the flight attendant to cover his scrutiny of the other passengers. At the rear of the cabin, he ducked into the lavatory and tallied his results. There were three possibles, one of them a woman.

His weapons were out of reach in the cargo bay of the airliner. If security was working, the passengers he suspected would also be unarmed. But like the rest of the world, Bolan had lived through twenty years of terror. Security or no, he wished he had a buck for every gun that made it into the main cabin of a civilian airliner during those two decades. It would be better than a pension.

He splashed some cold water on his face, then returned to his seat. On the way back, he checked each of the possibles again, and made up his mind. It was the woman, he was sure. And her handbag just might have more in it than tissues and a wallet. She was four rows behind him, on the opposite side of the cabin.

She seemed confident she hadn't been nailed. That was good. It meant she wouldn't do anything foolish. As long as she was undetected, she could wait and pick her spot, probably in the terminal at Dallas, where she'd have a chance to escape. It was also likely she'd have backup at the terminal. The fat guy was for sure.

Back in his seat, Bolan took a pair of sunglasses and a handkerchief out of his pocket. Breathing on the lenses, he polished them, then held them up to examine his handiwork. The woman's reflection was clear in the slightly curved surface. The green lenses did her complexion and blond hair a disservice, turning them a faint, sickly green. But she was attractive even in the distorted image. Her dark blue suit was a little too severe, but flattering all the same. On the rack over her head was an attaché case, small enough to be more likely hers than that of the man in the window seat. She looked for all the world like an eager young M.B.A. on the way to an employment interview.

But Mack Bolan knew she already had a job.

Him.

16

During the remainder of the ninety-minute flight, Mack Bolan had more on his mind than an attractive blonde. He knew there was nothing on her mind but keeping tabs on him or, more likely, taking him out altogether. But the puzzle was getting more complicated, and an inventory of its pieces was crucial. The latest surprise was that the chopper being used to ferry Kuscenko to Dallas belonged to the CIA.

If Albright was telling the truth, and gut instinct told Bolan he was, there had to be someone inside the Company using it for currently unfathomable motives. Ditto the chopper. And it took some clout to move that kind of hardware around. Not to mention the balls to do it so brazenly. Whoever was behind it was either crazy or desperate. It was not the sort of move you could walk away from later. Not unless there was a conspiratorial cabal of considerable size involved. And a group of that size meant almost certain discovery. You can't hide an elephant in a doghouse.

Bolan felt more alone in this than he had ever felt before. It wasn't possible to tell the players even with a scorecard. And Bolan's card was already full. There had been more pinch hitters than in any fifteen-inning game. The questions that overrode all others, though, were "Who is Yuri Kuscenko?" and "Why is he here?"

And Mack Bolan didn't have the answers.

During the flight, the blonde left her seat twice, the fat man once. They made no contact but still they were locked in some indefinable embrace, with Bolan held firmly in their tangled arms. As the plane neared Dallas-Ft. Worth, Bolan grew thoughtful. He would soon have to face the delicate task of extricating himself from their snare. If he could get to the luggage carousel before they made their move, it would be easier. Without his weapons, he felt their presence like a strap around his chest, constricting his breathing.

So much was riding on him. More than he could be sure of, in all likelihood more than anyone would ever know. With the dissonant chime of the seat belt warning the plane began its descent. It was beginning. Where it would end was anybody's guess.

Touchdown came with the usual screech of reluctant rubber, the nose wheel came down, and the long, slow taxi into the terminal began. Cleaning his sunglasses again, though it was still before dawn, Bolan watched the slender blonde reach up for her attaché case. She cradled it nervously in her lap, fingers playing with the clasps. Her long, brightly polished nails drummed brittlely on the dark leather, a thin, scratchy staccato that meant more to Bolan than she could know.

If she was on edge, she would be carrying the ball. Knowing that gave Bolan a leg up. Not much of one, but no help was to be disregarded in such circumstances. At the docking area, the seat belt sign remained lit, but the passengers were, as usual, emboldened by the contact with terra firma. The blonde got to her feet, but remained standing in front of her seat. The man in the window seat next to her was asleep.

Sometimes the best move is no move at all. Bolan stayed in his seat. The woman and the fat man would have to move first or betray a secret already known to the man they followed. When the plane shut down its engines, the floor of the cabin rumbled once, then all was whispered conversation and the scratch of luggage being moved. Bolan, alone in his row of seats, remained quietly in place.

As the passengers filed out, the noise died. Seeing she had no choice, the blonde left, followed soon after by the portly man. Ahead of Bolan now, they'd have to wonder what he was up to. Doubtless they had been briefed, but not too fully. No one knew all there was to know about the Executioner. They might panic and give him an additional opening.

Waiting a few beats after they disembarked, Bolan slowly made his way to the front of the plane. In the accordion tunnel, his feet tapped on the metal planking, their echoes bouncing off the ribbed plastic tube that led into the receiving area. Ahead, loitering with no apparent interest in anything around him, the fat man stood off to one side. The blonde was nowhere in sight. She must have gone straight to the luggage carousel.

Bolan stepped past the fat man and began to run. One thing they hadn't counted on was a direct challenge. The sudden sprint took the large man by surprise. He had no choice but to follow, but he was well behind and falling farther back by the time Bolan reached the first escalator to the lower level.

A broad flight of stone steps separated the up and down escalators, and Bolan sprinted into the staircase without missing a beat. Taking the slippery steps two at a time, he slid his hand along the metal rail dividing the steps in two. The short landing halfway down was more slippery than the stairs, and he almost lost his balance. Regaining it in midflight, he stutter-stepped the rest of the way to the lower level.

The universal green direction signs pointed him toward the carousel with a full quiver of broad white arrows. Down a long corridor lined with shops, his feet slapped against the stone with dull claps that bounced off the plate-glass walls on either side. The carousel area was brightly lit. Most of the passengers from his flight had already gone.

But not all of them.

The blonde was there, waiting. Her attaché case at her side, she leaned against a stone column, watching the entrance. As Bolan swept through the opening, she started, taken by surprise at his rapid pace. Bolan made straight for her.

She wrestled with her purse, got it open and plunged her hand inside. Bolan knew why. Less than ten feet away, he launched himself through the air, his shoulder crashing into her midsection. The purse went flying, spilling its contents onto the hard floor. As he rose quickly, Bolan heard a shout. He turned to see a security guard heading for them.

Just to be sure, he checked the strewn contents of the blonde's pocketbook and, sure enough, there was a gun. Two of them, to be exact, neither impressive in bulk. But both were deadly, especially the Colt Woodsman .22 caliber. A favorite of Mafia hit men, it packed a punch far beyond its caliber. The guard yelled again, but Bolan ignored him. He was in no mood for arguing with a cop, however well intentioned.

Checking the carousel, Bolan saw his bag and case emerge from the bowels of the terminal. He raced to the huge wheel, grabbed one in each hand and headed for the exit. The guard yelled a third time as he realized Bolan was making for the door.

Bolan heard the unmistakable sound of a gunshot. Instinctively, he dropped to a crouch. Turning, he saw something he hadn't expected. It was not the guard firing a warning round. The fat man had just dropped the security man. He fired again, shattering a window just behind Bolan's head.

His own guns inaccessible, Bolan had no choice. He got to his feet and zigzagged to the door and through. A third slug tore through the glass of the door and slammed into a steel column just to his left. Angling away from the doorway, he hailed a taxi with the raised attaché case, slamming the cab door as the fat man burst into the taxi bay. Watching through the rear window, Bolan saw the bewildered man as his eyes darted from place to place. Not until the cab was well on its way did the fat man connect his prey with the moving vehicle. By then, it was too late.

A short time later, in the early-morning sunlight of a November day, an eerie feeling of déjà vu swept over Mack Bolan. In the middle of Dealey Plaza, he looked around him as agog as any tourist. Most of the buildings still looked as they had in that other November of 1963. And like most Americans, he felt as if he'd always known them. He overcame the wave of emotion that threatened to tow him under. There was work to be done.

To make sure another generation didn't relive the same nightmare. Tomorrow.

His job, he knew, was next to impossible. The plaza was an assassin's dream. Wide open in the middle, it was surrounded by towering stone walls. Hundreds of windows, any one of which was ideal. A dozen roofs, full of nooks and crannies. The place was the quintessential box canyon from cowboy movies. And if an assassin had enough help, nobody could ride through the plaza unscathed.

The Secret Service knew that, of course. But then, it hadn't been helpful before. Putting himself in Kuscenko's shoes, Bolan stood in the middle of the grassy park at the plaza's heart. Split in two by a road running right through the middle, it was a broad expanse from which he could casually survey the perimeter. There were so many opportunities.

In thirty hours, the place would be thronged with cheering people. The current President was far more popular in Texas than JFK had been. That made Bolan's task a little simpler. He knew an assassin would not want to trust to luck. You never knew what people were going to do, or where they would stand in order to get a good view. That meant elevation was a prerequisite—the higher the better.

Looking up at the Book Depository, he realized the truth that lay behind something that had always bothered him. That vantage point was not the first choice. Or even the third. There were too many impediments to clear sight, and shooting time would be minimal. Unless the entire thing were a charade, a flesh-and-blood reenactment for some doubtful dramatic purpose, or in service of an obscure political point, Kuscenko would not choose it. But there were other possibilities.

Several of the buildings involved a heavier than normal police presence, like the Criminal Courts Building and the Dallas County Jail. They were unlikely choices, though better than the depository. The first place Bolan would have chosen was the Dal-Tex Building. Among the tallest that lined the plaza, it was also among the most public. Lightly guarded, as most public-access buildings are, it would be easy to get into and out of.

Walking up the middle of the plaza, Bolan crossed Houston Street and headed for the entrance of the Dal-Tex Building. The building was stately, bordering on stodgy, constructed before the go-go spirit had infused the former cowtown and made architectural flamboyance the order of the day.

The building was eight stories high. The high-ceilinged lobby featured a bank of elevators, and Bolan strode purposefully toward it. Pressing the button, he turned to watch the lobby traffic while he waited for the car. The soft chime announcing the arrival of the elevator was barely audible over the hum of conversation in the lobby.

Bolan turned and stepped in, followed by several other visitors, mostly businessmen, some affecting the J. R. Ewing fashion while others could have been from any place in the country. Some of them probably were. Bolan stepped to the rear of the car without pressing a button.

As the car rose, it slowly emptied until, with only three floors to go, Bolan was alone. Pressing the button for the last floor, he waited nervously for the car to climb the last thirty feet. For a brief instant, he realized the absurdity of his situation. The fate of the republic hung high above the ground on a slender steel cable. He suppressed a shudder and stepped out into a quiet corridor.

Largely law offices and import firms, the businesses that occupied the floor were announced by small signs of identical style. At the far end of the corridor was a heavy steel door leading to the emergency stairwell. Bolan made for it, keeping a casual eye on the office doors. The door to the stairs was open, and Bolan stepped through into the gloom of bare bulbs and battleship gray.

The flight led upward to a second door. Bolan mounted the steps and pushed out into the bright sun. Overhead, huge clouds floated as oblivious as ever of what was happening below. The roof was graveled tar, the small stones crunching softly underfoot. A jungle of conduits and shafts, steel ladders and windowless cupolas sprouted out of the tar as if it were fertile soil.

Affecting a casual demeanor, the Executioner stepped to the front of the building and looked down into the plaza, eight stories below. The view was commanding. The green expanse at the plaza's center, still damp with dew, gleamed as if recently oiled. Houston Street, directly below, was inaccessible to any shooter who wasn't a human fly, but the rest of the arteries that flowed into and out of the Dealey Plaza were in plain view. And traffic flow was such that, no matter how you entered the plaza, you had to pass under the muzzle of a gunman on the roof of the Dal-Tex Building.

This was it. Bolan knew it. It had to be.

He stepped back from the low stone wall that marked the roof's perimeter. Turning his attention to the structures behind him, he began a methodical search. There were nooks and crannies everywhere. Some were too small to hide a man, and others were tailor-made for that purpose. Even a chopper hovering above the building would be hard put to find a man determined to conceal himself on the roof.

Undoubtedly the roof would be sealed off sometime before the motorcade. Even the Secret Service wasn't that dumb. But Bolan couldn't take the chance. He wanted to know every conceivable hiding place by noon, and he'd be back later to spend the night.

A small steel cube housing a ventilation fan caught his eye. It had been recently painted, yet there were scratches at the edge of its grating. Stooping to look more closely, Bolan noticed its mounting screws were absent. He tugged the grating and it came away easily in his hands.

Inside, there was a long, thin package, wrapped in canvas and secured with two leather belts. Noting the exact position of the belts, Bolan undid them, and unrolled the canvas. The package was heavy, and he knew roughly what he'd find.

The reality took his breath away. It was a Walther WA2000. The very latest in sniper rifles. Bolan had seen one before. Its unique contours made it unmistakable. There was a box of 7.62 shells and a superb scope. Bolan handled the gun admiringly. Listing at more than four thousand dollars, it was a killing machine an artist could admire. And one only a top-drawer assassin could leave lying about so casually.

Kuscenko was coming.

And Bolan would be waiting.

17

Sunset.

The day's heat still hung in the air, the baked tar of the roof doing its best to throw it off. It would be a long night, but Bolan was prepared to wait. The motorcade would enter the plaza at approximately 9:00 a.m. the following morning. Sometime before that, Yuri Kuscenko would again put in an appearance. The rifle he'd found was all the proof Bolan needed. A plant is one thing, even as a diversion, but you don't use a rifle like the WA2000 as a throwaway. Not when a cheap Italian rifle from World War II would do the trick.

As he watched the rags of color bleach out and disappear along with the sun, Bolan couldn't help wonder what made a man like Kuscenko tick. The blond man he had seen at the rooming house had appeared to be young, not more than twenty-five or -six. His entire life had been directed toward a single purpose. As a trained assassin of the KGB, he had had the best available schooling from the most ruthless instructors imaginable. Balashikha was not a school you dared flunk out of. You got a diploma or you just disappeared. Kuscenko had graduated summa cum laude. Conjectural, of course, but nonetheless obvious.

And in a matter of hours, Bolan would once again be face-to-face with him, this time at close range, and this time with all the stakes in the pot. The sky began to darken and Bolan grew watchful. The building, like most office buildings, would be open, and sparsely populated, for several hours before closing down tight for the night. Kuscenko could show at any time.

As the darkness grew deeper, the sounds of traffic from the street below grew thinner, more distant. The quiet hum of machinery, the life support system of the Dal-Tex Building, grew more dominant. Eventually Bolan would be alone with the sky and the mechanical symphony to keep him company.

He'd dressed for the occasion, and had come armed, but not as heavily as he would have preferred. Big Thunder and the 93-R were all he could hope to get into the building easily. Too much was riding on him to risk discovery with a larger weapon. Kuscenko had managed, but he'd had help. How much and from whom were unknown, but Bolan was solo and it didn't much matter if Kuscenko had the Red Army on his side. The Executioner would have to take him out alone.

With the traffic all but gone, Bolan had nothing but his own mind to keep him alert. There was nothing to listen to but the night, and nothing to see but an occasional airliner winking through the sky. The deep blue-black directly overhead was smeared with stars. An occasional meteor flashed and disappeared in the city-bred haze at the horizon. At that point, even the brightest stars were only faint specks, dimmed by the urban glare.

As he sat in the quiet darkness, Bolan's upper arm, where Kuscenko had shot him the night before, ached a little. He had had it attended to that afternoon. The wound had been superficial and would heal quickly.

Alone in the November night, Bolan remembered his own history, his first encounter with assassination. Like most Americans, he had been young...and naive. The war that seared him, that would tear the fabric of his life to shreds, was still to come. And that day, in this city, was something he'd never forget. The glazed eyes standing before the flicker of TV screens in shop windows, the hush in the streets, the ears jammed against portable radio speakers, all were images in a silent tableau that he'd seen replayed a thousand times. The overwhelming impression was one of quiet. It was as if the day had been captured by silent cameras.

In retrospect, he could see himself engaged in conversations, but the words were lost. Even the first couple of hours, when people were crying in the streets, were silent. People wept soundlessly in memory, the tears bright on their cheeks. Their mouths were open, sagging shoulders shaking, but their voices had vanished. Preserved in utter quiet, like living insects in soundproof amber, people did what they had done, again and again, and not a whisper could be heard, as if the ears had no memory. Or as if the country had been stripped of noise by the awful reverberation clattering once, and once only, through the plaza, taking all sound with it as it faded into history.

This night was unlike any other he had spent. And as it deepened, Bolan wrapped rags of depression around himself to ward off the chill of reality. Wallowing in a national grief vividly recovered, the Executioner wondered why he bothered. His war was endless, the body count climbing ahead of the Dow Jones average and, unlike it, irreversible.

Killing had never come easily to him, but he seldom permitted himself to wonder about those to whom it did. Understanding them might lead to a recognition he considered with dread . . . that he was no different. It was easy enough to say killing for a cause is fine, if it's your cause. But is it really? he asked himself sometimes. Did anyone have the right, for whatever reason, to do what he did? The answer was easy to formulate, but impossible to accept without accepting with it a heavy responsibility. And he knew that as long as freedom mattered to the American people, someone had to be willing to shoulder the enormous burden of fighting fire with fire.

The center will not hold if the margin is a no-man's-land, he reasoned. He was determined that, as long as Mack Bolan drew breath, it would be one man's land. The moral desert others had created was a place where he would wander as long as it was necessary. Like a more traditional executioner, a solitary man who acted in the name of all the people, Mack Bolan stalked the wilderness in search of those who would impose that desert on everyone else.

The night grew chilly. A wind whipped around Bolan, unimpeded by anything but his clothes. The dark clothing would have blended with the shadow against the wall, if anyone had been there to see it. The shadows were where Mack Bolan had chosen to live, and he had grown accustomed to darkness of all kinds. It almost seemed as if he were forced by circumstances beyond his control to be his own source of illumination. High overhead, anomalous among the tall buildings, a bat squeaked as it whirled and dipped. Bolan suppressed a smile of kinship. It was too close to the truth.

His muscles were growing cramped from the inactivity. A glance at his watch showed it to be only 2:00 a.m., probably too late for Kuscenko to come now until dawn. Most likely the assassin would arrive as the building opened, disguised in something appropriate, perhaps as a workman. Such a cover would allow him to gain access to the roof without raising eyebrows.

Getting to his feet, the warrior stretched his arms over his head, reaching high to the edge of the elevator housing against which he had been sitting. A few quick calisthenics helped him shake off the cramping that had been making him uncomfortable. He also knew that limberness, the ability to move swiftly in the blink of an eye, might be crucial. He couldn't afford to stiffen up.

Walking to the parapet, he looked down into the street. Like any large American city, Dallas had a night life. Far from the bustle of New York of L.A., it was tame by comparison with either, but a few cars waited at the stoplight below. On the Stemmons Freeway across the plaza, there was a more steady stream of traffic. He walked toward the opposite side of the roof, to look at the buildings behind him.

Lights were on in several of the offices. Cleaning staff worked their way through the suites, office by office, their nights spent in thankless labor cleaning up the mess left behind by the busy and the indifferent. Here, too, Bolan found an analogy for his own career. It was remarkable how much people were capable of taking for granted. If something could be sloughed off on someone you never saw, it was easier to be thoughtless about those who came later to set things right than it was to take a few precautions as you went.

It was care for the future, for those who would come along later, that motivated Brognola, and it was perhaps the aspect of the big Fed's character that Bolan most admired. More than once, for the sake of a future that perhaps no one but he believed in, the man from Justice had staked his own future on a man who was tolerated reluctantly by some, passionately despised by others and ignored by all but a very few.

Living in the dark as he did, Bolan sometimes saw Brognola as a beacon, the one ray of light he could steer by. In a very real way, Bolan recognized, Brognola was as callously abused as the Executioner himself. Exploited, utilized, used...none of them very pretty words. None of them inaccurate. It might have been this shared, but unspoken, recognition that had initially bound them together. Bound them so tightly that now it would not be possible to break the bonds, themselves grown into something so complex that they rivaled a spiderweb for intricacy. And for its ability to hold them, whether they would or no.

There was a difference, too, between Bolan and the night crews that kept things neat. It did not escape him. No one pushing a broom, with whatever urgency, for however many thankless nights on end, had to watch his back. No one wanted to make the cleanup man part of the mess, leaving him on the trash heap for someone else to clean up. Bolan never knew when it would happen to him, but he knew that one day it would. Some cop would stand there, hands on hips, shaking his head. One more bloody mess in an endless string. And if Bolan bought the farm, who would carry on? Johnny?

Maybe.

But he, too, would have his turn. And then?

Bolan turned and walked back to the cranny where he would spend the night. The hard stone against his back felt solid, reassuring. For the night, at least, he didn't have to watch behind him. He looked up, and a streak of light, so quick that he might have imagined it, tore the dark curtain aside for an instant, flashing low and disappearing almost before he saw it. And the darkness returned, this time for good.

Bolan slept.

THE FIRST LIGHT OF DAY was cold. Bolan felt the brightness of the rising sun and flickered his eyelids. In an instant, he was wide awake. His watch said 6:05. The depression of the night before was still with him, but scurried back into its own shadows like a night creature with its hatred of the light.

Bolan stood and stretched. He checked his weapons and made certain the extra clips for each were readily available. His jacket felt heavy, and drops of dew glittered in the folds of the leather where they had collected. Like small, ephemeral jewels, they sparkled as he moved, slipping across the smooth surface, sundering and recombining, then dropped silently to the tar and were gone.

Behind him, he heard a hum. Felt it, really. The elevator was running as the Dal-Tex Building made ready for the workday. From this point on, Kuscenko's arrival would be a constant possibility.

And he would not be the only threat. If the Secret Service had learned anything at all since 1963, there would be guards, heavily armed, on a few of the buildings around the plaza. They couldn't cover them all, but their presence, visible and vigilant, would be a deterrent.

Bolan would bet a bundle that the Dal-Tex Building would not feature a guard of its own. Too much had been going Kuscenko's way for it to be coincidence or dumb luck. The sniper rifle in the ventilation housing meant Kuscenko had chosen this spot, and he probably had done so with the help of inside information.

Maybe I'll just ask him about that, Bolan thought. At six-thirty, Bolan heard a thud in the stairwell. The door scraped on its concrete jamb, and swung back. Yuri Kuscenko had arrived.

Bolan waited as the tall, slender blonde, dressed in crisply starched coveralls obviously purchased for the purpose, stepped through the door onto the tarry gravel. His work shoes crunched the small stones. He closed the door behind him, pressing it home with the flat of his hand.

Struggling against his urge to nail the assassin, Bolan pressed back against the stone. And waited. Kuscenko might have help. Bolan had to be sure what he was up against before he did anything.

The young Russian looked around appreciatively, maintaining the charade of a workman beginning his day. At the same time, Bolan knew, he was scanning the other roofs for early guards. Satisfied that he would be unobserved, Kuscenko crossed to the ventilation housing and lifted the cover, just as Bolan had done the day before.

The assassin reached into the housing and withdrew his package. He dropped to his knees and undid the leather straps that bound the canvas closed. When he had unscrewed the lens covers on either end of the scope and sighted through it, he made a last-minute adjustment, sighted again and, satisfied, opened the box of shells. Kuscenko detached the magazine and slid five cartridges in, carefully checking each one before inserting it. When he had loaded the magazine, he rammed it home with an audible click.

It was obvious he was on his own and planned to make the hit by himself, from this very roof. Satisfied, Bolan slipped behind the elevator housing and moved to the other side. Peering out, he watched Kuscenko replace the rifle under the ventilation grate and replace the cover.

As soon as the cover was in place, Bolan unharnessed Big Thunder. The silver AutoMag glistened in the early sunlight as the Executioner stepped out from behind the elevator housing. He had taken a half dozen steps when the door sprang open with a bang, slamming against the wall behind it. Out of the stairwell stepped two heavyset men, guns drawn. One wore the uniform of a Dallas policeman. The other was almost completely bald.

"Hold it right there, pal," the older guy in civvies said. "J.D., arrest him and read him his rights."

Bolan was dumbstruck.

The cop waved a hand at the other guy, as if to shut him up. "Put the cannon down on the roof. Use your fingertips, and do it slow. You move too suddenlike, and you're gone."

Bolan did as he was told, bending slowly to place the AutoMag on the gravel. As he straightened, J.D., the cop, stepped forward and frisked him. He whistled when he found the Beretta, and held it aloft for Baldy to see. "Nice gun," he said. He meant it.

Bolan gestured with one hand toward Kuscenko. "He's the one you ought to be concerned with."

Baldy turned to look. "Him? How come? He's just up here doin' his job. Ain't you, there?"

Kuscenko nodded at the guy, then at Bolan. "Yes, sir. Just doing my job."

"Let's go," J.D. said. Baldy mumbled and pushed Bolan in the small of his back, urging him forward.

Bolan began to move toward the door. He turned to look over his shoulder at the Russian.

Kuscenko smiled.

18

Baldy and the cop ignored Bolan's plea and pushed him
again, more roughly now, toward the doorway. Kuscenko
watched, the smile slowly fading into a contemplative study.
His eyes lingered on Bolan, reluctant to break contact.

Bolan dug in his heels. "Look, I'm telling you that man
is an assassin. In a couple of hours, all hell is going to break
loose down there, and you can stop it. Right now."

"Oh, yeah?" Baldy followed the question with a shove.
"And I'm telling you to move it. Now."

"Will you listen to me, dammit! Look under the grate
there, right next to him. There's a rifle."

"Sure, sure. I know all about it. As a matter of fact, I
know it's your gun. I even know you're going to try to escape, and . . ."

"Shut up, Mike. Your mouth is too damned big." J.D.
turned to the baldheaded guy, whose drawn gun was wavering uncertainly between J.D. and Bolan. Obviously J.D.
was the leader here, with hairless Mike providing backup
muscle and an extra gun.

Now Bolan knew for sure. These guys were part of it.
They had to be. Mike had given the ball game away. And
Bolan was unarmed.

"Okay, read about it in the papers, then," Bolan said,
seeming to give up his argument. He shrugged and began
walking to the doorway again. When the three men reached
the door, still open and swinging on its squeaky hinges in the

breeze, J.D. stepped through first. Bolan came next, then Mike.

When all three had reached the bottom of the stairs, Bolan moved toward the door from the stairwell to the floor itself and was about to pull open the door when J.D. stopped him. "Hold on there, son. We'll take the stairs. No use in wasting electricity on you. Besides, it's a long walk, and you might make a break for it."

"I'm not going anywhere," Bolan said. He smiled at the cop.

"You got that right, son."

"You're overdoing the 'son' stuff, aren't you?"

"How so?"

"You're about as Southern as I am."

"It don't matter where I'm from. Or where you're from, neither. What matters is where you're goin', and that's down them stairs. Right now." He gestured with his gun, a Colt Python .357 Magnum. It wasn't standard police issue, but Bolan knew many cops had taken to using them. Upscaling their firepower to match that of their opposition, they took every opportunity to pare down the odds. And some of them, like this one, were no better than the criminals they were supposed to be combatting.

Bolan moved slowly toward the head of the stairwell, dropping his hand reluctantly from the corridor entrance doorknob. He wanted his captors loose, relaxed. If they thought it was over, they might get careless. If he was going to have a chance, they damned well better.

Once again the three set out down the stairs, J.D. in the lead and Mike bringing up the rear.

Four flights down, Bolan glanced at his watch. It was 8:55. The motorcade was due in five minutes. He couldn't wait much longer. Breaks were for making, anyway.

As they started down the next flight, Bolan made his move. Halfway down, he pitched forward in a dive, catching J.D. just above the hips with his shoulder. He hung on as the cop fell forward, riding the man's body the rest of the way down the stairs like an imperiled surfer. The big man's body took most of the bumps, smoothing out an otherwise rocky ride.

Mike shouted but held his fire. Bolan had counted on that. The baldheaded man was easily rattled. He wouldn't freeze for long, though, and Bolan twisted as they reached the landing between flights, bringing J.D. into the line of fire. The cop's Magnum and Bolan's guns had been sent flying by the initial impact, and the Magnum had rattled to a stop against the wall, just beyond Bolan's reach.

Using his legs, Bolan wormed his way toward the gun, keeping the struggling policeman atop him.

"Dammit, Mike, don't just stand there," J.D. yelled. "Shoot the son of a bitch. Get down here." Mike began to run down the steps. With all the strength he could summon, Bolan launched himself backward, releasing his hold on J.D. in order to reach for the barrel of the Python.

Both Bolan and J.D. dived for the gun at the same time. Mike fired once.   As Bolan grasped the Python, J.D. gave a little gasp and fell forward. Blood pooled under his blue uniform. Mike's bullet had found the wrong target, and Dallas had one less crooked cop. Mike wasn't as dumb as he'd seemed, however; at least he had good reflexes. In an instant he started to sprint back up the stairs, turning into the next flight before Bolan could fire a shot.

Leaping to his feet, Bolan raced up the first flight. At the landing he stopped to make sure he didn't run right up the barrel of Mike's gun. But the footsteps still rang as the bald guy continued his climb.

Bolan raced after him, glancing at his watch. 8:58. Two minutes.

An eternity.

With one more flight to go, Bolan heard the door slam back against the wall, and Mike was on the roof. The crowds below could be heard, as the cheering in the distance came closer. It seemed to swell like a breaker rushing toward shore, its hiss and thunder unsteady in its progress.

Then the sound faded. Mike had closed the door. The darkness on the stairway seemed thicker than it was, with the sun cut off. Bolan reached the last landing and stopped at the doorway. He pushed, but the door stayed closed. Either Mike had jammed it, or he was using his body to keep it closed. The door was heavy-gauge steel plate. There was no way to fire through it. Bolan braced his shoulder and strained. The door groaned. It still held, but it was beginning to yield. Bolan shoved a second time, and the door sprang open, slamming into the stone wall behind it once again.

The first shot was Mike's. It glanced off the doorframe above Bolan's head and clanged down the stairwell. And then Bolan heard it. The shot he'd been trying to prevent. Followed quickly by three more.

He had to stop Kuscenko from getting away. It might be too late to stop him from killing, but there was no way he could get away. Not now.

Bolan dived through the doorway onto the gravel, hit in a shoulder roll and sprang to his feet. He raced to the nearest cover, just ahead of Mike's next shot. There was other movement on nearby roofs. A blur of khaki on the Criminal Courts Building told Bolan there were police snipers present.

Where was Kuscenko?

Bolan scanned the roof, keeping his head low, but saw no sign of the assassin. It dawned on him that he was in a box. There was a dead policeman in the stairwell below, Bolan had known about the assassin's rifle, and he had even touched it. Now he was flat on his stomach on the roof of the very building from which four shots had been fired at the President of the United States.

If they caught him alive, something they would try to avoid, no one would believe him—if he even got a chance to tell his story. Without Kuscenko, he had no proof. As far as anyone else would know, Mack Bolan, the Executioner, had become Mack Bolan, presidential assassin. In the public mind, it would be a logical progression.

Mike was biding his time. Wherever Kuscenko was, the longer Bolan waited, the more likely the assassin would get away. In the streets below, there was chaos. The cresting wave of adulation had become a steady roar of confusion. In the distance, sirens keened, some approaching and some fading away. Bolan wondered who had been hit, if anyone.

The sirens nearing the building seemed to surround the place with their sound. It spiraled up into the sky, reverberating eerily among the tall buildings. The background roar below began to dim. Time was running out. Bolan flattened himself even further against the gravel. A shot could come from any direction. And time was on Mike's side. All he had to do was lie low and wait.

In the current situation—shots fired at the President and a man in black engaged in a gun battle with a policeman— no one would think twice if Bolan were blown away by the police marksmen who were converging on the adjacent building roofs. As for the dead cop downstairs, it was Bolan's word against Mike's —and while Mike might be no genius, Bolan was sure that whoever arranged for J.D. and Mike's arrival on the rooftop had made certain that Mike knew what to do or say in the event that things went badly for J.D.

Bolan was in a box.

A neat one. Yeah, very neat. He even admired it. But so far nobody had closed the trap. As long as there was daylight, he had a chance.

A whining sound was followed by the rain of broken mortar on his shoulder. Only then did he hear the crack of a distant rifle. The supersonic slug had struck just inches above his head. It was time to move out.

He fired the Python twice in Mike's direction. Wheeling around the stone wall behind which he had been hiding, he got up and sprinted for the doorway. Mike saw him and poked his head out. Too far.

Bolan fired on the move. The shot missed.

But the ricochet didn't. The battered slug tore through the baldheaded man's right eye, blasting away the side of his face. He was dead before the bits of bone stopped bouncing on the gravel. Bolan dived through the open doorway and landed on the slick floor inside. He rolled sideways, just ahead of four slugs from the marksmen.

The worst part was over. Getting out of the building would be easier than getting off the roof. Or would it? The whup-whup of a police chopper overhead made him guess again. This was no picnic.

The building would be surrounded. The stairs were already beginning to echo with a search party from below. The elevators would be watched. And Bolan's problem was more complicated than his pursuers knew. He knew he was innocent, but they didn't. They would kill him on sight, but he couldn't kill a guy doing his job. Surrender was out of the question. He had no idea of the scope of the plot, but he was a dead duck in the eyes of the plotters. Jack Rubys were a dime a dozen. And not just in Dallas.

Back on the roof, the chopper was about to land. He couldn't go up, and he couldn't go down. At least not in any conventional manner. He retrieved his weapons from near the wall of the stairwell and, looking desperately around, noticed the second door on the top landing. He ran to it just as the chopper touched down.

He turned the handle and yanked. At first the door resisted. It groaned as he yanked again. On the third tug, it opened. Inside, he could see the pulleys and greased cables of the elevator system. He was at the top of the shaft. It was a long way down.

And it was his only chance.

The shaft was dimly lit by sunlight coming through the grimy skylight above. Far below, a sliver of light marked the presence of the car. It was slowly rising toward him. He wasn't dead yet.

Bracing himself, Bolan reached out to grab the cable with one hand. With the other, he pulled the door to the stairwell shut behind him. He let go of the doorframe and grabbed the cable with his other hand. His gloves weren't made for this kind of heavy duty. And if there were cable slivers sticking out, he'd be in big trouble. He ran his right hand tentatively along the tight cable. It was slick and sliver free. But it got its least wear at this height. He checked the other strand and it was slick, as well.

Down the shaft, the car was still rising toward him. He would wait. Unless the door to the stairs opened behind him, he was safe. Sooner or later, the elevator car would come to the top floor. When it did, he could land lightly on its roof and ride down to the basement. Sooner or later.

Failing that, he could slide down the cable to the basement on his own. If he had to.

The car continued its slow rise. Behind him, he could hear heavy footsteps on the roof. The whirring pulleys groaned and squealed as the cables paid out. Bolan's grip on the girder above was not as secure as he'd like, one glove slippery with grease from the cable. His recent shoulder wound began to throb. The elevator was about forty feet below, still rising. It wobbled slightly in the shaft, rose another twenty feet and stopped.

This was it.

He swung his legs out into the shaft and wrapped them around the cable, then let go of the girder with the hand wearing the greasy glove. Grasping the cable as securely as he could with the other still-dry hand, he let go and began to slide. He pressed his knees tightly together to slow his descent, and held on. A sharp pain in his left hand told him he'd found a sliver on the cable.

The twenty-foot descent was quick and ended quietly. Bolan let go of the cable and settled himself on the roof of the elevator. He listened, but heard nothing from within the car. He moved to a squatting position, trying to look through the ceiling of the car. But although a dull glow of the car's lights could be seen through the translucent plastic, he could see nothing else.

A mechanical hum signaled the opening of the elevator door. Two shadows moved in the illuminated box below. Their voices were muffled, but intelligible.

"I don't know what the hell's going on. But I know there were two men on that fuckin' roof."

"J.D. says there was one, a big guy in black."

"J.D.'s so full of shit his eyes are brown. I was on the Criminal Courts Building roof. There was a guy in coveralls, too. I saw the bastard."

"Probably just a workman."

"Then where the fuck did he go? Why didn't he hang around, get himself on TV?"

"What difference does it make?"

"One of those bastards tried to kill the President, Buddy. Okay, he didn't, but it was close. Too close. I want to know who the other guy was. Are we chasin' two guys or one? It's the difference between a lone nut and a conspiracy. To me, that's all the difference in the world."

"I still say it don't matter, Captain."

"You're young yet, Buddy. You was hardly born in '63. I was a cop then, and I'm a cop now. I can tell you, I never swallowed the official story about Oswald. Didn't then, and don't now. Now, I'm not sayin' I know what happened, 'cause I don't. No more'n I know what the fuck happened on that roof this mornin'. But I'll tell you, I ain't lettin' it happen again. Not this time, Bud. I'm goin' to find botha them fuckers, and I'm gonna get the truth out 'em iffen I hafta hold a cattle prod to their nuts. This time, it's *my* turn, Buddy.''

''Whatever you say, Captain.''

Bolan listened with appreciation. The captain sounded like a good man. For a minute, he thought about dropping into the car to tell him what did happen. But he couldn't. Kuscenko was still out there, on the loose. He'd missed the President, and that was a plus. But how could he have missed? Bolan wondered. There had been no distraction. Dolan hadn't even reached the roof when the assassin fired.

But, like the captain in the car below him, Mack Bolan was determined to get the truth.

Any way he could.

Any way he had to.

Sorry, Captain, Bolan thought, but this time it's *my* turn.

19

The elevator opened at the lobby, and the two men got out. A moment later, it descended one more level. Bolan sat atop the car for an hour. He had overheard no further conversation, and the elevator remained where it was. He had heard creaking cables in an adjacent shaft and guessed security had closed the building down, leaving one elevator running for controlled access.

At last Bolan decided it was time to move. He had waited long enough; now he'd have to take his chances getting out of the building. The metal grating that provided access to the roof of the car from below was held loosely in place by a pair of friction clips. Bolan pressed the grate downward, then turned it on an angle and pulled it up through the square hole.

The Plexiglas sheets used to diffuse the light from the single fluorescent bulb were a little tougher. It would be simple to break one, but the noise might attract attention. Wrestling with one sheet, he managed to get a fingernail under an edge and to pry the sheet up far enough to get his fingers under it. He slid the sheet sideways. The resulting hole was large enough to admit him.

Carefully balancing his weight, he leaned forward and looked into the car. As he had feared, the door was closed. He tried to see if it was locked, but he was too far away. If he descended into the car and anyone heard him in there, he'd be finished, but there was too much at stake. Grasping the rim of the car's superstructure, he swung over the hole and dropped through. The soft thud of his feet on the car floor sounded to him like thunder.

Bolan held his breath. He heard a profusion of mechanical noises, but nothing else. No voices. It seemed probable the basement was deserted. He moved to the lock and found it was not engaged. Power was still available. He pressed the Door Open button and the door slid back to release him.

Outside the car, the basement was dimly lit with bare bulbs and low wattage fluorescents. Anybody with work to do would know where the power switches were for better light or, more likely, would bring his own.

Moving carefully, Bolan made a tour of the basement. It was high ceilinged, to accommodate the building's heating and cooling plants, emergency power and other heavy-duty equipment. He noted several heavy steel doors, but he didn't try to see where they led. Not yet.

He hoped he was alone in the basement. Had to be. If they caught him here, it was finished. The war, his career, everything. Himself included. The perimeter tour finished, he knew what he had to do. Several windows were mounted high in the wall, just above ground level, but they were covered with heavy steel grates bolted into place. The elevator was one route, but it would take him right into the lobby, or back to the roof. Neither was a place he cared to go.

That left the stairs. And there were several to choose from. On his inspection of the building the previous day, he had noticed a freight delivery dock at the rear. It was just the ticket. But he couldn't just walk up the stairs, dressed as he was.

He tried the door to the custodial staff room. It swung back silently. Probably the best-oiled hinges in the joint, Bolan thought. He felt for the light switch and clicked it on. The room glowed dully under a circular fluorescent. Inside, there was a large, scarred wooden desk, with a banker's desk lamp on it, and a doorway. Through the door, he could just make out a row of lockers. Maybe he'd get lucky. It was about time.

Keeping an ear tuned to the outside, he slipped through the door. He felt for a wall switch and came up empty, but there was enough dim light from the outer chamber. Moving swiftly, he tried several lockers. Nothing. Those without locks were empty. And breaking into the locked ones would cause more noise than he could afford to make.

He was about to leave, when he spied a heap in the corner. At first glance, it looked like rags. He walked over to the pile and poked it with his toe. It was stiff and its starch rasped as the cloth gave before the pressure. He bent down and picked up the bundle. It felt new, and smelled new.

Carrying it to the outer chamber where the lighting was better, he realized why. It was new all right, and he had seen it before, just that morning. The assassin must have left through the basement. He was holding Yuri Kuscenko's coveralls.

Bolan stripped off his jacket and hung it on a hook behind the desk. Removing Big Thunder and its harness, he placed them on the desk. He struggled into the coveralls and noticed they were a good fit. The assassin must have been bigger than he'd seemed. Bolan took the jacket from the hook and put it in an empty locker. It might not be discovered for days. The Beretta bulged a bit under the coveralls, but not noticeably.

Out in the basement again, Big Thunder slung over one shoulder, he crossed the floor to a workroom he'd seen on his circuit. Opening the door, he clicked on a light and entered. He was in luck—there was a toolbox on a workbench. He opened the box and removed a few tools, coiled its harness around the AutoMag and tucked it into the box. Not exactly handy, but at least he wouldn't have to leave it behind. And if anyone got close enough to see it, he'd already be in big trouble, anyway.

Crossing to a stairwell he figured would take him near the freight dock, he opened the door carefully to listen. When he heard nothing, he started up the stairs, trying to act as casual as he could. He whistled softly as he climbed. At the ground floor, he whistled a bit louder and pushed the door open.

He was in the freight receiving room. There was a guard on the door. Bolan headed straight for the guard. He nodded.

"Big doin's, today, huh?" Bolan said.

The guard nodded. "Bet your ass. Anybody else down there?"

"Nope. Like a tomb down there."

"You lock the door?"

"No. No keys."

"Well, hell . . . guess I'll have to. You take it easy, now, hear?"

"Easy as I can," Bolan said. He walked on through the access door adjacent to the big corrugated roller door for freight reception, and out into the street. There were cops everywhere. Small knots of people still stood around, talking, their eyes glazed.

As near as Bolan could tell from the scraps of overheard conversation, the President hadn't been hit. More than that, he didn't know. And he wasn't about to hang around and talk about it. He crossed the street at the rear of the Dal-Tex Building and walked the two blocks to his car. Reaching inside the coveralls, he got his keys to unlock the trunk, threw the toolbox inside and closed the lid.

He cranked up the rental car and pulled out into the traffic, still snarled by the morning's disruption. Working his way carefully to the nearest side street, he hung right, leaving the confusion behind.

He still had a problem. He didn't dare enter the hotel lobby with his torn and dirty clothes, and the coveralls he wore on top of them would just call attention to him. He'd have to carry on the charade a little longer. Parking near the hotel, instead of in its lot, he got the toolbox out of the trunk. He'd want it in any case, because he didn't want to be more than an arm's length away from the AutoMag. Lugging the heavy box, he walked to the rear of the hotel and found the maintenance entrance. He nodded to the security man on the door and stepped on in.

After climbing the stairs to the fourth floor, he entered the main corridor and crossed to the elevator. When it came, he stepped in. There was a man at the rear of the car, the flower in his lapel all the evidence Bolan needed that he was a hotel employee. Bolan stood near the door, ignoring him.

"Who are you with?" the man asked, tapping Bolan on the shoulder.

"What?"

"I want to know who you're with. What company?"

Bolan looked blankly at his interrogator.

"Who do you work for? I've told vendors a hundred times, use the service elevator. That's what it's for."

"Sorry, I'm new on the job. I guess they forgot to tell me." The man's inquisition was irritating, but Bolan kept his cool. He turned back to face the elevator door.

"Well? I'm waiting...." The man was persistent, Bolan had to give him that.

"Phoenix Air Conditioning," Bolan said, stepping off at his floor.

"Well, you haven't heard the last of this, fellow...." The man kept on prattling as the door closed, muffling his voice. As the car continued to rise, Bolan could still hear him ranting.

Bolan went to his room and entered it with a sigh. Closing the door, he leaned back against it. He felt a thousand years old. And he still had work to do.

Bolan turned on the television. While he got ready for a shower, he listened to the endless chatter of the newscast. The reporters, as usual, were struggling to fill time. They knew very little and had been given a great deal of time to prove otherwise. They failed.

Already, in one of the favored techniques of broadcast journalism, they were trotting out the typical pantheon of paid consultants to develop a psychological profile of the alleged assassin. Not bad, since they didn't have a clue who it was.

The old clichés about disaffected loners, envy, and so on, were crackling over the airwaves. Not once did he hear the word "conspiracy" mentioned. Americans seemed to be pathologically afraid of the word when it had something to do with their own political process. Nobody seemed to remember that the first American President killed by an assassin had been a conspiracy victim. Not to mention the most recent.

In the shower, Bolan mulled over the facts known about that morning's attack. They were scanty, at best, but heartening. At least to the general public, they were. The assassin had fired four shots at the motorcade, a senator had been wounded, but no one had been killed. The President was unharmed. Comforting.

But not to Mack Bolan.

He kept asking himself how a highly trained mechanic, with the best equipment in the world and more help than he could use, could have missed. Missed not once, but four times. So far, according to the media, the rifle had not been found. When it was, it would be interesting to see what was made of it. For public consumption.

After the shower, Bolan felt better. It was time to get Brognola on the horn. He dialed the big Fed at his office. It was still early, and the man from Justice was sure to be having a busier day than usual, what with the morning's events.

The secretary recognized his voice. "Just one moment, please. Mr. Brognola will be right on the line."

He was as good as her word. "Striker, what the hell *happened* down there? Dammit, man, I thought you were on top of things."

"Hal, you know better than that. We don't even know who's behind all this. But I'll tell you one thing—it's a lot bigger than we thought."

"How do you know?"

"Because I was on the roof this morning."

"You were where? How the . . ."

"That's right. I saw him. It was our boy, Mr. Kuscenko. At least that's what Albright's friends call him. I think this is a Company op, Hal. I'm convinced of it. I want to know what the hell is going on. I want to talk to Albright."

"I'll call him. What's your number there?"

"No! No phones. I want him in the flesh, down here. Tonight. You tell him to meet me in the Carousel Club at 9:00 p.m. sharp. Alone."

"Sounds like you don't trust him, guy."

Bolan sighed before responding. "Hal, I'll tell you something. Right now, I don't trust anybody."

There was a long moment of silence on the other end. Some muffled sucking noises told Bolan Brognola was fiddling with a cigar. When the Fed spoke, it was through clenched teeth. "I can understand that. I guess I can, anyway. I'll tell Albright."

"You do that." Bolan couldn't remember the last time he had spoken so harshly to him. He knew it hurt Brognola, but feelings could be soothed, time permitting. Right now, it didn't.

"Striker? You be careful."

"Uh-huh."

"Hear me?"

"Yeah. Talk to you later, Hal."

He hung up without ceremony. He could catch a few hours' sleep before meeting Albright. It would be most welcome. He crossed to the bed and lay down. The sheets felt cool on his skin. He closed his eyes and was asleep before the lids met.

AFTER TOSSING FITFULLY FOR A WHILE, Bolan realized he was awake. He sat upright. The digital clock on the nightstand read 7:00 p.m. He'd been asleep for five hours. He was still tired, bone tired. But something had awakened him. Some sixth sense. He reached for the Beretta on the night table. Once the gun was in his hand, he felt better. He strained his ears to listen for a repetition of the noise that had wakened him.

A scratching sound, so soft that he barely heard it, at the door to his room. The dead bolt was thrown and the chain latch on. No simple burglar with a shim or a credit card would be able to get into the room. If there was someone there, he was either serious or about to be disappointed. Bolan listened carefully while slipping on his pants, moving the gun from hand to hand as he zipped and belted them.

He tiptoed to the door and placed his ear against the frame. A soft hum, like a man whispering, was followed by a renewed rasping. It was metallic, and getting louder. They had switched to a key. Bolan, hoping to throw them off guard, reached across and unfastened the chain, careful not to let it bang against the door.

When the chain was off, he went into the bathroom and closed the door three-quarters of the way. All the lights were off and the curtains drawn. Whoever came in would be framed in the doorway, silhouetted against the corridor lights behind.

Suddenly the door opened. Two men stood in the doorway, their faces in shadow.

One of the men whispered loudly, "He ain't here, Joe. Put on the light." The other did as he was told. Amateurs, both of them. Bolan waited until they were both facing away from the bathroom, then stepped out with the Beretta ready to roll.

It was party time.

20

In the bright light, Bolan figured his callers were cops.

"You looking for something?" he asked.

"Dallas Police," the one called Joe said, reaching behind him to his hip pocket.

"Hold it right there. Close the door softly."

The cop did as he was told.

"Now place your weapons on the floor. And I mean *all* your weapons. I'm going to check, and if I find you holding, you're dead men."

The young cop pulled a service revolver from a hip holster and placed it on the thick carpet, butt first. He took a second weapon, a small automatic, probably a .22 and placed it next to the first.

"Now assume the position, against the door." When the cop had done as he was told, Bolan gestured at the second man with his Beretta. "Now you..."

The second man looked at his partner, as if for instructions, but Joe was looking at the door panel. Hard. The man followed suit, placing a service revolver and an automatic, this one a .25 caliber, on the carpet.

"Now join your partner."

The man turned around and placed his hands flat against the wall, next to the door. Bolan stepped close and patted him down. He found a switchblade in the man's jacket pocket and tossed it on the bed. "You don't hear too well, do you? Or is it that you just don't listen?"

"I thought you were talking about guns," the man said. His voice broke. He turned to look at Bolan out of one eye. Bolan saw drops of sweat on the man's brow, and decided the guy was too scared to have been planning to try something.

"Next time, listen."

He nodded eagerly, grateful he'd been spared. Bolan moved to Joe and patted him down more carefully. This one was trouble—obviously the leader of the pair, and most likely the more dangerous of the two.

As Bolan patted him down, Joe seemed nervous, too, but his was a different kind of nervousness. He fidgeted restlessly. He was holding something, Bolan was sure of it. One hand was much higher on the door than the other, as if he wanted to keep something out of Bolan's reach. Of course, a wrist harness. Probably a small-caliber palm gun. Maybe even a single-shot job. Bolan tugged the sleeve on that arm, and the guy turned suddenly, slamming his elbow into Bolan's arm.

The Beretta flew loose, and Bolan smashed a forearm into Joe's neck, knocking him to his knees. The second man seemed uncertain what to do. Joe turned and dived for Bolan's legs, hitting him hard just above the knees. The impact carried both men to the floor.

Bolan reached out and caught Joe around the hips, flipping him over and sending him crashing into the wall at the foot of the bed. Momentarily stunned, Joe groaned. Bolan grabbed his Beretta a moment too late for everyone concerned. The other man, thinking he had to make his move, dived for the pile of weapons on the carpet.

The Beretta spit, sending a burst of three 9 mm parabellum slugs on their way with a barely audible hiss. The three slugs impacted in a tight circle just below the diving man's throat. He gurgled and reached for his neck, his fingers swimming upstream against the fatal tide gushing from his ruptured arteries. The blood splashed against his fingers and ran down his hands onto his cuffs.

Joe was on his knees now. Desperate, he threw himself at Bolan, knocking him over. He grabbed the Executioner's gun hand at the wrist, shaking it violently in an effort to dislodge the gun. Bolan kneed him in the chest as they rolled over, and the blow forced the breath from Joe's lungs.

Gasping for air, he scrambled toward the guns on the floor, his fingers closing around the barrel of one of the two service revolvers. He flung the gun toward Bolan, narrowly missing his head. While Bolan ducked Joe grabbed the second .38. Before he could aim, Bolan shot him, the Beretta nearly obliterating his face with the 3-shot burst. The guy fell backward, his legs stiff, his feet kicking on the soft carpet. Then he lay still.

The room smelled like death. It was a smell that seemed to follow Bolan wherever he went, one he knew only too well. One he had grown to accept. But never to like.

Once again, he had been flushed from a hole. This time, he knew, the tip could not have come from Albright, because the CIA man didn't know where he was staying. Convinced he had not been followed back to the hotel from the Dal-Tex Building, he could conclude only one thing: they had known where he was all along. Coming here for him must have been their fallback plan, in case they failed to nail him at the scene.

But who were they? What did they want with him? The questions were beginning to eat at him. Obviously they wanted to frame him in Kuscenko's place, but that didn't explain why Kuscenko had missed. Why frame a man for attempted assassination when you can nail him for the actual deed?

Then Bolan understood. He had spent a good part of the previous day and all last night and early this morning trying to prevent Kuscenko from killing the President. He had spent several hours thereafter trying to escape from the frame. They had wanted him preoccupied, and they had got what they wanted.

It was all beginning to take shape now, like a ship looming out of the fog. Kuscenko had missed on purpose. He hadn't been after the President at all. But if Bolan had been arrested for the shooting, he would have been out of the way, unable to prevent Kuscenko's actual mission, whatever it was.

That might just mean that Albright's friend Mitchell was right. Kuscenko was after one of the two defectors, and somebody inside the Company was helping him, as much to cover his own ass as to assist the KGB.

There was a mole. High up in the CIA. And Bolan was going to dig deep enough and fast enough to get on his tail and chase him right out of the ground. That had to be his first priority. And the only way to do it was to stop the assassin and protect the defector he wanted to kill.

But which defector was it? Even Mack Bolan couldn't be in two places at once. And to get the defectors into one place, he would have to alert the Company and tip his hand. No, he decided, all he could do was follow Mitchell's hunch.

But first Bolan had to get rid of the bodies and get the hell out of the hotel. He'd have to leave the blood. It would not be an easy job, and it had to be quick. For all he knew, Joe and his friend had backup downstairs. Slipping on his shirt, Bolan opened the door and looked out into the corridor. It was empty, but he knew it was dinnertime and there was bound to be traffic in the hall. Leaving the door slightly ajar, he sprinted down the hall to the nearest service area.

The laundry room door was unlocked. He yanked it open, dragged a laundry cart into the corridor and pushed it down the hall, its squeaky wheels protesting loudly. Just as an elevator opened at the other end of the corridor, he dragged the cart into his room after him and closed the door.

After pulling the laundry out of the cart and tossing it on the bed, Bolan hefted Joe and tossed him into the cart. The other body followed Joe. Bolan threw some laundry in on top of the two dead men, opened the door and found the hall was again empty. As he pushed the cart, now infinitely heavier, down the hallway, its wheels groaned under the added burden.

At the laundry room, he shoved the cart in, then peered back into the hall. A man and woman were approaching, but were too far away to be able to notice which door he came out. He stepped into the hall.

Rattling some coins in his fist, he walked toward the couple, smiling amiably as he asked, "Excuse me, which way is the soda machine?"

The man pointed back over his shoulder. "That way. An alcove at the end of the hall, past the elevators."

"Thanks," Bolan said. He smiled at the couple again and walked past them. Behind him, he could hear the rattle of keys followed by the sound of a door closing. He reached his own room and closed the door behind him. One more step and he could get out of here.

It would be none too soon.

He grabbed his things and jammed them into his bags, snapped them shut and threw on a jacket. By the time he reached the lobby, his nerves were jangling. The Carousel Club was a fifteen-minute drive, and he'd have to wait more than an hour for Albright if he left immediately. He toted the heavy bags to the car. Leaving them with a bellman until he drove back for them would call attention to him. And he had had enough of that already.

The car was where he had left it. It was the only one on the street. He tossed the bags in the trunk, closed the lid and got behind the wheel. It was getting dark, and when he threw on the lights he noticed the paper, stuck under the driver's side wiper. He rolled down the window and grabbed the paper.

He expected it to be a ticket and was preparing to toss it aside without a glance when something—maybe the light-weight paper—made him look at it. Turning on the dome light, he read the handwritten scrawl with some difficulty. The author had used a stubby pencil, smearing the fat letters across the page as a child would have done.

Mr. Bolan,
I'm glad I missed your President. It is what I was paid for. When we meet again, I'll kill you. That, too, is what I am paid for. See you in New Mexico.

                                                    Yuri

So it was getting personal at last. It always did. Bolan had been wondering when they would get down to cases. Toe to toe. Survival of the fittest, Darwin said. And so it would be. And, as a prudent man might, Mack Bolan wondered who would survive this time.

He didn't doubt for a moment that the note was genuine. There was no reason for it not to be. Kuscenko knew that the impersonality of their meetings up to now was unsatisfactory, to him and to the man they called the Executioner. There was pride at stake in this, the kind of pride a true professional takes in his work. And Bolan knew that Kuscenko was, above all else, a professional. Just how good he was, only time would tell. But it wouldn't be long now.

Not long at all.

Bolan pulled away from the curb and drove at a leisurely rate, as if the note had solved all his problems. In a way, it had. All but one. And Albright would settle that matter as soon as they met.

At the Carousel Club, he left his car in the lot and walked around to the side door. As he opened the door, the sound of country swing blew out on a blast of alcoholic wind. There was no smell like that of a bar. The band inside was playing full volume, and Bolan wondered what the door was made of, to be able to contain the sound so thoroughly. He turned to look as it closed behind him It was covered with a thick layer of sound-absorbent material, wrapped in bright red cloth that glistened as only artificial satin could.

He walked to the bar and ordered a diet soda. A lanky brunette in skintight jeans ambled over and asked for a light. Bolan pulled out his lighter, flicked it and turned away as soon as the butt flared into life. She asked where he was from and, when he ignored her and her question, shrugged and walked away. There were other pebbles on her beach.

Bolan sipped at the soda, watching the room in the large mirror behind the bar. Nobody was paying any particular attention to him. At least, nobody he could see. That meant that, at last, the amateurs were out of it. He wouldn't relax until Albright came in, but he knew nobody was going to make a move on him in the crowded bar.

Bolan nursed his soda until the bartender started hovering. He tossed back the remains, mostly melted ice, and ordered another. The bartender grumbled, knowing his tip was going to be small. When he slapped the second soda onto the bar, it sloshed over the edge of the glass. Bolan gave him an icy stare, and he blinked, then wandered down to the other end of the bar.

Bolan had been watching the door and breathed a heavy sigh of relief when Albright finally showed. He was a half hour early, but the wait had still seemed like an eternity. Bolan left the bar and walked to meet the young agent. Taking him by the elbow, he steered him to a vacant table in one corner and, none too gently, urged a chair on Albright.

Bolan sat down, too, and leaned toward his guest. "Listen carefully. I don't have much time, and I don't want any bullshit. Understood?"

Albright gulped. "Yeah, understood."

"Do you know anything about a note sent to me in New Orleans, signed with your name, and telling me where Yuri Kuscenko was hiding?"

"No, I didn't. I already told Brognola—"

Bolan charged ahead. "Did you leave a note on my car this evening, signed by Yuri Kuscenko?"

Albright shook his head.

"Do you know anyone in the Dallas police department? And if not, does the Agency have a pipeline to the department?"

"No, I don't know anyone. Somebody might have a pipeline, though. The Agency trains a lot of guys, you know, in counterterrorist techniques, that sort of thing. Lines get opened, they have a tendency to stay open. SOP. Listen, what's this all about?"

Bolan ignored him. "I want names and addresses in New Mexico."

Albright started noticeably. "New Mexico?"

"You heard me."

"But I . . . how can I tell you what you want to know, if you don't tell me what you're trying to get at? Where in New Mexico? What for?"

Bolan pulled the note from his jacket pocket, flattened it out and pushed it across the table toward Albright. He knew its contents by heart. He watched as Albright read it by the dim red glow from the overhead lamps, holding it at an angle for a better look. The young man wrinkled his brow, either confused or faking. But he couldn't be that good an actor, Bolan decided.

Albright read the note a second time, than looked at Bolan. He shrugged in bafflement. "I don't know what this means, unless . . ." He tried to snap his fingers, but the gesture was silent. "That must be it . . . it has to be."

"What?" Bolan's voice crackled through the noise around them.

"Those defectors I told you about. Remember?"

Bolan nodded.

"They're both in New Mexico. Kuscenko must be after one of them."

"Which one?"

"I don't know I . . . Alan might know. I'll call . . ."

"Sit down. No calls. You tell me, and you tell nobody else. *Nobody!*"

Albright swallowed hard, his Adam's apple bouncing with nervous energy. "Okay, my guess is Korienko. He's in a compound outside of Taos. It's in the mountains, pretty desolate. I'll tell you how to get there."

"Like hell, Albright. You'll *show* me. You're going with me."

Bolan stood up, waiting for Albright.

For a long moment, the young man stayed where he was, avoiding Bolan's steady gaze. Then, getting to his feet, his voice breaking, he said, "Let's go."

21

Face-to-face at last. Yuri Kuscenko had been doing the man's bidding for several days. Finally he had got to meet him. And he didn't like what he was learning. The man wasn't as unpolished as his KGB counterparts, but he was no less ruthless. And no less offensive.

He was tall, looked like a college professor and handled himself like Ivan the Terrible. "You've done very well for yourself so far. You're to be congratulated."

"Did you have reason to expect anything less?" Kuscenko was irritated. Who was this pompous ass, to speak to him as though he were still a student?

"No, of course not. Still, it is a complicated series of, shall we say, exercises that confronts you. I am very pleased with your performance so far."

Kuscenko bristled. "You keep saying 'so far.' What does this mean, this 'so far'? Do you think you could have done better with someone else?"

"Don't be so full of yourself, my young friend. There is quite a bit left to do, you know. You have a long way to go yet. And the most difficult part lies ahead."

"Difficult?" Kuscenko laughed, a slight chuckle breaking into full-throated enjoyment. "Difficult? Tell that to the bargain basement help you've been using. I understood I was simply to lead Mr. Bolan along for a while. Your hired hands would take care of the rest at the proper time."

"That is correct."

"It seems to me the proper time has come and gone. More than once. At the moment, our Mr. Bolan seems interested in me, but unopposed. Is the proper time imminent? Or should I continue to interest him, for your benefit?"

"You are in too much of a hurry. You don't know everything. Timing is paramount in this sort of endeavor."

"Perhaps. But I don't mind telling you, Bolan is not going to be easy, even for me. He is an extraordinary man. I would feel more comfortable if he were out of the way."

"All in due course. Soon you will not be just leading Mr. Bolan on a merry chase. You will have to kill him. But first things first. You will have to take care of another matter. When that has been attended to, we will let Mr. Bolan know where you are, and you can take care of him then, hmm?"

The buffoon. Kuscenko smiled to himself. If he had it to do over again, he would have written Bolan a better note. He was coming to have a great deal of respect for Mack Bolan, and less and less for the man who was paying him to do his bidding. Still, the pay was good. A new name, money and freedom in the U.S.A. were worth a few risks, Kuscenko realized.

If he got the chance, once he was secure in his new identity, he would pay this man an unexpected visit. That would be a pleasure. Kuscenko smiled at the thought. No one would ever suspect him. What reason could he possibly have? Still, this man could be dangerous. He was, after all, working for two masters, so he said. Kuscenko was beginning to suspect he worked for no one but himself. The man seemed overconfident, bordering on megalomaniacal. He could get them all killed. And there was no reason to trust him. None at all.

"What am I to do now?"

"An old acquaintance of yours, and of mine I might add, has preceded you to these shores. I can't allow that. He knows...certain...things, which could prove embarrassing, to say the least." The tall man began to pace nervously, stopping once to light his pipe. When he got it going, he puffed vigorously a few moments, then resumed his walking.

"Are you going to tell me, or do I have to guess?"

"You have a disconcerting habit, my young friend. You are far too impatient for someone of your tender years. I have waited a long time to get where I am, and I am not about to act precipitately. I have too much to lose."

"That may be, but you can hardly expect me to read your mind. That, surely, is a skill beyond one of my tender years." Kuscenko's tone bordered on insolence.

"Perhaps you underestimate the value of experience."

"Perhaps I do."

"I'm not surprised. My own superiors have been less than forthcoming. I have worked a long time for very little reward. Now at long last, when I am in a position to reap the benefits of my labors, I am in jeopardy of losing it all. I can't have that, you see. I *won't* have it. I've worked too hard. I'm tired."

"You are not exactly an idealist, I see. Political or otherwise."

"You are hardly in a position to impeach my motives, Mr. Kuscenko, not at all. It would be most inappropriate."

"For one of my tender years, you mean?"

"Not at all. For one of your precarious circumstances. That's much more to the point, you see."

"Are you threatening me?" Kuscenko got to his feet. The tall man flinched, losing for a moment the icy superiority that had marked his demeanor since the beginning of their discussion. The man was afraid, Kuscenko realized. He was soft. And he was scared. Scared to death. "I have done very well for you," Kuscenko went on. "Better than you have any right to expect. And I will not be intimidated or threatened."

"I'll keep that in mind, Mr. Kuscenko." The tall man turned his back for a moment and reached into his jacket. When he faced the younger man again, he found himself staring into the muzzle of a small-caliber automatic. Kuscenko's gaze was unwavering. The other man chuckled nervously. "Now, now, no need for theatrics. I merely want to give you this." He held a crisp envelope in his hand.

Kuscenko watched the shiny paper flutter in the older man's hand. He waited a moment before accepting the envelope, just long enough for the older man to know that Kuscenko had seen the tremor, knew how nervous he was.

"What is it?"

"Everything you need to know in order to complete your assignment successfully."

Kuscenko started to open the envelope.

"That can wait until you leave," the tall man said.

Kuscenko put the envelope on the desk in front of him. He looked expectantly at his employer, who asked, "How much trouble do you think you'll have with Mr. Bolan?"

"Some, I expect, but not more than I can handle. He is very good. In the Soviet Union, we have heard stories about him. He is almost a figure of folklore in the KGB. No one believes the stories, of course. He has always seemed more like a creation of our teachers, a figure used to bring home the dangers of our chosen profession. Now I am not so sure the stories do him full justice. Of course, I am his superior, but time will tell. Why do you ask? Are you getting nervous?"

"Not at all. You are not the only egg in my basket, you know."

Kuscenko laughed. "Yes, I know, I have seen some of your other eggs. Unfortunately they were scrambled before I was in a position to assess their true worth."

"Your humor is inappropriate, Mr. Kuscenko."

"Really? Why is that?"

"Because from this point on, you are on your own. There is nothing else I can do without giving away our little secret. I have already extended myself too much. I think it would be best if we not meet again."

"And my compensation?"

"That has been arranged. You'll find all you need to know in the envelope. I have made provisions for everything I promised you. All you need do is complete your assignment successfully. The rest will be easy."

"Mr. Bolan is surely suspicious of you by now. Your other eggs were not exactly untraceable."

"Not at all. He is suspicious of the Agency, of course, but he has no way of connecting me with anything that has happened. As far as anyone knows, I am on holiday in Spain."

"What about the people you have used? Can they not incriminate you?"

"Do you take me for a novice? I was running agents inside Nazi Germany before you were born. I have never lost a man. And it isn't luck . . . it isn't even skill. It is an art and a science. I mastered it then, and I am its master still. I know what I'm about. I only hope you do."

"I have seen precious little of your expertise so far. And things are not what they used to be when you were a boy. The craft was in its infancy when you learned it. I am beginning to suspect that time may have passed you by."

"Don't worry, my young friend. I am not some backwoods teacher using the same lesson plan for fifty years. I have kept abreast of my trade, even pioneered a little. I can still teach you a thing or two."

"I suppose we shall see, shall we not?" Kuscenko smiled.

The smile reminded the tall man of the flat, unblinking stare of a cobra, its lidless eyes focused on its prey. He suppressed a shudder and wondered if, after all, it might be too late to save his skin. Maybe the best thing he could do was run.

But where could he go? He'd be damned if he would spend his last days wasting away as a Kremlin oddity, like Kim Philby. He was not going to be stuffed and mounted like a prize trout, he resolved, to hang on someone's wall and be pointed out with pride two or three times a year. He had wasted the better part of his life in thankless service. His family had broken up, victim of his demanding profession, and he was not interested in women or drugs. A little peace and quiet, away from everything he'd known—that was what he wanted. And he'd be damned if he would settle for anything less.

No, the Soviet Union was not where he belonged. It was time for retirement, but it was going to be on his terms, at a place of his choice. If he had to sacrifice a life's work to do it, what difference did it make? he asked himself. It was his life and his work. No one else seemed to give a damn, so why should he?

If it were true that his reach exceeded his grasp, then that was just an unfortunate consequence of his ability, he reasoned. To have the mind he had, the insight into human affairs, was not just a skill, it was a gift. And the gifted, far too often, are exploited by their societies and tossed aside like so much used Kleenex. He had decided that was not going to happen to him.

As the tall man watched the young Russian leave, he puffed contemplatively on his pipe. A tool, when it has outworn its usefulness, is something to be replaced. Kuscenko would be useful a while yet, but he would be expendable soon. In a way, he admired the young man's brashness. It reminded him more than a little of his own youthful enthusiasm. He was not a specialist like Kuscenko, but after all, he thought, it was easy to kill. It was in some ways demeaning. He himself had always taken more pleasure in manipulating people, in outmaneuvering his foes. Victory was so much sweeter when your defeated opponent was alive to acknowledge your superiority.

Such a sweet victory he hoped to experience just one more time. Dissatisfied, he had chosen to serve two masters, doubling his pleasure and his fun. The fact that his pay had more than doubled was a secondary consideration. To serve two masters, he understood, was to serve none. More than that, it was to make yourself their master. Calling the tune yourself was so much more satisfying than dancing to someone else's.

When this was all over, he would be able to sit back on the porch, an old man, secure in the knowledge that he had survived all they could throw at him, survived and triumphed. In some ways, this victory would be his masterwork. It would, of necessity, go unacknowledged. But he would know. Someday, he promised himself, when it was too late to harm him, they, too, would know. They might not have appreciated him when it mattered, but he sure as hell was going to leave them something to think about.

No one had ever managed what he was about to achieve. Misleading both sides and walking away with no one the wiser was the aspiration of every double agent. But he would do more than aspire. He would carry it out. He would write the book others would only read and marvel at. He could see them now, shaking their heads in amazement that this stuffy academician with his pipe and his rumpled tweeds had made fools of them all. He only wished he could be there to watch the enormity of his coup dawn on their faces, like sunlight breaking on a summer morning. He could not, of course. But he could imagine it.

And imagination had always been his long suit, he mused. After all, wasn't that what had made him so valuable, if insufficiently prized, a possession? Of course it was. And all the blood-and-thunder types, the Mack Bolans of the world gathered the glory.

Well, he would put a stop to that, too. It was not often you got a chance to defend yourself and to take the initiative at the same time. That was what made the plan so attractive. If he could arrange the ideal conclusion to his little epic, he would have no victors in the clash of ideological assassins. Such a conclusion, unfortunately, was beyond even his ability to orchestrate. The idea was pleasant, though, to contemplate.

Refilling his cold, dead pipe, packing the bowl with that meticulous attention that was his hallmark, he smiled. There was such an imposing universe of possibility, all created from the smallest details. That had been his great insight. Knowing the minuscule gave you command of the cosmic. While others had wasted time scheming, elaborately reshaping the world with the vanity and vision of Alexander the Great, he had done the real work. He had slogged through the petty, seeing the universe in every grain of sand he came upon. The schemers had reaped the rewards, the power and position. Not that he was envious. But still, he had made their success possible. The least they could have done was say thank-you.

Well, it was too late now. He was through waiting for appreciation. They could all go to hell. He would show them the way. He would even lead them. Then he would sit back and watch them while they burned.

He reached for his lighter, and smiled again as the small flame caught hold in the bowl, soft clouds of fragrant smoke wreathing his brow.

He was content.

22

On the way to New Mexico, Bolan and Albright kicked around a variety of possible scenarios for Kuscenko's next move. None of them could be ruled out, and none seemed more likely than any other. Bolan drove most of the way, his jaw set in a way that Albright took personally. He knew things had gotten out of control, and he knew the CIA was not looking too good to Bolan at the moment. For that matter, it wasn't looking that good to him, either.

He understood Bolan's reluctance to trust him, but he wanted the big man to know there was no reason not to. The drive across Texas gave him ample time to consider his strongest argument, but he kept stumbling over the one incontrovertible fact in the entire Kuscenko affair: Kuscenko had inside help.

When he looked back on the sequence of events that had started the whole business, the exchange at the bridge, he even felt somehow responsible that the Agency had brought the assassin into the country. It didn't matter that other departments of government had initiated the exchange. It didn't even matter that Kuscenko could have been smuggled in any number of other ways, most of which neither required nor could have utilized CIA assistance. The bottom line was red ink. The Agency had fucked up, either in its handling of the assignment, or in its internal policing or, probably, both.

Belonging to an agency that had so badly mishandled its responsibilities was hardly cause for celebration. As the New Mexico border drew close, Albright took the wheel, letting Bolan get a few hours' sleep. The solitude gave the young man time to reflect on possible ways he could balance the books. Bolan was suspicious of any further Agency involvement. Albright couldn't blame him at all for that. But if Bolan was really concerned about stopping Kuscenko, and there was little doubt in Albright's mind that he was, then he should accept any help as long as it wouldn't compromise the mission. The odds were too long as it was. Refusing all assistance was tantamount to throwing in the towel.

What frightened Albright the most was the notion that they might never know what Kuscenko's mission was. It was not beyond the realm of possibility that he would carry it out and they would not even realize it. For all anyone knew, Kuscenko's target was unknown. Sure, the defectors, both of them, were logical possibilities, but they weren't the only ones.

The attack on the President had been a success, if it were meant to serve as a diversion. Nearly everybody in the federal government was looking under rocks and tearing up floors. They were all searching for something, and they didn't have a clue what it was. Security on the President had been doubled and redoubled. Intelligence agencies were busy pointing the finger at one another, trying to fix blame for the failure to anticipate and prevent the attack. As far as Albright could tell, only three men understood that the assassin had missed the President intentionally. The trigger man was one of them. The other two were tearing across Texas on the craziest chase Albright could have imagined.

Even Brognola, for whom Albright had come to have the highest regard, had been skeptical of Bolan's theory, when Albright had contacted him for details of the security at Korienko's compound. He seemed to lean toward the two birds with one stone approach. As far as he was concerned, Kuscenko and his puppetmasters had meant to kill the President, but as only one of two or more goals. Whoever the puppetmasters might be. On that point, Brognola was no closer to home than he had been four days ago. The CIA, as was its habit, was proving less than cooperative in dealing with what everyone else clearly saw as the presence of a mole within it.

As soon as it had become evident there probably was a mole, even those who had been arguing for that very point began to pull in their horns. Agency integrity seemed to become more important than reality. Those two notions, as Albright had been forced to concede, were often more distant from each other than the antipodes. Never more so than now. An attack on any agency seemed to rally its troops in a way that nothing else, even a threat to national security, could.

As long as agents were free to indulge the illusion that theirs was the noblest calling in government, free of taint and misunderstood by all but themselves, they would be critical of one another, and petty squabbles would be the rule rather than the exception. But suggest that one of their number might be disloyal, and you had to deal with them all. The ostrich mentality kicked in, and you couldn't see a thing for miles, what with the clouds of smoke from burning files and confetti storms from the paper shredders.

Albright had gotten an education in the past few days, he had to admit to himself. He hadn't liked much of what he had learned, and he liked the circumstances even less. But he still felt he had a job to do. In his own way, he was no less dedicated than Mack Bolan. And he figured he owed the big guy a debt. It wasn't Albright's way to excuse the Company and walk away from problems just because he wasn't personally responsible for them.

The moon was out, nearly full, and the prairie ahead seemed infinite in its expanse. As the car bored through the pale night countryside, Albright made himself, and Mack Bolan, a promise. Yuri Kuscenko was not going to walk away from this. There were things you could overlook and things you didn't dare overlook, not if you wanted to face yourself in the mirror. Okay, things were fucked up. But they didn't have to be. Not if everybody pulled together.

Bolan's one weakness, Albright thought, was his insistence on working alone. Albright didn't know all the circumstances, but he couldn't imagine any that would require such willful independence. Sure, he knew the outline, the bare essentials. You couldn't be in intelligence and not know some of the story. Albright figured he'd heard the worst, and that whatever he didn't know was probably just more of the same.

But Albright was a young man. There was much more to living, and dying, than he could appreciate. Bolan had recognized a quality in him from the very first that, for lack of another word, he labeled innocence. Albright had it in abundance. The young agent knew it, and he didn't try to plea-bargain the charge.

For all his enthusiasm and good intentions, Don Albright could not imagine the depths of despair and heights of exuberance witnessed by the man who dozed now beside him in the passenger seat. In one way, the situation was a metaphor for Bolan's very existence. A solitary man, relying on the kindness of strangers, traveling through an endless night in a rented car. For Albright, it was a kind of adventure. For Mack Bolan, it was a way of life.

The dreams of self-vindication that danced in the young man's mind as he considered and discarded one scenario after another were romantic nonsense. And a part of him knew it. The dreams were proof of his good intentions and clinched the case for his innocence. The world Bolan moved through had no room for heroic grandstanding. When the hellfire burned, you got your ass in gear and moved. If you didn't, you didn't get a second chance. Albright should have known as much—maybe a part of him did—but he felt the betrayal of the sleeping man by someone in the CIA more keenly, more personally than he should have. That, too, was a sign of innocence. Only the innocent can afford excess baggage like unnecessary guilt.

Feeling guilt was, in Bolan's world, not only unthinkable, but fatal. Guilt slows the hand, causes the eye to blink. It was in such split-second timing that Bolan's edge lay. Stop, even for an instant, to wonder, and the edge was gone. Without it, survival was a matter of days or weeks. Given the intolerable length of his private war, Bolan would have been dead a dozen times over if he had allowed himself the luxury of second-guessing.

Mack Bolan had never killed anyone who didn't deserve to die. Brognola had told this to Albright, and the young man hadn't quite believed it. The notion of Bolan as a swashbuckling vigilante, roaring out of the night and shooting from the hip, had been a powerful one. It died hard. But it *was* dead. The complexity of the man had killed it. Brognola couldn't destroy the notion for Albright, and Bolan himself couldn't have if he had tried. But just watching the man work, believing his statement that he had taken his own first experience with death as hard as Albright had done, made that image impossible for the young agent to maintain. Heroics, no; a hero, damn straight. And Don Albright wasn't going to let him down. Not as long as he could do anything about it.

He looked over at Bolan, and noticed that the man's features, even in repose, were not at rest. He wondered what nightmares prowled behind those closed eyes. And even as he wondered, he realized he didn't really want to know. He also realized that, before this was all over, he was liable to have firsthand knowledge of those nightmares. He was prepared to do without that knowledge. If he could. But he knew there was no way to escape it.

Not in this life.

The moon began to dip, and gray was everywhere. Albright knew the sun would come up almost full-blown, behind him. The vast prairie was smothering in its expansiveness. Ahead lay the mountains of New Mexico, but they were still below the western horizon. The day's heat would raise hell. And Albright needed some sleep. They had a long way to go and a lot to do. He reached into the console between himself and the sleeping man for a cigarette.

He pushed the lighter in. When it popped, he lit the butt, took a long drag and exhaled deeply. It was his first in several hours, and only his ninth overall, for smoking was a bad habit newly acquired. The recent events had been tearing at his nerves. The cigarettes didn't help much, but he didn't know what else to do. The nicotine rush hit him, making him dizzy. The road blurred for a moment, and he shook his head to clear it.

"You shouldn't even start. It's a nasty habit."

He turned to catch the smile fading on Bolan's lips. "Hell, bad habits are a dime a dozen. What's one more?"

Bolan reached for the pack and knocked one loose for himself. He pushed the lighter in, waving off Albright's cigarette in favor of the more reliable method. When he had taken a couple of pulls on the Marlboro, he exhaled with a sigh.

"I think I've been pretty hard on you."

"Naw. I can take it. Hell, I deserve it. Those assholes I work for have screwed up royally. I have to take a piece of the blame."

Bolan nodded. He didn't say anything, but he knew he didn't have to. The kid was all right. He had a lot to learn, but he was a man. He was willing to own up to his errors and do something about them. That was a rare attribute, making him almost an endangered species. There was no place you could protect that kind of sense of responsibility, nurture it, guarantee its survival for another generation.

"You got any ideas on what we can expect?" Bolan asked.

"Well, as you suggested, I got a little information about security from Brognola. I've never been to the compound, never seen pictures, either, the whole thing's so hush-hush. Alan gave a rough idea of the layout, but he'd only been there once. And when I found out that's where we were going, I couldn't risk tipping off him or anyone else besides Brognola that we're going there. Things have been so crazy, I'm beginning to wonder whether *I* might be the mole."

"You're not the only one," Bolan said. His voice was dry and raspy. If there was humor intended, it didn't show. Albright responded in kind.

"Look, Mack, I know you must be pretty pissed off. I don't blame you. But I was thinking a lot about it while you slept. It seems like the only thing we can do from here on out is stay down and watch our backs. You don't quite know whether you can trust me, and I understand that. That means you'll have to watch your own back. Okay. But I'm telling you, I'm going to do whatever I can to help. Whether you like it or not."

"Fair enough."

"No argument?"

"None."

"I appreciate that. Really, you don't know how much."

"No big deal. If I'm right, it'll work out. If I'm wrong, chances are I'll never know it."

Bolan lapsed into silence. It was almost time to switch places with Albright. He wanted a bit of time to think things through for himself. There wouldn't be much of that in the foreseeable future.

"I'll take over when we cross the state line."

"You got it."

Both men stared straight ahead, through the debris of mashed insects on the windshield. The sky was now almost light, a reddish glow from behind them tinting everything they saw. The coming day would be a hot one. In more ways than one. Each man wanted to deal with that reality in his own way.

Bolan had wondered how long it would take the kid to wise up. It hadn't taken him long. That was another mark in his favor. In a pinch, he thought, the kid would be there. He might not know the right thing to do. He might even get them both killed. But there were worse things than dying. Especially when you've lived with the possibility for as long as Bolan had.

As he stared straight ahead into the glare of the new day, that possibility was just as strong as ever for Mack Bolan. It always would be, or he'd be doing something wrong. Some things don't ever change.

23

Bolan and Albright rode silently with the full glare of the late-morning sun beating down on the roof of the car. The roar of the engine was barely audible over the rush of wind past the open windows. Each man knew what the other was thinking and neither felt the need to talk. Nor could have if he had wanted to.

Bolan struggled against a sense of despair. He ticked off the odds in his head, and they were not very good. The stark beauty of the New Mexico countryside was no consolation. Where, in another time, he might have seen in the landscape an austere, rigorous assertion of life against overwhelming adversity, now he saw life hanging on by its fingernails, desperately trying to avoid extinction under the baking sun and encroaching sands. He recognized the point of view as the age-old question of whether the glass was half empty or half full. The way things were going, it was definitely half empty, and going down. He thought ruefully that he could have watched water evaporate before his eyes if he had the time.

Albright was hardly more sanguine about the coming hours. He knew the compound where Korienko was being detained was a highly prized secret installation. Its security would be as tight as humanly possible. Few in the Agency even knew of its existence, fewer still had ever seen it. Albright had heard some stories and got some details about security from Brognola. He was keeping his fingers crossed that would be enough. Enough to get them close, and enough to nail Kuscenko before he killed Korienko. They had fewer than twenty miles to go now, and at their current speed they'd be there in less than fifteen minutes.

When they crossed the New Mexico border outside Dalhart, Texas, their situation had suddenly seemed irreversible and inevitable. As they pushed on, the magnitude of their dilemma seemed to grow geometrically, as if they were rushing headlong toward it through a telescope.

By the time they reached the foothills of the Turkey Mountains, the sun seemed to have grown cold. Its light was undiminished, but its heat seemed to recede. The quality of the air was different, thinner, as they rose, and colors took on an unearthly pallor. Their richness seemed to leach away into the arid mountain air. It was late November, and there was already snow on many of the peaks ahead of them.

The compound was high, nearly thirteen thousand feet, and Bolan knew exertion at that altitude was quickly exhausting. Although Albright was young, he was out of shape, overweight. Too much desk duty, or no personal inclination toward fitness, it didn't matter. When push came to shove, he would be little help. One more notch in the odds. Kuscenko's chances were looking better all the time.

The Sante Fe National Forest lay just ahead. They would cut through its northernmost part and head due north, into the no-man's-land of the Cristo Range. If the CIA had been looking for a lunar landscape, this was it. The place couldn't have been more like a moonscape if it tried.

"You nervous?" Bolan asked, turning to his contemplative passenger.

"Yeah, very. You?"

"No. I'm worried we might not get there in time. I'm worried he might pull it off. But I'm not nervous. I think my synapses must have overloaded a long time ago."

"Yeah, I suppose you can't afford it, either. Not in your line of work."

"No, I can't afford it, and neither can you. Not today. We are looking for a fast-moving needle in a gigantic haystack. We'll be lucky to find Kuscenko before he gets off his first shot. You said security was airtight."

"It is."

"How large is the compound?"

"Twelve acres. But the security perimeter is a hell of a lot larger than that. We are talking drum tight here. And nobody stays long enough to get lazy. The guards are rotated in and out every two weeks. It's the same pool of men, but they get two weeks on and four weeks off. With full pay, I might add."

"Sounds like you're envious."

"I guess I am, a little. At least they get to do something important."

"I'd say important is an understatement. All of this is just for the sake of isolating one man?"

"Yeah, but like I said, Korienko is special. So special that nobody knows what the hell to do with him. If he's genuine or if he's a disinformation agent, he's still the weirdest thing CIA has ever gotten involved with. Almost four years, and nobody knows what to make of this guy. He's got to be Kuscenko's target. There's no two ways about it."

The trees rushing past were gray-green in color, their tall trunks rising as if they wanted to leave the barren wilderness behind. High above, their crowns seemed to strain against gravity. Mack Bolan lost himself in contemplating the increasingly sparse growth. They were climbing steadily now, the engine racing, struggling in the thin air.

Albright looked out the window, watching a pale, ghostly image of himself in the glass. He wondered what had become of all his aspirations. The life he had chosen, one supposed to offer the satisfaction of public service and the glamour of international intrigue was starting to taste dry on his lips. There was something so oppressive in the surroundings that he began to slide down into a pit of depression, again blaming himself for the current situation.

Kuscenko had become an embodiment of his dilemma, a deadly grail he pursued because he had no choice. In ten minutes, they would be leaving the car, and plunging into the arid upcountry wilderness. It would be no less a separation than a space walk, leaving the safety and relative comfort of the car behind in order to track a solitary man with a rifle whose mission they only dimly understood.

Nagging at the back of Albright's mind was the suspicion that this time, too, they would come up empty. They had been running on blind faith for days. They had guessed often and not well. Like a tapeworm, something had crept into the bowels of Albright's Agency and taken root. Living a lie, it fed on nourishment intended for its host, draining the host of energy and waiting, quietly, for its death. Then it would move on, offended by the very corruption it had nurtured.

The road began to get rougher, long stretches of pavement broken into corrugated rubble by the weather. Soon it would give out altogether, and they would move ahead on foot. They were climbing at a steep angle, now, the car wheezing its discontent. And then the pavement ended.

Albright had informed Bolan that transportation in and out of the compound was by chopper and ORV. The security patrols used jeeps to ride the outer line. The terrain was too rugged to bother with routine chopper surveillance. Bolan pushed the car along, raising a heavy cloud of dust that settled quickly in the lean atmosphere. They bumped and bounced over the pitted dirt and, finally, Bolan packed it in.

He pulled off the scarcely discernible track they had been following and shut off the engine.

"Shank's mare from here on in," he said.

Albright said nothing. They quickly gathered weapons and clothing, locked the car and started trudging on up the slope ahead. The crest of the ridge was only a thousand yards farther on, but the going was tough. The thin air made any exertion costly.

Bolan slowly drew ahead, pausing once to look back over his shoulder at Albright as if he were a wayward child, lollygagging to avoid some distasteful visit. He hoped the young CIA man wouldn't be a liability. Whether he could possibly be an asset seemed unlikely. He had got them this far; Bolan expected little more of him.

At the top of the ridge, Bolan paused and waited for Albright. He studied the valley below them, a broad, sweeping saddle-shaped depression between two high ridges, with peaks higher still at either end.

The thin forest swept down and away from them, growing thicker at the deepest part of the bowllike valley. The heart of the trees had been cut out there, and Bolan could see a sprinkling of Spartan structures straggled across the dust-colored scar. A faint black line marked the edge of the scar. It was a fence of some sort, but it wasn't readily apparent what it was made of. Bolan unslung a pair of Zeiss field glasses, shook them from the leather case and popped the lense covers.

He swept the perimeter of the compound, zeroing in on the fence. It appeared to be razor wire, strung in loose coils to a height of eight or nine feet. It wasn't possible to estimate the height more closely because the fence was too far from any structure to provide scale.

One by one, he checked the buildings, seven in all, for signs of life. Six of the buildings were military-style quonset huts of corrugated sheet metal, readily disassembled for quick transport. The seventh structure was more substantial, apparently the only permanent building of the seven.

It was a good-sized cabin, made of heavy logs and concrete. A plume of smoke rose from its pair of fieldstone chimneys, but there was no sign of life. A four-wheel-drive vehicle was parked at one end of the cabin and partially hidden by it.

Three more jeeps were parked near the most distant of the quonset huts. Moving his glasses back to the fence, Bolan looked for a gate, but if there was one, it was well concealed.

Albright straggled up behind him as he finished his preliminary survey. "Tell me everything Brognola told you about security for this place," Bolan grunted.

"Why? We don't have to get inside, do we? I mean, aren't we going to look for Kuscenko from outside?"

"Sure. But you know as well as I do that if anybody spots us, we're in big trouble. They aren't going to bother asking us polite questions, are they?"

"No, I guess not. Well, there should be thirty men in the security detail. They work in teams of ten on three shifts. Four stay in the compound while the other six cover the perimeter. I think there's regular rounds, but I'm not sure."

"They have any backup?"

"Not much. The best they can hope for, if they need it, is Army at Los Alamos. That's nearly a hundred miles away. By chopper, we're looking at a half hour minimum. I guess they could use the state police, but I think they'd have to be pretty desperate to go that route."

"And where do they keep the man of the hour, Comrade Korienko?"

"Alan says he stays in the main cabin. The huts are for the security people, the counterintelligence team, support personnel, medical team and so on."

"Does he have a regular outside exercise period?" Bolan asked.

"Brognola says he goes out twice a day, early mornings and four-thirty to five in the afternoon."

"What about other access roads? Is there more than one way in?"

"Yeah, there's two more. There's a more direct route than the one we took, but it's guarded, and there's another that's not much more than a hole in the woods. It's where they trucked in the materials to put this place together. After that it was abandoned. In four years, a lot can happen. It's probably overgrown now."

"You're saying nobody even thinks about using it, right?"

"Yeah, why?"

"Because if our boy has the help I think he does, he'll know about it. And he'll know nobody worries about it. It's just what he's looking for."

"Maybe you're right."

"I'm betting I am. Where is it?"

"It comes in at the other end of the valley. Let me have the glasses a minute."

Albright took the glasses and began sweeping the far side of the compound. He didn't know what he was looking for, other than some sign of disturbance to the normal growth of the forest beyond the razor wire. His friend, Mitchell, had just mentioned the road in passing, dismissing it more cavalierly than Albright had to Bolan just now. Albright told himself he should have known. He should have realized what he was up against.

"I don't see any... Wait a minute. There, I've got it." He handed the glasses back to Bolan and pointed with an unsteady finger. "There—see that notch just above the last hut on the left? That's it."

Bolan looked where he was told, and saw a break in the forest wall. If there was a road there, it came in at an angle, and was camouflaged by the trees and underbrush on either side. It looked clogged with scrub growth, but might be passable to a four-wheel drive.

"It doesn't look like much."

"Like I told you, it's not used."

"I'm not so sure. I'm going to get a closer look. Let me have one of the walkie-talkies. Keep yours handy. I'll fill you in when I get down there."

"But that'll take hours."

"Two—at the most three."

"Do we have the time?"

"Do we have any choice? You want to walk down there and tell your buddies what's happening?"

Albright shook his head. "No, but I think this is the most likely place."

"Fine, that's why you're staying here. But I've been at this line of work a whole lot longer than you, and I think we can't afford to overlook any possibility. You keep checking the road behind you. You see anyone, you give a shout." Bolan pointed to Albright's walkie-talkie. "I'll do the same."

"Remember, the guy we're waiting for is a pro. He also knows as much about what goes on here as we do. Probably more. They may unpredictably move Korienko from one building to another, so the only regular parts of the routine are likely his exercise periods in early morning and late afternoon. I'm betting Kuscenko will be here by this afternoon. He'll try to take him out this afternoon or maybe tomorrow, if he wants a dry run. I'm betting he won't wait long, though."

"And you're coming back, right?"

"Yeah, I'm coming back. You just stay here and do what I told you."

Albright nodded. Bolan moved down the front of the slope, kicking some loose scree with his feet before finding more solid ground about a hundred yards down. He moved behind some boulders and he was gone.

Albright was alone. And he wasn't happy about it.

24

Albright watched Bolan grow smaller and smaller as he popped in and out among the rocks below. The big man moved quickly, and Albright was impressed with his agility. Bolan was heading to the right, on a line that would bring him down to the valley floor not far from the compound fence. It was obvious he planned to get a close look at things inside, as well as check out the other access road.

Soon he was out of sight altogether. Alone with his thoughts, Albright decided to take stock of the situation and find some way to make himself more useful than he had been so far. There was no need for him to stay put. He could keep an eye on the road and still cover some ground. At this distance from the compound, the amount of territory to be covered was enormous.

The forest was sparse on the ridges, but even so there was plenty of cover, with boulders strewn haphazardly across the loose earth. There were raw outcroppings of rock tilted at crazy angles, as if the earth here had been fractured. Thinking back to his college geology classes, he realized that was exactly what had happened. The San Cristo range was part of the same mountain-building process that had left behind the Rockies and the Sierra Nevada.

They weren't as lush as the Rockies to the north, or as knife-edged as the Sierra Nevada to the west, but they were impressive nonetheless. The towering peaks to the north and west approached thirteen thousand feet, possibly even topped it here and there. The panorama from the ridge was starkly breathtaking.

"I'm thinking like a goddamned tourist," Albright muttered. "That's all the use I've been on this whole damned thing."

He shook himself as if he were just waking up. He took his own field glasses and ran a quick scan of the highway he'd left behind him, following it to the point where it became broken asphalt, then along the dirt road that succeeded it. When he reached the spot where their car was parked, his hand jerked. He thought he had seen something moving.

The spasm had yanked the glasses off the car, and he had to scramble to get it back in view. The car seemed undisturbed, but Albright was sure he had seen something. Some motion, maybe a shadow, maybe not. He waited patiently, propping his elbows against his rib cage to hold the glasses steady. If he had seen something, he'd see it again.

Several minutes went by. Nothing. He moved the glasses in a wide circle around the car. In a stand of tall pines, fifty yards off the road, he saw movement again. This time he was sure of it. Just a hint of shadow, moving against the dark trunks. He zeroed in. Again something moved, and this time he saw it clearly. A deer, grazing among the underbrush, stopping here and there to tug at some late-fall greenery. That must have been what he had seen. He shrugged, feeling a bit foolish, and resumed his scan.

When he reached the point on the approach road he could see clearly with the naked eye, he turned his attention to the slope on either side. It was desolate, to say the least, the line of the ridge all but naked, as if seeds were blown free before they could sprout or as if carried by the wind to this height, they were moving too fast to stop and continued on down the slope a hundred yards before losing speed.

The last fifty yards of the slope, on either side of the ridge, was little more than bare earth and clumps of grass. He wondered how the soil stayed put under the brisk winds that blew almost unceasingly, whistling among the rocks.

Checking the road again, satisfied that no one was coming, he walked along the ridge, keeping just below the crest on the side away from the compound. Bolan had told him to carry an M-16, and he felt ludicrous. Even stationed in Berlin, he had seldom packed as much as a handgun. He was reminded of playing war as a child. The heavy weapon slung over his shoulder had no more reality than a toy.

Idly kicking the gravel, Albright moved in a shambling slide. He had gone about fifty yards when he saw something in the scree ahead, about twenty yards lower on the slope. It seemed out of place, its bright color grabbing his eye and holding it. He sprinted toward the object, half buried in the loose soil. He kicked it loose. A Diet Pepsi can. What the hell was it doing up here?

He kicked at the earth again and found several more pop cans, as well as empty cigarette packs, wrappers from candy and junk food and some chicken bones wrapped in newspaper. The cans looked brand-new, and the papers were still crisp and dry, their colors bright. Either a picnic, which seemed unlikely, or some sort of surveillance team had been on the slope. Recently. The newspaper was the *Albuquerque Tribune*, dated only two days ago.

But who? And why?

His first instinct was to get Bolan on the walkie-talkie, then he realized it was pointless. Bolan would be back in a couple of hours. He could tell him then. In the meantime, it was more important to see what else he could dig up. He started back up the slope, puzzling over his find. That someone had been watching the compound recently was beyond question. He doubted if the refuse had been left behind by compound guards. They might come this high on the ridge occasionally, but they would have no reason to bring meals here, or to leave garbage behind.

Albright moved ahead on the ridge, traveling another 150 yards, but saw no further evidence of surveillance. Doubling back, he retraced his steps to the point where he had been standing when he first saw the trash, and moved toward the road again, kicking at the loose soil. Nothing.

The date on the newspaper meant it couldn't have been brought by Kuscenko, because he was in Dallas then, if the paper were placed there on the same day it was printed. But if not Kuscenko, then someone else was watching the compound. An advance team? Someone mapping the place and recording its routine for Kuscenko's information?

Or was someone else interested in Kuscenko? He wished Collingsworth were available. He had never liked the man, but he did respect his judgment. He was not in good odor at the moment, his current assignment a gentle nudge toward retirement. Collingsworth knew it, but he did his job. He knew more than anyone Albright had met in the Agency. He'd be able to puzzle it through with him, see things Albright missed, obvious things revealing deep secrets, if you knew how to interpret them.

MACK BOLAN was fifty yards from the fence, and on the other side of the compound from the point where he had first seen it. All the way down the slope, he had been watching the compound and had seen little that suggested anyone was aware of an impending threat. That was the way he wanted it, but he wondered now if he had been too cautious.

Maybe it would have been better to warn them and take the chance that it wouldn't leak. Caution was only a step away from paranoia. On the other hand, as the old joke said, even paranoids have enemies. The risk was too great. The threat to the defector had to be kept close. Bolan felt the strain of his decision, knowing that if he miscalculated, or if he simply blew it, Kuscenko would win. He had carried heavy burdens in the past, but this one was special.

His resentment of this assignment was gone. In its place was the recognition that his usual war wasn't the only one being fought. Others were on the line, too, every day. Kids like Albright, rookies, giving up a hell of a lot to fight an enemy as old as their grandfathers. It was a fact easy to overlook in the heat of his personal conflict.

He wondered if he was too arrogant, too confident that he could make all the decisions and fight the most meaningful battles. The weight of those days out ahead of the firing line was getting heavier every day. Pointman for life, that was what he had become. In Nam, it had been the riskiest place in the column. You were the first one into the line of fire, the first one to pass through a sniper's cross hairs, the first one to step on a mine or fall on a pungi stick.

Now, not as cocksure as he once was, and a hell of a lot wiser, Mack Bolan felt as if he were standing on the edge of a precipice in the dark. He had no idea what he was up against. These were untested waters for him. The skills were the same maybe, but the vision was broader. You had to look past the end of your own gun to know what was going on. Well, hell, he thought, I've grown before, I'll keep on growing.

The compound was still, even in the middle of the morning. The sun overhead seemed farther away than he was used to. It seemed ironic, in a way, that he would feel the distance magnified by being closer. In the marshy lowlands and the dense jungles of Vietnam, he had been closer to the center of the earth, the air had been thick, the sun a lead weight on sticky shoulders. Here, the air was as rarified as the quest for Kuscenko. Two miles high, and higher, he struggled under a sun that might as well have been the moon. Even its light was diffused, as if the thin air had somehow absorbed it on the way down. The quiet was overwhelming. And the death. He had seen no signs of life, unless a vulture could be counted. Bleached, white bones were not uncommon in the waterless soil. Signs that there once had been life. He wondered whether the compound was the agent of destruction, whether it might symbolize something to the less passionate animals who lived beyond the wire.

The cut in the forest was just ahead. He wanted to check it out quickly but thoroughly. He sprinted through the thin stand of trees on the edge of the clearing beyond the wire. Running parallel to the cut, he moved fifty yards farther in, then stopped to get his bearings.

The cut was no more than fifteen feet wide, just wide enough to admit a heavy truck with a little clearance. It was riddled with small boulders and the stumps of trees cut off a few inches above ground level. Limbless trunks lay along both sides, stripped of branches and tossed out of the way. Straight as a pipe, the cut ran uphill to the ridge above, a no-nonsense kind of slash-and-burn approach to road construction. Bolan moved up the slope, keeping to the edge of the cut against the tree line.

When he had gone three hundred yards, he realized Albright was right. The cut might be accessible by FWD, but there was no way to drive down without being seen. The cut ran into one corner of the compound where two huts stood. A casual glance out a window was all it would take to spot a vehicle approaching.

Even crossing it on foot was risky, but he had to take the chance. He wanted to make a complete circuit of the compound. The amount of ground they had to cover was too large for a squad of men . . . or for carelessness. If they were going to have a chance, they had to have an edge. Anything they knew about the terrain might be useful.

From what Albright had found out, Korienko would be out in the open, exercising, between four and four-thirty. Bolan glanced at his watch. It was twelve-thirty now, and Kuscenko would have to have some time to get into place. He would have to figure on getting only one shot or, if he was lucky, two. If he missed the second time, the guards would be hustling the Russian to cover, and every man on the security detachment would be pouring into the forest. Kuscenko couldn't afford to miss, and he couldn't afford to wait around to see whether he had. He would not be permitted a second chance.

Bolan realized the best angle was on the crest of the first ridge. It would give the assassin the clearest shot and maximum choice of the moment. Korienko would be in the clear for a half hour, relatively unobstructed the entire time.

Bolan dodged across the cut, keeping as low to the ground as he could manage. The big Weatherby was slung over one shoulder, and the walkie-talkie and field glasses over the other. The glasses banged against a rock as he neared the other side of the cut. When he reached the trees, he looked at the case and noticed it was badly damaged. He opened the case and pulled the glasses out. One objective was shattered, the tube crumpled in as if it had been... No, he thought, no impact with a rock could have done that much damage. He shook the glasses and something rattled inside. He screwed off the damaged objective, and a slug rolled into his hands.

He hadn't heard a report, but someone had seen him and had taken a shot. If he had been a little less cautious, he might be lying in the middle of the cut with a hole through his head. Bolan looked around carefully, listening intently. He heard nothing.

He closed one eye and looked through the glasses, using the undamaged tube as a telescope. He scanned the forest across the cut, but it was deserted. Trying as best he could to reconstruct the angle of fire, he realized it had not come from below in the compound. Someone was above him, across from the cut. Someone with a gun, who knew how to use it. Compound security wasn't likely, since they would have no need for silenced weapons.

Kuscenko?

But why would he bother? It would compromise his primary mission. Bolan didn't doubt that the assassin would take him out if he got the chance, but not until he did what he had come to do. Korienko was his first target, Bolan was gravy. But then the thought came to Bolan, maybe there was a bonus in it for Kuscenko. There was no doubt the puppetmaster wanted Bolan involved, or they wouldn't have gone to such lengths to lead him across the country like a wayward child, tugging his nose now and then to keep him moving, till they got him out here at the compound. They had had their chances to kill him before now. But they hadn't. Bolan wondered whether they hadn't wanted to, whether they figured they could take him down anytime they chose.

Maybe, he thought. Just maybe.

But now it's my turn.

25

Bolan looked up at the sky. The sun was well past its peak and the day would rapidly disappear. The afternoon exercise session would be coming up, and Kuscenko was already here. Using the single functioning tube of the binoculars, Bolan searched the slope for some sign of the marksman. His paranoia was running full tilt now. There had been so many near misses. Could he feel certain the assassin had meant to hit him just now? But if not, what was he to think?

Albright was alone on the opposite slope, much closer to the shooter. Bolan tried to raise him on the walkie-talkie but got no answer. Rather than waste time in what might be fruitless attempts at communication, he hotfooted it around the far end of the compound.

Even though the trees were sparse, the going was rough. Strewn rock made footing treacherous, and stiff thorny branches tore his clothing every foot of the way. Bolan was cutting in tight at the end of the compound, but the place seemed quiet, and he could shave twenty minutes off his return trip by doing so.

Once he rounded the point on the distant end of the fence, he would be moving away from the buildings. He could pick up his pace a bit then without fear. His breathing was labored. The thin air was shorting him on oxygen, and the exertion was draining his energy.

As he began to move uphill, heading toward the place he'd left Albright, Bolan had to slow down again. If he kept up the pace he'd been setting, he'd be useless for an hour when he finally got where he was going. Stopping for a brief rest, he tried the walkie-talkie again, this time getting a crackling response after a few seconds of static.

"Bolan, is that you?"

"Yeah, I'm coming back up. Listen, be careful. Keep your eyes open. He's here."

"How do you know?"

"He took a shot at me. Almost nailed me. Fucked up my field glasses."

"I didn't hear anything."

"Neither did I, but he's on your side of the valley. I was in the cut when he fired. The only way he could get a clear shot is if he was below you, to your right. Check it out. I'll call in in ten minutes. But if you see anything, let me know right away."

"Check."

Bolan reslung the squawk box and resumed his sprint. The thin underbrush was less tenacious as he got higher on the slope. There were more rocks, but they were smaller and easier to go over rather than around.

He kept one ear on the walkie-talkie, hoping, but not expecting, Albright would have something to report. The odds were that Kuscenko had been aware of Albright's location when he got off his shot. The guy was trained for that sort of thing, and could work rings around a greenhorn desk jockey like Albright.

The thin stand of trees was less an impediment to movement than to vision. Bolan opted for a straight push to the crest of the ridge. From there, he could make a beeline toward Albright. If his luck held, he'd be above Kuscenko with plenty of time to spare. From that point, he could figure where the assassin would position himself for the hit.

While he climbed, Bolan wondered whether he'd rather have two Albrights along or none at all. He decided the latter seemed preferable.

Then, for a moment, Bolan thought he had fallen into a warp in time. The sun disappeared, and the slope above turned gray in the diminished light. He looked up in wonder, just as the sun came out from behind a thick gray cloud. Just over the lip of the ridge, he saw a mass of similar clouds. It was going to rain.

Great.

Maybe Korienko wouldn't even come out to play. Kuscenko would have to wait until the morning exercise session. There was no way he would dare try to crash the compound.

Unless he was still getting inside help. That was a possibility Bolan didn't care to consider. It made his job all but hopeless, and there was precious little hope left as it was. Bolan reached the crest of the rise as the first raindrops fell. Large, half-gallon icy-cold bombshells, they stung the bare skin when they hit. Bolan realized they were lucky it wasn't snowing. At least his luck wasn't all bad.

Not yet.

The rain fell in fits and starts, dampening patches of the dry earth in dark brown stains. The soil crusted with the moisture, then erupted into tiny moonscapes as a further flurry of large drops pocked the dark dirt, throwing small, dry puffs into the air on impact. Bolan was only a hundred yards from the ridge line now, and none too soon, he thought. If the clouds burst, the slope would be a slippery morass in nothing flat.

When he reached the top at last, Bolan paused to check the terrain below him. He dropped to the damp ground and peered through the single tube. He had no depth perception through the maimed binoculars, but at least could bring things into sharper focus.

He paid particular attention to the area from which the shot had to have come, but there was no sign of Kuscenko. He was scanning across the lower half of the slope when the walkie-talkie crackled.

"We got company."

Before he could respond, he heard the sound of an engine running flat out. The sound came from behind and below. He spun around and spotted a jeep with three men in it, charging up the last stretch of pavement, then jouncing into the dirt portion of the road.

Their clothing was nondescript, but that meant nothing. Uniforms could be faked as easily as anything else, and the absence of one made a man no less a threat, no matter whom he worked for. The chances were these guys worked for Uncle Sam. They had probably been riding circuit and spotted Albright or the car, or both.

Whoever they worked for, Bolan needed them the way he needed a broken arm. There was no time to explain to them what was going on, if they were compound security, and if they weren't he would have to take Kuscenko with these guys at his back.

Bolan swung the broken glasses toward the jeep and noted the .50-caliber machine gun on a detachable mount at the rear of the jeep. Two of the men sat in front, each armed with an M-16. The third man sat on a jump seat, one arm draped over the breech of the MG to keep it from swinging as the jeep roared over the broken road.

"Albright, I don't think they've seen me. Stay down. Get away from the ridge line if you can. I can't tell who they are, but we don't have time to fuck around with them."

"They're probably Agency guys from the compound. They waved back when I signaled them."

"You what?"

"I signaled them. We need all the help we can get. Don't you think?"

"Don't *you* ever think?" Bolan rasped. "You don't know who the hell they are. Dammit, man, hired goons have been dogging me all the way from Washington. You know that. What the hell's wrong with you?"

"I . . . uh, I'm sorry. I guess I thought . . ."

The walkie-talkie crackled and went silent. As the echo of the static faded, Bolan could hear the rattle of fire from the MG. Whoever they were, they weren't going to ask questions. Not as long as their ammunition held out. He yelled into the mouthpiece of the squawk box, but there was no answer.

Bolan swung the glasses to the point where he'd last seen Albright. He saw nothing at all. Except the butt end of the walkie-talkie, lying flat on the crest. Albright was nowhere to be seen.

The machine gun stopped its angry rattle, and the jeep roared to a halt about fifty yards below the ridge top. The man in the passenger seat leaped to the ground while the jeep was still skidding on the slippery muck. The rain continued to fall heavily, and soon even the rugged tread of the jeep tires would be unable to pull the vehicle out of the mire.

The running man looked to be about six feet four or five. Bolan kept the glasses trained on him as he sprinted to the top of the ridge. He halted just over the crest. Turning to his companions, he shouted something, but his words were carried away by the rising wind. He turned back and bent to pick up the walkie-talkie, tapping it thoughtfully in his palm as he looked for the man who had, just a minute before, been using it to talk to Bolan.

Bolan was wishing they hadn't found it. A man alone doesn't need a walkie-talkie; it told them Albright had at least one companion. If they couldn't find Albright, they would sure as hell start looking for his friends.

Bolan was in a quandary. He didn't know who the men were, and he wasn't about to start shooting until he was certain he had reason to. The way they had opened up on Albright was nearly reason enough, but they might just be jittery. Before he struck, he had to be sure. And he had to get to Albright. If the agent had been hit, he might bleed to death before anybody found him.

There was only one thing to do. Clicking on the walkie-talkie, Bolan tried his somewhat rusty Russian on the big man holding the other end of the wire, saying what could be roughly translated as, "Your mother sleeps with a goat." The lightning response was too rapid, and too chokingly incensed, for Bolan to understand it all. But the way the big man spun around, looking for a throat to wrap his huge hands around, spoke volumes.

These guys were no CIA agents.

Extra innings.

Bolan pressed himself down into the sloppy muck, behind a medium-size boulder. He pulled the Weatherby to his side and took off the safety. The big guy was the easiest target, but Bolan chose a more difficult shot for his first. He wanted the MG out of action, fast.

The shot boomed across the ridge, the big gun barking and biting almost simultaneously. The slug had ripped through the machine gunner's chest, just below the collarbone. He had been thrown violently backward, sprawling out of sight on his back. He was dead before the sound of the shot reached his companion's ears. His own never heard a thing.

Bolan zeroed in on the second man in the jeep, who seemed stunned by the disappearance of his mate. His bushy mustache, Stalin-style, needed trimming. Through the scope, Bolan could see steely blue eyes looking nervously around as he wondered which way to run. But the man never moved. He didn't have time. Bolan squeezed once, then again. The thunder of the Weatherby was drowned by a peal of natural thunder, a sound like the earth cracking in two, beginning as a high-pitched rending then exploding with a megaton rumble.

The big man was smart, but a little slow. He dived headlong down the slope, hitting on his stomach and sliding in the soupy muck for several yards. He rolled sidelong another fifteen feet, plunging behind an outcrop of rock just as Bolan squeezed off his fourth shot. The .460-caliber slug slammed into the stone and whined away into the void. A rain of chips fell silently into the mud.

The guy wriggled, trying to flatten himself behind the rock. He peeked once, then ducked back. He knew whoever was after him had a scope. He didn't want to give his adversary the added edge of an easy shot. The muzzle of his M-16 poked out from behind the stone, and the prostrate man squeezed off a burst.

He was guessing, but he wasn't far wrong. The deadly fire chewed the wet soil a few feet to Bolan's left, the slugs whumping into the earth and spattering mud in every direction. The muddy rain poured down on Bolan's head and shoulders. A thick gob of the brown goo splashed on the objective of the Weatherby's scope. Bolan reached out to wipe it away, just as a second burst tore up the ground to his right.

Either the guy was zeroing in or he was a lucky guesser. Bolan didn't want to find out. He cleared the lens as best he could and peered through the scope into a beige cloud. The big man was hardly visible behind his rocky cover. The Executioner was patient. He could wait.

But not forever.

Bolan figured he had the whip hand. The big gunman had just lost two allies. If he was human, he had to be feeling spooked. And he had made a mistake in his giveaway reaction to the insult over the walkie-talkie. Bolan kept the scope trained on the rock, its field just broad enough to cover either side. Whichever way the guy moved, Bolan would see him.

The M-16 sneaked into the clear again and barked. Its muzzle flashed, but the sound was tinny and distant under the pouring rain. As he waited, Bolan knew the edge was slowly becoming his. The downpour would wash the haze of mud from the scope. As visibility improved, Bolan's chances got better, and the guy's luck got worse.

The sky had gotten still darker, and it was almost like twilight. A rag of lightning flapped briefly, brightening the sky for an instant, then, by contrast, plunging the slope into deeper gloom.

Like a horse made skittish by the elements, the big enemy was getting nervous. He was peeking out more frequently, and for longer periods. Another minute, Bolan knew, and he would bolt. All it would take was another thunder clap or bolt of lightning. When he ran, he would be coming straight at Bolan.

Holding his aim over the heart of the outcrop, Bolan waited for the mistake he knew was coming. There was another flash, not as bright as before, and the guy was on his feet. Through the scope, Bolan could see his mouth wide open, as if he were yelling something. If so, the words were torn aside by the wind. His mouth never closed, even when he swallowed the big Weatherby slug. Bolan could see the flash of lightning that followed starkly etched against the ragged hole torn through the back of the big man's skull.

He fell heavily, the impact strangely muted by the mud. The body skidded downhill a few yards.

Bolan got to his feet and began to run. If Albright was alive, he had to find him. It might already be too late, and three for one wasn't good enough.

Not by half.

26

Bolan scrambled through the rain, his feet slipping in the soggy mess. Another bolt of lightning threw the ridge line into garish relief. The flash bleached all color out of the scene so that it looked like an old black-and-white movie. Bolan's movements were jerky as he struggled to keep his footing.

Skidding down the slope, he passed the carcass of the big man, flat on his back. The guy's sightless eyes stared up into the rain unblinkingly. Bolan paused for a second and looked up at the sky, as if to see what the man was looking at. The rain beat down incessantly, its heavy drops slashing through the wind and stinging Bolan's cheeks.

As he watched, the clouds seemed to rip apart, showing patches of dark blue. It grew lighter, the clouds turning yellow around their edges, the way the edge of a sheet of paper turns brown before breaking into flame.

Shafts of light flew in every direction, like beacons pointing nowhere. The beams looked solid enough to touch as they fanned out across the heavens. The clouds grew wispy as the sky brightened and then, as quickly as it had come, the rain was gone. Scudding on the high winds, the clouds fragmented and scattered. The sun returned, its light harsh and uncompromising. Bolan glanced at the dead man again, and found him unimpressed by the fiery spectacle above.

Leaving the staring corpse in the mud, the Executioner slid farther down the slope, each step he took carrying him forward in a torrent of slippery earth. His shoes were heavily caked with mud, and each foot seemed to weigh a ton. There was still no sign of Albright. When he reached the approximate point he had last seen the young agent, Bolan knelt to scrutinize the soil. There were no signs at all that anyone had been there. He had hoped to see some evidence, a track in the mud, some sign of hurried flight. But there was nothing at all.

"Albright?" The question trailed off in thin air, reverberating down the slope in diminishing echoes. He called again, his voice ringing, but there was only silence. Twenty yards away, at an angle down the ridge, was the only possible cover.

If Albright had been hit, and it looked more and more like he had, that cluster of large rocks would have been his haven. Encouraged by the absence of a body, Bolan walked deliberately toward the rocks. He was looking for blood, but knew it would have perked into the soil with the heavy downpour.

Reaching the rocks, Bolan moved slowly around the uppermost of the large stones, hoping to find Albright cowering behind them. The young man was there, lying on his back beside the stones. A dark red stain had soaked into the right leg of his corduroy slacks, making them look old and stiff. Albright's eyes were closed.

"Albright? Are you okay? Don?"

Bolan stepped around the rock and knelt beside the prostrate form of the young agent. He felt for a pulse, and was gratified to detect a faint throb under his fingers. He chafed the wrist between his palms, then tapped Albright gently on both cheeks. The closed eyes flickered. Albright groaned.

"Albright, it's me, Bolan."

The eyes finally opened, and Albright starment. "Where'd the sun come from? What …

Bolan did not answer right away, but ripped the pant leg from cuff to thigh and pulled the sundered material away from the wound. A .50 caliber slug was no joke, often tumbling as it tunneled through flesh. This one had missed the bone and arteries of the leg, but it had torn two ugly holes in the lower thigh, just above the knee. The cloth had suppressed the bleeding somewhat, allowing it to clot, but Bolan's action had reopened the wounds.

When Albright struggled to sit up, Bolan pushed him firmly back against the rock. "Lie still. I have to wrap this leg before you do anything. Stay here. I'll be right back."

He sprinted up the slope to the fallen gunner and ripped the dead man's shirt from his body. Scrambling back down to the rocks, he split the shirt and rolled the rain-soaked fabric into a makeshift compression bandage.

Expertly, almost tenderly, he wrapped the wound. It had been some time since he'd had to do anything like this, but his history was indelible. It was not for nothing he had once been known as Sergeant Mercy. That was in another war, for another kind of victim, but blood was red any place he'd been.

And he'd seen more than his share.

When he had knotted the cloth securely around Albright's thigh, he told the young agent to sit up but not to try to stand without help.

"You know, I've been thinking about this whole thing," Albright said. His voice was weak but steady.

"So have I," Bolan answered, "but we don't have time to think right now. Kuscenko is down there, remember?"

"I'm not so sure—"

"I am. Now shut up and listen."

"But—"

"Dammit, Don, we don't have time for this shit. Can you make it down to the compound?"

"I think so, but I'm not sure I ought to try. They probably think a small war has started up here."

"No, they don't. There hasn't been any movement at all. I doubt they even heard the firing, with the thunder, wind and rain."

"What about the guys in the jeep?"

"What about them?"

"Wouldn't they have called in before they jumped us?"

"They don't have anything to do with the compound. They were KGB."

"How do you know that?"

"Trust me. They weren't on our side. And they weren't just trigger-happy, they wanted to kill us both. That's why they were here in the first place. Here, stand up, lean on my shoulder for a minute."

Albright reached up and Bolan, rising, took his hand and yanked him as gently as he could to an upright position. Albright winced as he put his weight on the injured leg, and would have fallen if Bolan hadn't reached out to catch him.

He sat down heavily, holding on to Bolan's arm.

Bolan said, "Wait here. I'll be right back."

Moving quickly, he bounded up the slope to the top of the ridge and raced to the jeep. The keys were still in the ignition. The vehicle was undamaged, and rain was certainly nothing new to the workhorse. He ripped the MG from its mount and tossed it to the floor, then climbed in the driver's side. He cranked it up, and the engine coughed, resisting the labor of its starter. He pumped the accelerator a couple of times, then tried again. This time, the engine caught with a reluctant rumble.

Popping the clutch, Bolan wrestled the steering wheel and gave it some gas. The wheels spun in the mud, and the jeep started sliding backward. He backed off on the gas a little, and the heavy-treaded tires caught, stopping the slide. The wheels spun in place a moment, then reluctantly the jeep began to edge upward. The engine groaned as the wheels fought for traction in the slime. At the crest of the ridge, Bolan yanked the wheel hard right and headed downhill. He knew Albright wouldn't be able to work the pedals, but on the slope, neutral might be enough.

He half slid and half drove to the cluster of rocks. When he braked, the jeep slid a few feet farther before coming to a halt. Bolan jumped out and helped Albright to his feet. He nearly had to carry the wounded man, dumping him as gently as possible into the driver's seat.

"You're going to have to try this, Don. Think you can manage?"

Albright grinned, gritting his teeth to keep from losing it all. "Hell, yes. Besides, what choice do I have?" he asked.

"None."

"See?"

"You'll have to stay up to steer, but keep as low as you can. Kuscenko will blow you away if he can."

Albright nodded that he understood.

"When you get down the slope, just lean on the horn but keep out of sight. Get as close to the entrance as you can. They'll come and get you."

"What'll I tell them."

"The truth. Tell them there's somebody out here trying to kill Korienko, and somebody else trying to stop him. But that's *all* you tell them. Got it?"

"Who's Mack Bolan? Never heard of him."

Bolan grinned for an instant, then patted Albright on the shoulder.

"What are you going to do?"

"I have to see a man about a dog." He slipped several cartridges into the magazine of the Weatherby and cleaned the scope with the remnants of the tattered shirt he had used to make the bandage.

"I still think you ought to listen to my idea."

"Later, Don. There's no time now. And listen, when you get inside, call Brognola and tell him what's going down. There's probably no such thing as a secure phone in there, but we don't have many secrets left. Good luck." He slapped Albright's shoulder again, and the young agent gave him the thumbs-up.

Albright reached down to release the brake, and the jeep started to roll. He kept his head just high enough to look through the steering wheel and the lower portion of the windshield. Like a skier on a new slope, he zigzagged, using the changes of direction and the brakes to keep the jeep's momentum under control.

Bolan looked at his watch and realized it was after three-thirty. So far, no one in the compound knew anyone was here. If Albright didn't make it in time, they'd be trotting Korienko out for his afternoon constitutional in less than thirty minutes. As he watched the jeep grow smaller in its descent, something nagged at him. He wondered whether he had been too hasty in brushing off Albright's idea.

The kid had a head on his shoulders. Maybe he'd hit on something. It was too late now, though, and time was wasting away. He raised the broken glasses to scan the slope below, hoping Kuscenko might show himself in order to take a shot at Albright. The slope seemed deserted, but there was someone out there, hiding in the rocks, quieter than a rattler, and a hell of a lot more deadly.

Letting the glasses fall, he headed downhill, his feet sucking into and out of the mud with regularity. They sounded like some perverse heart-lung machine, pumping away against all odds to keep a moribund patient alive. And, Bolan realized, that was an apt comparison. If he failed, Korienko was a dead man. Right now, the defector was oblivious to the threat on his life, could not have been more so if he'd been comatose. It was ironic, Bolan thought, that the man's life depended on the Executioner.

When Bolan had gone about seventy yards, he caught a glimpse of movement among the sparse trees near the bottom of the valley. It was too brief to be certain what it was, but it was large. Of that, Bolan was sure. If it was the assassin, he had moved in tight, as if he wanted to make sure of the kill. His field of vision would be narrower, but the shorter range made him a bigger threat.

Bolan looked for the jeep and found it, a blocky stone tumbling slowly downhill in its erratic course. He trained the broken glasses on the vehicle and noted with approval that Albright was all but invisible. Even for a crackerjack like Kuscenko, he would be a tough shot. And then as Bolan watched, he saw the windshield star and spatter color as a web of cracks diffused the sunlight on the glass. As with the previous shot at Bolan, no sound betrayed the location of the gunman. An instant later, and the windshield was gone altogether, raining down into the front seat of the jeep and out of sight.

The vehicle was still zigzagging, so Albright was still in control. In another hundred yards, it would reach the bottom of the valley. It was a short hop from there to the fence. Albright wouldn't be able to make it on foot, but Kuscenko probably didn't know that. Bolan began to run.

His feet felt leaden with their burden of mud, which was now beginning to dry and becoming stickier as the glutinous muck congealed under the sun.

The jeep was on the flat now, still rolling toward the compound fence. Bolan could hear the distant blare of the jeep's horn, a steady wail carrying uphill on the wind. The jeep lurched sideways and seemed to limp. The assassin had gotten one of the tires in a desperate attempt to stop its progress. Apparently he didn't realize gravity was all that kept it moving, since Albright couldn't work the pedals.

The flat tire slowed the jeep's progress, and it bumped to a halt about twenty feet from the fence, and some distance along from the gap in the razor wire. Then Bolan saw motion outside one of the huts. Two men, running into the open, spotted the jeep and ran toward the camouflaged gate. They were safe for the moment; Kuscenko would not betray his presence with a shot.

The first man was through the wire, about ten yards ahead of his slower companion. They still had some distance to travel along the fence, and Albright was staying put. But if Kuscenko nailed the young agent, the security people wouldn't have any idea what was going on. As soon as the thought flashed through Bolan's mind, he realized Kuscenko must have known it, too.

He saw the assassin as he stood among some rocks, not a hundred yards from the jeep. Bolan skidded to a halt and unslung his Weatherby, throwing it to his shoulder. He zeroed in just as Kuscenko ducked among the boulders.

Bolan looked for the jeep through the Weatherby's scope and found it. But he couldn't see Albright.

27

The jeep sat like a monument to futility. The men racing toward it were ignorant as yet of Albright's message, and Bolan couldn't tell whether the agent was alive or dead. The assassin had scrambled from sight after shooting out the windshield. When Bolan trained his damaged glasses on the spot where he had been, there was no sign that anyone had been there.

The shooting at the jeep had been silent, but the men running toward it knew from the shattering glass that something had happened. Bolan's job was now infinitely tougher. For all the men from the compound knew, he was the shooter. He would have to stay out of their sight, and still try to close in on the assassin's lair.

Bolan knew Kuscenko was preparing for his final assignment. Time was slipping by. It was 3:55. The men had reached the jeep. As he ran obliquely across the slope, Bolan caught a glimpse of them through the trees. One of the men was bending over the driver's seat. He turned to his companion, and was lost to Bolan's view as the Executioner pushed on through the trees and into the brush that tangled the last hundred feet of the slope.

When Bolan passed into another clearing, the man from the compound was no longer visible. The jeep appeared to be empty. Bolan paused to scan the razor-wire fence but saw no one. If they had carried Albright in with them, they had made good time. Bolan had to make time himself. Korienko would soon be in the yard. Crashing through the brush made Bolan's task doubly difficult, for there was no way for him to watch for the assassin as he ran. His vantage point kept shifting, and more often than not was obscured by the vegetation.

At 4:15, Bolan made a decision. He ran straight toward the fence, bursting into the clear, still three hundred yards from the spot he had seen the assassin. Charging ahead, heedless of the possibility of discovery, he sought to close the gap between himself and the shooter. The compound was on his right, and he could sense movement, rather than see it, behind the wire.

He heard a shout. Someone fired a weapon into the air. He ignored the uproar, and closed to within one hundred yards of the rocky niche where Kuscenko had been hiding. So far, there was no sign of movement among the jumble of boulders. There was a second shot, and an engine roared.

Turning to look over his shoulder, Bolan saw a jeep full of armed men racing straight toward the fence. A burst of automatic weapons fire shredded the earth behind him. He dived into the brush, narrowly ahead of the rain of death.

He rolled to his knees and peered through the sparse shrubbery. It would hide him from the men's eyes, but not from their bullets. The trees behind him were shredded by the continuing fire. He glanced at a stand of firs and saw the bark splinter and fly off in all directions. Dropping to his stomach, he started worming his way through the undergrowth. If the guards chose to aim a little lower, they could nail him blind.

Where the hell was Albright?

Bolan had only a minute before Korienko came out. It was possible the disturbance in the compound might prevent his outing, but Bolan had seen too many things go wrong in his life to count on it. The fire from the compound was diminishing, whether because the guards had given up or because they thought they had hit him, he didn't know.

The pile of rocks was in clear view now, and Bolan continued to inch forward on his belly, pinning his eyes to the summit. If Kuscenko was going to show, it would be there. The Weatherby was all but useless now. Fifty yards and closing, but still a long shot for the AutoMag. Scrambling to his feet to make better time, Bolan crouched as low as he could and pushed on. He worked his way from tree to tree, the AutoMag in his fist, glinting orange in the sun.

In the mountains, sundown would come as quickly as had the rain. The shadows had begun to deepen among the trees. Twenty-five yards from the boulders, Bolan stopped. He braced himself against the rough bark of a Douglas fir. Waiting for an opening, he sighted on the tops of the rocks. He could sense something happening in the compound, but he didn't dare look.

Suddenly, quietly, the barrel of a rifle appeared over the foremost boulder. The front of a scope was also visible, but Bolan could not identify the gun. He knew only that it wasn't the pricey item he had seen on the roof of the Dal-Tex Building. He wondered at the balls of a man who would leave a killing machine like that behind and trust the most important assignment of his relatively short life to a deer rifle.

A second later, the top of a man's head came into view. Judging by its position, the assassin was peering through the scope.

Bolan leaped high to grab a broken stub of a branch protruding from the barren trunk of the fir. Wrapping the trunk tightly with his legs, he shinnied higher, hauling himself to the stub and resting his weight on the precarious support. He had a steep angle now and could see the man's head down to the ear. He was wearing a black knit cap.

Bolan steadied the AutoMag against the trunk of the tree. He had to be sure, because one shot was all he'd get. As he set himself to squeeze the trigger, the bark above his head exploded. The sound of hellfire screamed in behind the bullets. The men in the compound had spotted him.

The assassin ignored the gunfire. Patiently he waited for his target to appear. Bolan knew that the odds against that appearance were lengthening. As the number of men in the compound who realized something was amiss grew, the chances increased that one of them would realize Korienko had to be kept inside. That improved the odds on the defector's survival, but diminished the possibility that Bolan himself would survive.

In the reverberating gunfire, Bolan recognized Albright's voice. The young man was calling to the shooters to stop. They seemed to understand what he was trying to say, and the firing died as suddenly as it had commenced. As if he realized something was wrong, the man in the knit cap moved his head abruptly.

Bolan caught the movement and squeezed before his target had a chance to duck behind the rocks. He squeezed a second time. The watch cap seemed to explode in a dull red haze. Bolan dropped to the ground, landing heavily and twisting his right ankle. Ignoring the flashes of pain, he ran toward the rocky pocket of protection, keeping low and ducking behind whatever cover came to hand.

At the back entrance to the assassin's lair, he paused and listened for any sound of movement. He heard nothing. Then a roar caught his ear from somewhere in front of him. A jeep was racing along the razor wire, heading straight for him. His first instinct was to jump for cover, but the men in the jeep were holding their fire. He dropped to one knee and peered around the corner of the rocks. He recognized the slightly overweight figure in the rear of the jeep as Albright.

The jeep roared to a halt just below the pocket of boulders. Albright leaped from the jeep, landing heavily on his wounded leg and falling to one knee. He grimaced from the pain and turned white. One of the other men in the jeep jumped down beside him and helped the injured agent to his feet.

He gritted his teeth and waved to Bolan. "Wait, you have to listen to me."

Bolan stepped out from behind the boulders and moved toward the jeep. He didn't give a thought to the assassin behind him. He was convinced the man was dead. There was no way he could have made a mistake about the significance of the dark red halo that had risen over the dark woolen cap. All that remained was to verify the identify of the assassin. That could wait. Albright had a bug, and Bolan wanted to know what it was.

When he reached the jeep, he extended his hand to the young agent. "Thanks, Don. We did it."

"I'm not so sure."

Bolan was nonplussed. "What do you mean? Kuscenko is over there in the rocks, dead as he's gonna get."

"Maybe so. But it's what I wanted to tell you before."

"Okay, tell me now."

"Well, put yourself in the mole's shoes, or even the KGB's shoes, for just a minute. If somebody has enough on you to blow you out of the water, what do you do?"

"You whack him, what else?"

"But what if you don't know what he's already told the other side? You can't take the risk of whacking him, because that would be the best confirmation they could ask for. You don't whack him, he hangs you. You do, and his will hangs you. A hell of a fix, no?"

Bolan nodded. He saw what the young man was driving at, and it was starting to make a lot of sense. "You mean the best thing you can do is whack the *other* guy. That makes everybody think *he* was genuine, even if he's a plant.''

"Yeah, that might work, but these counterintel guys are weird. That might just be what they would conclude, so by trying to throw them off, you'd be playing right into their hands. No, the best way is one we never considered. You whack them both. Now there's two dead defectors who contradict each other, instead of two live ones. You can't break a dead man, and there's no point of trying to confirm anything, because you can't ask follow-up questions of a corpse.''

"That's all very pretty, Don. Except for one thing. Right from the beginning, we were betting on Korienko as Kuscenko's victim. Well, here we are, and here Korienko is, and here was Kuscenko. Now Kuscenko's dead, and you can ask all the follow-up questions you want, because he didn't get to whack his man this time.''

"Maybe.''

"What do you mean, maybe? I nailed the bastard.''

"But there's still Balanov. I put in a call to the other compound, where they've got him under lock and key. Nobody's going to get to him, unless it's an inside job. And I don't think there's any chance of that. The guard is too heavy. But we have to get over there. Quick.''

"If you say so, but I think it's a waste of time. Those crazy counterintel guys are always building castles in the air, as far as I'm concerned. They spend so much time gathering information and constructing fancy theories that nobody ever gets to do anything at all. They're always waiting for one more piece of the puzzle. I sometimes think they wouldn't jump out of the way of a runaway truck unless they stopped to see what make it was. And what year.

"That's all bullshit, as far as I'm concerned. There's a real war on, and while your fancy boys play intellectual games, people are getting blown away in Beirut and Athens, Rome and Rio de Janeiro. I say you get what you can when you can get it. Those games are for somebody else. Me, I'm not playing.''

''Maybe you're right, Mack. But we've come this far. Let's just see it through another day or two, all right? We'll wrap things up here and go have a look at the other compound. If somebody's sniffing around, you can find him.''

Dolan nodded his assent. He walked away from the jeep a few steps and looked at the sky, now beginning to darken rapidly. He turned back to Albright. ''Okay, I guess you're right.''

He walked toward the boulders. Albright hobbled after him. Stepping into the niche for the first time, Bolan stooped to look at the fallen assassin. The black knit cap lay against one rock, a bloody smear marking its passage down the rough face of the stone after it had been blown off the assassin's head, along with much of the top of his cranium.

The assassin lay on his stomach, one arm by his side, the other splayed out beneath him. Bolan grabbed the corpse by its one free arm and tugged, rolling the dead man onto his back. Despite the damage done to the man's head, his face was unmarked. Peaceful in repose, as if the man were simply sleeping, his features were slack. There was only one thing remarkable about the face.

It wasn't Yuri Kuscenko's.

Bolan had never seen the dead man before.

28

Mack Bolan looked at Don Albright. "Who the hell is he?"

"I have no idea," Albright said. He was speaking between clenched teeth. Obviously in pain, he was showing the big guy something. "We can try to get a fix on him, but I don't think it'll be easy." Then Albright threw up on his shoes.

"You all right?" Bolan asked.

When his shoulders had finished bobbing with the dry heaves, Albright nodded. He spit to rid his mouth of the sour taste. "Yeah, I'm all right. You sure you get used to this?"

"It gets easier, yeah. But you never really get used to it. At least I haven't."

"What do we do now?"

"I guess we go check on your other defector. I think this guy just proved you're right about paying him a visit. If Kuscenko isn't here, he sure as hell is somewhere, and he didn't come over here just to play hide-and-seek with me."

"You sure?"

"I'm not sure of anything right now. But I'm fresh out of answers, and I was wrong about Kuscenko being dead. So unless you got a better idea, I think we better look in on Comrade Balanov."

Albright nodded. "I've already called for a chopper. It's about twenty minutes by air. We'll get there after dark, though."

"Do we have any choice?"

"No, I guess not."

Bolan slipped the magazine out of the AutoMag. He replaced it with another, and slipped the partially exhausted clip into his jacket pocket. "When will the chopper get here?"

"Any minute."

Albright had barely closed his mouth when the familiar thumping of helicopter rotor blades started to pound in the deepening twilight. A moment later, the pilot clicked on his landing lights. The big chopper hovered in the air at the center of the compound. Albright gestured to two security men, sitting in the jeep. The driver pulled the vehicle over next to the young agent.

"Let's go. Our ride's here."

Silently Bolan stepped into the waiting jeep. He stood on the running board for a second, glancing back at the dead man among the rocks. In the gloom, the body was no more than a lump of shadow. As he watched the big guy, Albright realized every detail of the dead man was starkly etched in Bolan's memory. He understood now that Bolan hadn't been kidding when he said he had never got used to the killing.

Albright hobbled to the jeep. One of the guards helped him up into the other rear seat, and the hiss of Albright's breath told Bolan how much pain he was feeling.

Albright sat down heavily, keeping his wounded leg extended straight before him. He tapped the driver on the shoulder. "Let's get to the chopper," he said.

The driver popped the clutch and the jeep lurched through the thickening mud. The driver revved his engine, shifted to second gear and cornered roughly around the edge of the razor wire. Albright reached out to grasp Bolan by the shoulder, squeezing tightly to keep his balance. The grip was painful, an indication of how much the wound was hurting the younger man.

Inside the wire, the driver didn't bother to shift into third, choosing instead to wind the jeep out in second. They bounced over the rough ground, the engine whining and racing as the rear wheels made and lost traction repeatedly. Just outside the sweep of the rotor blades, the jeep skidded to a halt.

Bolan bounced out and turned to Albright. "The pilot know where to go?"

"Yeah."

"Okay, I'll be in touch."

"Wait a minute, I'm going with you."

"No, you're not."

"Why?"

"Because you're a liability. You can't walk, and you sure as hell can't run. And I can't baby-sit."

"I'll be better in the morning, and you can't do anything until then."

"No you won't, and yes I can."

"But—"

"Look, Don. I can't afford to have you along. You can't afford it, either. Besides, somebody has to coordinate things here. You have to get on the horn to the other compound and make sure Balanov doesn't stick so much as his nose outside. Then you have to get Brognola and tell him what's going down. But *only* Brognola. No assistant, no secretary. You talk to the man himself, or you don't talk to anybody. And that includes your own people in Langley. Understood?"

Albright nodded gamely. He knew Bolan was right. It didn't change his mind about wanting to go with the big guy, but he recognized the justice in his position.

Bolan climbed into the chopper and strapped himself in, the Weatherby cradled in his lap. He tapped the pilot's shoulder, gave Albright the thumbs-up, and the rotor blades spun faster. The helicopter wobbled as it reluctantly broke contact with the earth. Once it had cleared the ground, it rose quickly, then wheeled off into the darkness.

In a moment, the chopper was gone. Albright stood watching as blinking lights rapidly dwindled to tiny points, then disappeared altogether. Then he shook himself, as if awaking from a deep sleep. He leaned in toward the driver and the jeep roared into life, its engine straining to compete with the recent thunder of the big helicopter.

The driver sped across the compound to the command center, where Albright stepped stiffly to the ground before the engine died. He hobbled to the door, turning once to look back over his shoulder as if he half expected Bolan to change his mind and come back for him.

BOLAN WATCHED the compound fade away behind him. Its lights cast ghoulish shadows as the security men scurried around, hustling everyone inside. As the chopper cleared the ridge, Bolan turned his attention to his weapons. He was coming down to the wire, and his only friend was hardware. He felt bad about leaving Albright behind. The kid meant well, but there was no way Bolan could afford a millstone around his neck, and that was just what Albright would have been.

Bolan had not been lying when he told the kid he was more useful handling communications than he could ever have been with Bolan in the mountain darkness. The second compound was only forty miles away by air, but it might have been on another planet. Kuscenko was surely lurking somewhere nearby, just waiting for his chance to nail Balanov. And Bolan was not about to let that happen.

Kuscenko and the puppetmaster had been leading Bolan around by the nose for so long, he thought he must look like Pinocchio. The thought struck him as funny when he caught himself scrutinizing his profile in the chopper's canopy, the garish glow of the cockpit lights sketching him in its soft, reflected green.

Timing, of course, was everything. And something had gone wrong with Kuscenko's timing. The surest way to make sure there wasn't a fuck-up was to synchronize the hits at the two defectors. The first thing either compound would have done if attacked was get on the horn to the other. The Langley clowns weren't total ignoramuses. They would have suspected something, some concerted action, or at least defended against the possibility, as soon as someone tried to get to either one of the Russians.

Maybe the schedules of the two defectors didn't allow for simultaneous hits. Maybe the KGB, and their internal ally, were counting on just the assumption Bolan had made at first—that there was only one assassin. If an assassin was nailed at the scene of the crime, he could not very well get up and move on to the next assignment. Maybe, maybe, maybe...

Bolan was drained. For a week now, uncertainty had been slowly chewing him to a fine pulp. He was beginning to second-guess himself at every turn. It didn't surprise him. It went with the territory. But he'd never been so unsure of what he wanted to do, of what he had to do. Lost in a wilderness of mirrors, he saw himself at every turn. Passing judgment on his own performance, he had begun to censure himself in the very heat of action.

Now, with the final heat approaching like a bolt of lightning, there was no time for such ambivalence. He knew it. And it scared the hell out of him. Out in the cold for so long, he had become a law unto himself. Like the lone wolves who had wandered through these mountains well into the present century, and some of whom were still out there, howling at the night sky for their own amusement, he was isolated beyond comprehension. But unlike the wolves, he was capable of reflection.

An anachronism, he thought, that's what I am.

And it hurt like hell.

The thought that his useful time had been consumed, that he had outlived any reasonable function, burned in him like fire. The pain was deep, magnified by his conscience and stoked by the limitless fuel of reality. Everywhere he looked below was darkness. He was floating above a landscape that had no more use for him than it had for the wolf. And what haunted him most was the question of whether he could work in a pack any longer. Had he been on his own too long? Was he, as so many people claimed, an ungovernable liability, a lumbering troglodyte who belonged nowhere?

Maybe, just maybe...

The pilot reached back and tapped him on the knee. Bolan followed the man's gloved finger, pointing straight ahead and down. There it was, the second compound. Only dimly lit. They must have heard from Albright. Bolan reached for the second headset and put it on.

"Have you heard anything over the radio?"

"No, sir." The pilot shook his head.

"Are they expecting us down there?"

"No, sir. My orders are to drop you in the meadow just beyond the compound. You're on your own from there."

On his own, Bolan thought. When had he not been? And when had being on his own become a liability? He nodded, and removed the headset. The pilot glanced sideways at him for an instant, his face expressionless.

The chopper was closing rapidly on the compound. The marginal illumination revealed little, but Bolan could determine that its layout was almost a carbon copy of the other. The same nondescript quonset huts, the same razor wire. For a second, he wondered whether the pilot was playing some elaborate game with his head, circling through the night sky and coming back to their starting point.

And if so, what was the game? Would they spiral end-lessly through the darkness, finally to plummet earthward, the fuelless engine coughing to the last shattering contact?

Paranoia, Bolan thought, is the flip side of caution. The fine line between them had been eroding rapidly. Maybe the distinction was gone for good.

The helicopter started to climb as it neared the open space around the compound. As if on a string it rose almost ver-tically, then veered to the left and swept in a thunderous semicircle around the far end of the fence.

The buildings fell away behind them, and suddenly they touched down as the earth rose to meet them. Bolan looked out into a sea of waving grass, its foot-long strands bent double under the propwash, and struggling to rebound.

The pilot leaned toward him, yelling to make himself heard above the engine. "End of the line, sir."

Bolan nodded. "Where are you going now?"

"My orders are to report back to Mr. Albright, sir. In person only. No radio contact. This is pretty hush-hush, I guess."

"You better believe it," Bolan said, jumping down from the chopper. He reached back for the Weatherby and, on an afterthought, asked the pilot, "You got binoculars I can use? Mine got busted."

"Yes, sir, I do, as a matter of fact." He reached behind him to pop open a small storage cabinet built into the rear wall of the cockpit. He yanked a leather strap, and a case popped free, dangling in his gloved hand for an instant, then swung toward the canopy door.

Bolan caught the case in his left hand and reached in with his right. "Thanks," he said, shaking the pilot's hand. "I'll take good care of them."

"Doesn't matter, sir. They're GI. Good luck."

Bolan's answer was swept away on the wind from the quickening rotor. He stood watching the bird climb straight up. At about one thousand feet, it whirled in a graceful semicircle, banked sharply to the left and sped off. Its whumping rotor thumped into the darkness.

There was something about that sound that Bolan would never forget. He was ten thousand miles away, and years in the past. The grass around him smelled of rice and napalm. More times than he could count, he had stood listening to the hurtling steel as it disappeared into the darkness. It made his skin crawl. The nerve endings at the back of his neck tingled. The war went on.

And out there, in the darkness, a man was waiting.

For him.

29

The darkness overhead was total. The stars were bright pinpricks in a black garment, their light shimmering in the air currents sweeping up over the meadow. The compound lay below him, pale blocks of light scattered on the ground from dimly lit windows. Bolan had his work cut out for him.

Again.

There was no unusual activity in the compound. If Kuscenko had come and gone already, Bolan was sure there would be some evidence. If he was still here, Bolan had to find him. Before dawn. Once the sun rose, the assassin would make his move. The first time Balanov stepped into the Russian's line of fire would be the last.

Bolan watched the compound with his naked eyes for a few minutes, fixing its layout in his memory. Then, pulling the borrowed glasses from their case, he took a close-up look. One by one, he examined the buildings, checking each window. Those showing light were mostly covered with heavy shades, and any movement inside was little more than a poorly defined, blocky shadow on the heavy fabric.

The main building, where Balanov would be kept, was dark, except for one window. Bolan watched the window for several seconds, then fiddled with the focus knob of the glasses. What had seemed to be one more shaded window was actually a beige wall seen through naked glass. For some reason, the window shade was up or missing altogether. Bolan scanned the rest of the windows to make sure he hadn't misread any of them, as well. But a quick pass with the sharper focus confirmed his suspicions. The main building window was the only one uncovered. Its uniqueness was grounds for further scrutiny.

Moving through the knee-high grass, Bolan crept toward the lower edge of the meadow, stopping periodically to check the window. Without the glasses, it looked no different from the others. If there was a reason for its difference, someone was counting on the accidental similarity of the wall color to that of the shade.

When he was less than fifty feet from the lower edge of the grass, he knelt and zeroed in with the binoculars again. While he watched, he noticed a shadow moving against the dim rectangle of light. He couldn't tell whether it was someone moving past the window on the outside of the building, or the shadow of an occupant cast against the opposite wall.

Either way it bore watching.

Closely.

For several minutes, Bolan kept his eyes screwed onto the eyepiece of the binoculars. He began to wonder if the pressure was making him see things. Small flecks of light flashed and moved in orange smears, semicircles of sharply etched light danced at the corners of his vision. Twice, he thought he saw a cigarette being waved, as if to signal someone outside the building. He knew enough about the tricks played by night vision, especially the dancing phosphenes that bedeviled the sight of a midnight voyeur, to doubt his own eyes.

But that window gnawed at him. It was wrong in some way he couldn't quite define. It hadn't been left open for someone to sneak in, that was certain. It was too far across the compound. The distance from the razor wire to the window was more than a hundred yards. A man would be a fool to try and make it through the fence to gain access through that opening. And it wasn't likely that Balanov would decide to sit down and read a book anywhere close to the window.

Even so, it was wrong. There was . . .

And then, he knew the light he'd seen had been illusory. The window suddenly filled with shade too dark to be imaginary. Someone was there on the inside looking out.

Bolan put the glasses down and squeezed his lids tightly closed to clear his vision. When he opened them again, he elected to forgo the glasses, preferring a wider field to a close-up view of a small area. The shadow was nearly motionless. It was too distant for him to discern anything other than its general outlines. That it was a man was beyond question. Who it might be was impossible to tell.

Suddenly a bright light flared in the center of the dark obstruction and was gone almost immediately. The man had lit a cigarette and quickly cupped the flame in his hands. Or had he?

The flame started appearing and disappearing at regular intervals. Throwing the glasses to his eyes, Bolan peered through the night, straining to see more clearly. The regular pulse of the flame continued for another few seconds, then was gone. Bolan hadn't figured it out before it vanished, but the answer hit him moments later. It wasn't a cigarette at all. Someone had lit a pipe, puffing regularly, sucking the flame down into the pipe's bowl, letting it breathe, and drawing it in again until, satisfied the pipe was securely aflame, the lighter had been extinguished.

It could have been a signal, or just some damned fool taking an evening smoke. In an open window? With a Soviet assassin possibly within a stone's throw? How likely was that? Not very, Bolan decided. He dropped the glasses again.

He'd wait. As long as it took.

Yeah, he'd wait. What choice did he have?

He didn't have to wait long. Moments later, an answering glimmer appeared from the trees to Bolan's left. That the pipe had been a signal was almost beyond question. The flicker from the trees was repeated several times, then it, too, vanished. Debating whether to stay put or close in, Bolan held his ground.

A few moments later, he was glad he had. The blocky shadow in the window began to move. It rose up in the window, then seemed to collapse on itself and disappear, returning to view in seconds, but half its former size. For a moment, Bolan was stymied. Then he realized what had happened. The man in the window had climbed through it and dropped to the ground. He was leaving the building and heading toward the wire.

To a rendezvous.

But with whom?

The shadowy figure disappeared in the murk of the compound yard. A dim bulk against a dimmer background, it moved quickly to the wire. The man was tall and thin, but other than that, Bolan could discern nothing about him.

It was time to move.

Bolan slipped down into the underbrush, moving cautiously to avoid making unnecessary noise. The clinging tendrils of the thorny growth tugged him, as if asking to let well enough alone. Bolan had been beseeched by more compelling supplicants in the past. He hadn't paid attention then, either.

Another flash of light, so quick that it might have been an illusion, sparked among the brush in the general direction of the answering flash he'd seen from above. It was difficult to judge distance in the shadows, but he knew he'd cut the intervening space by half.

He reached the bottom of the brushy slope, and the land began to level out. It still dropped, but so gently that the descent could pass unnoticed. To his right, there was open sky. He was very close to the edge of the safety perimeter that circled the wire.

Resting for a moment, he tuned his ears toward the compound. At first he heard nothing. Then a series of sharp metallic clicks caught his attention. Plunging into the last strip of vegetation, Bolan reached the edge of the cover and peered into the night in the direction of the sound. It had stopped, and his movement had disoriented him somewhat. Even though he was looking for the source of the sound, when it recurred, it startled him.

He turned his head sharply, in time to notice a shadowed motion just beyond the wire. Another series of clicks was followed by another flash of light. About to rush toward the signaling figure, Bolan was warned by some sixth sense. He froze, as rigid as a jacked deer, and saw a second figure emerge from the dark line of bushes just ahead of him, directly across from the signal flash.

The second figure was also tall and thin. Either man could have been Kuscenko. And it was possible that neither of them was. The unidentified assassin at the first compound was all the proof Bolan needed that nothing was what it seemed to be. The new arrival, carrying a rifle in his left hand, bent double and rushed toward the fence.

The shadowy newcomer merged with the first figure. They seemed to be huddled in conversation. After a brief pause, both of them moved away from the wire. It was then Bolan realized what the clicks had been. The first man had cut the wire and was now ushering the second into the compound.

It was the inside man. And the outside man. The Bobbsey Twins had come home at last.

But not for long. As the two men sprinted soundlessly back toward the compound buildings, Bolan rushed toward the hole in the fence. Tempting as it was to take them down from where he stood, he had the feeling there was much more he had to know if any of this were going to make sense. He was determined to get the whole cancer, root and branch, metastasized as it might be. And he was going to cut it out tonight.

The surgery was imminent. Dr. Bolan was ready to operate. Now.

Bolan would wait until the last minute. If anyone else was involved, he wanted to know it. The hole in the wire was just large enough to accommodate him, and he struggled through, slicing the back of one finger on the knifelike blades of the wire. The delay allowed his quarry to widen the gap between them. He caught just a glimpse of one of them as they ducked into the darkness behind the main building. It was, Bolan knew, the building where Balanov lay sleeping.

Moving from one pool of shadow to the next, the stalkers were carefully approaching the dull outline of the dimly lit window. If they got inside unopposed, it might be too late.

Dropping to one knee, Bolan raised the Weatherby to his shoulder. In the pale light gathered by the scope, Bolan caught a shadow in his cross hairs. He couldn't tell which of the men it was, and his features were indistinguishable. About to squeeze the trigger, Bolan realized it would be better, if possible, to take them alive.

Aiming just a tad high, he squeezed the trigger. The big gun slammed into his shoulder. The slug hit the thick wood of the window frame, just over the head of the shadowy figure. It hit the deck. Both men were out of sight now, but they'd think twice before trying to climb in the open window.

Bolan sprinted toward the main building as a Klaxon sounded. Suddenly the compound was bathed in bright, scalding light. The abrupt reappearance of day, however artificial it was, shocked Bolan's eyes into momentary blindness.

The alarm blared with earsplitting insistence, a nerve-shredding sonic buzz saw. It was joined by the slam of several doors. The general illumination grew in intensity as lights flashed on in several of the buildings.

In the bright glare, the two shadows assumed individuality. Dressed alike in black nightwear, they were nevertheless distinguishable. The nearer of the two was obviously Kuscenko. A shock of blondish hair flashed like a beacon under his knit cap. Bolan threw the scope on him and caught the last vestiges of a grim smile. The features were starkly etched in Bolan's memory by the sardonic grin he had last seen on the roof of the Dal-Tex Building. Before the Executioner could live up to his name, however, the young assassin was gone.

His companion, seen through the unflinching eye of the Weatherby scope, was much older, perhaps twice Kuscenko's age. He, too, was wearing a watch cap, pulled low over his ears and forehead. He looked just a little foolish, like a dime store David Niven with a mustache that was so real that it looked artificial, or like an old man playing a young man's game.

Which he was.

Bolan, fascinated by the vision in the telescopic sight, relaxed his finger. As he watched, the older man wriggled along the base of the building, his features contorted by desperation. But time was running out. Bolan heard the slap of running feet as security men poured into the open compound.

He squeezed off a round. The Weatherby bucked, and the slug slammed the slender figure roughly into the wall of the central cabin just behind him. The bullet entered the chest wall just below the left arm, traversed the thoracic cavity and exited through shattered bone and tissue, burying itself with a dull thunk in the solid oak timber.

Bolan got to his feet and ran headlong toward the dead man. His companion had vanished, but of the two, he was definitely the more dangerous. A bright flash, followed by a sharp report, gave away the younger man's position. In the transitory glow, Bolan saw him huddled in a concrete well beneath the cabin.

Cutting sharply left, Bolan slipped out of his adversary's line of vision, then plunged straight toward the wall. He slammed into the planking and dropped to his stomach. He swung the Weatherby around the waited.

Skittering forward, the assassin heard the sound of security men approaching him on the run. Spooked by the commotion, trapped in a cul-de-sac, Yuri Kuscenko made his stand. He rolled on one shoulder out of the narrow confines of his sanctuary, got to his feet and squeezed the trigger of his .45-caliber automatic. The series of explosions seemed to freeze time.

Bolan saw the big pistol buck in the assassin's hand, as if in slow motion. The shuddering thunder rolled over him and was gone. Kuscenko then swung his rifle to his shoulder, as if seeing Bolan for the first time. But the Weatherby slug impacted precisely where the assassin's scope would have been. The young man fell backward, his head dissolving in a watery halo, pale pink under the bright light. His last expression, frozen in the instant of his destruction, was the same cocky grin he'd worn on the Dallas roof. Even Bolan had to admit Kuscenko had gone out in style.

The Executioner got to his feet as the first security men arrived. One of them bent over each of the dead men, checking fruitlessly for signs of life. Bolan identified himself to the lieutenant in charge. He was finished for now. Out of the cold for now.

The lieutenant extended his hand. "Nice work, sir. We heard you were coming. It's a pity you didn't get here in time to save Mr. Collingsworth."

Bolan didn't bat an eye. The dispensation, and preservation, of secrets was not his province.

The Executioner had other things to do.

Epilogue

Hal Brognola was subdued. He poured coffee for himself and Albright, added cream and sugar and passed a cup to the younger man. Bolan stood by the open window of the big Fed's office, his back to the other two.

Breaking the silence at last, Bolan said, "I still don't believe it."

"You'd better," Brognola replied, taking a seat behind his desk. "And that's only the half of it."

Turning away from the window, Bolan asked, "What's the rest?"

"We'll never know, Striker. And it's probably just as well. Collingsworth seemed to have been selective in recording his entries in his journals."

"But why me? I didn't know the man, not really. I met him once, a long time ago. But that's all."

"Look, nobody ever understands how these things happen, or why. The bottom line for Collingsworth was pretty simple. He'd been a double for fifteen years. He got used to it, maybe even liked it. When that threatened to come apart at the seams, he spooked. It's as simple as that."

"You're not answering me, Hal. Why me? Why set me up and jerk me around like that? What was he trying to accomplish?"

"He kept you busy, for one thing. You were too good to be led around by the nose without some real threat to keep you interested. You were also being set up to take the fall.

He was giving you a high profile. Somewhere, somehow, Collingsworth settled on you because you were everything he wasn't. He was a desk jockey with dreams of grander things dogging every step he took. If not you, it would have been someone else. He happened to know about you, that's all. And you were the most critical link in the chain.''

"But why?"

"Because you were the ribbon on the pretty package. He was using you the same way he was using Kuscenko. It wasn't bad planning, actually. If he or Kuscenko nailed you at the Balanov compound, they had their assassin, gift wrapped. If you got Kuscenko, a difficult disposal problem was out of the way, and you were still a pretty good candidate as Balanov's killer. What he really needed was Balanov and Korienko dead. That would have solved all his problems. And even the agency wouldn't question your part in it. As far as they knew, you tried to hit the President in Dallas, for Christ sakes. You were a rogue elephant.''

"But *I* knew he didn't try to shoot the President," Albright said.

"That's right, you did," Brognola snapped. "And if you're smart, you'll give a little thought to the implications of that.''

Albright swallowed hard, but said nothing.

"Okay, but what about the other hitter, the guy who was supposed to whack Korienko?" Bolan asked.

"That's easy," Albright said, happy to change the subject. "He was a hired gun. He'd done some contract work for us in Europe. Collingsworth pulled out all the stops. He called in every chit he had, and during forty years in the spook business, he collected a lot of them. He had all the contacts, access to everything he needed. And the plan was pretty good, too. But you were better—that's all there is to it.''

"And that's basically why Collingsworth's plan didn't work. He couldn't accept the possibility that somebody might be better than he was." Brognola paused to sip his coffee. "Frustrated ambition, more than anything else, was what brought him down. It's why he was doubled, too, most likely."

"It's a shame, actually," Albright said. "I really admired the man."

"Did you ever tell him that?" Bolan's question cracked like a whip. His gaze bored into the younger man until the latter was forced to turn away.

"No, I . . . uh . . . I thought he knew, I guess. I mean, it never seemed necessary. He was *good*—you have to believe that. Everybody thought so, not just me. He knew so much. He was there at the beginning, for Christ's sake. OSS, you know . . ." His voice died slowly, the helplessness of incomprehension overwhelming him.

"The bottom line, however," Brognola cut in, "is that the guy went bad. He turned, and that's all that matters."

"I'm not so sure, Hal." Bolan left the window to sit on a broad sofa across from Brognola's desk. "I did a lot of thinking while I was out there this time. I think I know a little of what Collingsworth must have been feeling. After a while, you start to think nobody gives a damn what you do, or whether you even do it. Live or die, after a time, you're the only one who seems to care. It can make you bitter, and it can make you scared. I think that's what happened to Collingsworth."

"And what about you?" Brognola asked. "Are you bitter?"

"Yeah, I am, a little. More than a little. And I'm scared, too. Hell, every time I open a door, I expect it to be my last. How can I not be bitter?"

"But, dammit, Striker, you do what you do for a reason. You know why you do it. Doesn't that matter?"

"Of course it matters. I wouldn't be doing it at all, otherwise. But Collingsworth was just as certain, once, as I am. And I wonder if I'll ever be in his shoes, if a day will come when knowing why I do it won't quite matter enough anymore. And if that day does come, what then?"

Bolan's question hung in the softly lit office, right there for all of them to consider.

Nobody had an answer.

SuperBolan #8

ROGUE FORCE

AN EAGLE FOR THE KILLING

A covert clique within the U.S. military is set to launch an all-out war in Central America. This secret cabal of generals believes the American people are being betrayed by a soft U.S. government. Their idea is to stage another "Vietnam." But this time on America's doorstep.

There's only one way that Washington can neutralize these superpatriots: pit it's supersoldier against the very men who trained him!

SB8

4 FREE BOOKS
1 FREE GIFT
NO RISK
NO OBLIGATION
NO KIDDING

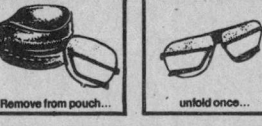